"What kind of sick fuck would do that?" T-Tommy asked. "Hack up these girls, patch them up, and then kill them?"

"The world's full of candidates," Stone said.

"Maybe some surgeon decided to dump his bad cases," one of the techs said.

Stone offered a grim laugh. "Probably an HMO."

T-Tommy returned his attention to the bodies. Cause of death? No way he could tell. He'd leave that to the MEs.

He stood and circled the corpses. He noticed the edge of a tattoo peeking around the side of one of the bodies. It was low, near the base of the spine. He tugged on a pair of latex gloves, dropped to one knee, and rolled the body on one side. The stiffness told him that death had been at least twenty-four hours or so earlier and not more than forty-eight. Fit the level of decay and the lack of visible maggots. Sometime Wednesday most likely. He could now see that the tattoo, a yellow rose wrapped in thorns, extended across the victim's lower back. "Shit."

"That's her," Stone said. "In report this morning we got a BOLO on a missing girl. Blonde, nineteen, rose tattoo on her back. I've got it in my car. I'll see who filed it."

T-Tommy stood. "Dub Walker."

"What?"

"Dub Walker filed it. He's looking for her." T-Tommy sighed and looked up. The sun approached its noonday zenith in the cloudless sky, and the temperature had begun its daily rise. "Nothing like a double homicide to screw up a perfect spring day."

HOT LIGHTS, COLD STEEL

D.P. LYLE

MEDALLION
P R E S S
Medallion Press, Inc.
Printed in USA

PREVIOUS ACCOLADES FOR D.P. LYLE'S
STRESS FRACTURE

"*Stress Fracture* is a cunning, imaginative thriller that will keep you up reading as I did, riveted from first page to last."

—Michael Palmer, MD, *New York Times* best-selling author of *The Last Surgeon*

". . . D.P. Lyle writes the perfect prescription for a psychological thriller."

—L. Dean Murphy, *BookReporter.com*

"D.P. Lyle's *Stress Fracture* is an intense, nail-biting adventure. The author's knowledgeable voice adds a fear factor that can't easily be found. A wonderful, thrilling read, an excellent work of fiction—and more!"

—*New York Times* best-selling author Heather Graham

"The writing is hard-edged and visually evocative, and readers of dark serial-killer thrillers will definitely want to read this one."

—David Pitt, *Booklist Magazine*

"Lyle writes what he knows—and what he knows is terrific. Dub Walker is a keeper."

—Lee Child, international best-selling author of the Reacher thrillers

"Cutting-edge forensics and a whip-cracking pace make *Stress Fracture* a one-sitting read. If you love *CSI*, this is the book for you."

—Tess Gerritsen, *New York Times* best-selling author of *The Keepsake*

"D.P. Lyle's *Stress Fracture* is just what I love in a book: lightning paced, brutally executed, dynamic characters, and a story that grips you by the throat. If Michael Crichton had written an episode of *Law and Order*, here might be the result. Simply brilliant!"

—James Rollins, *New York Times* best-selling author of *The Doomsday Key*

HOT LIGHTS, COLD STEEL

D.P. LYLE

Published 2011 by Medallion Press, Inc.

The MEDALLION PRESS LOGO
is a registered trademark of Medallion Press, Inc.

Typeset in Adobe Garamond Pro
Printed in the United States of America
Title font set in Cacavia01

Library of Congress Cataloging-in-Publication Data

Lyle, D. P.
  Hot lights, cold steel / D.P. Lyle.
    p. cm. -- (Dub Walker series ; bk. 2)
  ISBN-13: 978-1-60542-181-0 (alk. paper)
  ISBN-10: 1-60542-181-2 (alk. paper)
  1. Serial murder investigation--Fiction. I. Title.
  PS3612.Y43H67 2011
  813'.6--dc22
                                    2010049652

10 9 8 7 6 5 4 3 2 1
First Edition

ACKNOWLEDGMENTS

My wonderful agent, Kimberley Cameron of Kimberley Cameron & Associates.

My editors, Helen Rosburg and Lorie Popp, for their excellent insights and tireless work on this manuscript.

My parents, Victor and Elaine Lyle, and of course Nan, for their unwavering support.

All the great people at Medallion Press.

CHAPTER 1

IT HAD BEEN A NEARLY PERFECT DAY.

Got a lot done. Finished the final edits on my next book. This one about how evidence in criminal cases linked up, formed a chain, or maybe a noose for the bad guys. I titled it *Linkage: How Evidence Makes the Case.* With a keystroke I had fired it back to my editor. Few things felt better than final edits.

Time to relax.

Now, I lounged in a redwood Adirondack chair and worked the fret board of my Martin D-18. I bent out a few riffs and a couple of new turnarounds to "Red House," the original John Lee Hooker version, not the Hendrix electrified one. I added a backbeat with my bare heel against the wooden deck.

I'm Dub Walker, and I own a small cottage on the western slope of Monte Sano Mountain, one of the final remnants of the Appalachian chain. From the deck, I had a 180-degree view over Huntsville. The sun had settled beneath the horizon, and the city's lights were rapidly winking on. A warm breeze came up from the valley.

Earlier, around noon, an electrical storm had blown through. A real thunder-boomer. The kind that rattled windows and fractured the sky with pulse after pulse of lightning, some seemingly reluctant to let go. The kind that all too often spun off a tornado or two. But this one quickly moved eastward, leaving behind clean air, crystal blue skies, and now a perfect Southern spring night. The kind you wanted to go on forever.

Wasn't going to happen, though.

I leaned the Martin against the chair, went inside, poured a hefty glass of Blanton's bourbon, and flipped on the stereo. Buddy Guy churned out "Feels Like Rain." Back outside, I eased into the chair and closed my eyes. Buddy hit his stride, and I fell into the music.

I'm not sure whether I dozed or merely drifted with the music, but I sat up when I heard footsteps coming around the house. A woman stepped onto the deck and walked toward me.

A woman I hadn't seen in ten years. Still beautiful. Still unforgettable.

I stood. "Miranda?"

"Dub, you haven't changed a bit," she said.

"And you're as gorgeous as ever. What brings you here?"

"Sorry to barge in. I was going to ring the doorbell but then heard the music and guessed you were back this way."

I hugged her. When I broke the embrace, I noticed her eyes were red and her face drawn. "What's wrong?"

"I was going to call." Miranda sighed. "Truth is, I wasn't sure I would come here. I put it off. I sat out front for half an hour, trying to decide."

"What's wrong?" I asked again.

"Everything." She looked around as if uncertain what to do.

"Sit down." We moved to the redwood dining table, and I pulled a chair out for her. She sat. "Some wine?"

"What are you drinking?"

"Bourbon."

"Maybe that'd be better."

I retrieved a glass and the Blanton's from the kitchen and poured her a couple of fingers.

She took the drink with both hands, cradling it as if she feared she might drop it. I noticed her fingers trembled. She took a healthy gulp.

I sat across from her. "Tell me what's wrong. Something happen to Richard?"

Miranda shook her head. Tears collected in her eyes. "He died three years ago."

"I'm sorry."

"It's Noel." She sniffed.

I handed her a napkin, and she wiped her eyes.

"She's missing."

CHAPTER 2

"WHY YOU GOTTA BE SUCH A DICK?" ALEJANDRO DIAZ PEELED HIS damp T-shirt from his chest and flapped it. Didn't offer much relief. The flash thunderstorm that had rolled through earlier in the day had left behind sticky air and heavy soil. Made the digging hard. They had been at it for forty-five minutes.

"What?" Eddie Elliott took a pull from the pint of Jack. "Just because I'd rather be drinking a cold beer and watching the ladies dance?"

Alejandro tossed aside another shovel of dirt and then climbed from the hole. "Your turn."

Eddie stuffed the pint in his hip pocket, stripped off his T-shirt, and jumped in. He picked up the shovel and attacked the soil. "To hell with this. I'm tired of being the garbageman."

"You want your money? Dig the fucking hole." Alejandro lit a Marlboro with his Zippo, the flare reflecting off the surrounding trees. He took a long drag, then another, and exhaled the smoke toward the half-moon that peeked through the canopy.

"Fuck this," Eddie said. "Let's get done with it."

Alejandro looked down at the younger man. The moonlight silvered his shaggy, blond hair and sweat-slicked shoulders. "Dig the hole, or you don't get paid. Understand?"

Eddie jabbed the shovel into the dirt. It clanked against rock. "See. That's it."

"Shit," Alejandro said. "Get out."

Eddie did. Alejandro jumped in. He repeatedly poked the shovel into the soil, each time banging into chunks of limestone. This whole area was peppered with it. Should they start somewhere else? Waste nearly an hour's work?

"I need some beer and pussy," Eddie said.

"From that little *puta* at High Rollers?"

High Rollers was a strip joint off University Drive. Owned by Alejandro's boss, Rocco Scarcella. The guy paying for the hole.

"Carmelita's no whore." Eddie puffed out his chest. "She's my angel."

Eddie was such an ignorant little prick. Every time he made a couple of bucks, it disappeared on drinks and Carmelita's lap dances. "She's not yours. That girl belongs to anybody with a little *dinero*."

Eddie rotated his neck as if it were stiff. "She's got Eddie fever." He rubbed the crotch of his jeans. "I've got the cure."

Alejandro laughed. "You ever been with her, Edito?"

"Don't call me that."

"*Pobrecito.* You'd be better off to keep your money and fall in love with your hand."

Eddie glared at him, hesitated as if going to say something, but instead pulled the pint from his pocket and took a drink. He grimaced as the liquid went down. "You'll see."

Alejandro dropped his cigarette and crushed it with his boot. "Get the flashlight." He picked the butt up and slipped it into his pocket.

Eddie disappeared through the trees, heading toward Alejandro's pickup. He returned in a couple of minutes, shaking the light, clicking the switch on and off. Nothing. He banged it against an open palm. Still nothing. "Damn it." He flung the flashlight into the forest where the brush consumed it. "Fucking thing's broke."

Alejandro wrestled his temper under control. He had only brought Eddie into this as a favor to Ellie, Eddie's older sister and one of Alejandro's ex-lovers. He put up with Eddie's bullshit out of some vague sense of guilt for walking away from Ellie, hurting her, even though that was at least a year ago. The mothering and smothering she had heaped on Alejandro were now directed at Eddie. She had dragged her brother from the mean streets of Atlanta, away from the gangs, away from the drugs and guns, and away from an arrest warrant for armed robbery. Eddie the tough guy, wearing no mask, no disguise, not even a cap, had stuck a gun in the face of a terrified liquor store owner for a handful of cash and a six-pack of beer, all clearly recorded by security cameras.

"Go find it," Alejandro said.

"It's a flashlight for Christ's sake."

Alejandro stepped out of the hole and moved in Eddie's direction. At six feet to Eddie's five six, he looked down at him. "You want to fuck with me? With Rocco?"

"I don't want to do dirty work for that greaser pig anymore. Let him come out here and dig his own fucking holes."

Alejandro tightened his jaw. "Where else you going to get five hundred for a couple hours' work?"

"I did better pushing meth in Atlanta."

"That why you hit a liquor store for sixty-five bucks? Or was it the Budweiser you were after?"

Eddie offered no reply. He turned and headed for the area where he had pitched the flashlight.

Alejandro knelt near the edge of the excavation. The freshly turned soil smelled rich and fertile. He flicked his lighter to life and held it over the pit. Not deep enough. Needed another foot. Maybe two. Did he want to argue with Eddie? Do it himself? He looked around. They were miles from Huntsville, middle of nowhere, in a wooded patch sandwiched between a rural two-lane blacktop and a small, forgotten cemetery. Who would snoop around out here?

He heard a soft rhythmic whisper behind him and twisted on his haunches. The ghostly white form of a barn owl maneuvered through the trees above him. He watched until it faded from sight.

Eddie came from the darkness empty-handed. "It's not out there."

After tonight, Alejandro was going to dump this prick. He knew guys who would jump at this kind of money. Guys without an attitude.

Ellie would simply have to find her dickless brother different work. Maybe he could be a real garbageman.

"Let's finish this." Alejandro led the way out of the trees, across a narrow strip of wild grass, and into the cemetery. His pickup was parked beneath a gnarled oak tree on the gravel road that arced through the gravestones.

He lowered the tailgate and peeled back the tarp, revealing the two wrapped bodies. At least in the darkness he could no longer see the lifeless faces that earlier had stared at him through the clear plastic. After pulling on a pair of gloves, he heaved one of the bodies to his shoulder, feeling the onset of stiffness in the corpse.

Alejandro recrossed the open area, moved through the trees, dumped the body into the pit, and moved aside. Eddie did the same with the other corpse. But Eddie, he noticed, was bare-handed.

"Where're your gloves?"

"Lost them," Eddie said.

Fucking idiot. Alejandro considered making Eddie haul the body from the pit and wipe it down. Screw it. Get this done; get the hell away. "You fill it up."

"Why me?"

"Because I did most of the digging. Because I said so. You want to see your little *puta*, get to work."

Eddie took another slug of whiskey, set the bottle on the ground, picked up the shovel. He muttered to himself as he began filling the grave.

Alejandro fired up another cigarette.

Suddenly Eddie dropped the shovel and jumped into the hole, straddling the corpses.

"What is it?"

Eddie ripped the plastic, exposing a small, delicate hand. "How'd they miss this?" He tugged a ring from the finger and examined it.

To Alejandro it appeared to be silver with a large, dark stone.

"Saw it when you lit your cigarette. Should be worth something." Eddie slipped it into his pants pocket and climbed from the hole.

Fifteen minutes later, the grave was filled, packed down, and littered with pine needles. Eddie finished the Jack with a final gulp and tossed the empty into the night.

Alejandro stared at him. "You want to leave that behind? Let the cops find it?"

"How many times we done this? A dozen? More? They ever find anything?" Eddie shook his head. "You worry too much."

Alejandro closed his eyes, took a deep breath, and waited for his tightened jaw to relax. It wouldn't. His teeth ground all the way back to the truck. He threw the shovel into the bed and closed the tailgate.

"Let's get out of here," Eddie said, climbing into the passenger seat. "Carmelita's waiting."

Alejandro cranked the engine to life. The truck lurched forward, and he followed the gravel road out of the cemetery. Two lefts and a right put him on Jeff Road, the blacktop that led to the city.

Eddie opened the glove box and studied the ring in its light. "Bet I can get some pussy with this."

CHAPTER 3

"I don't know what to do," Miranda said. Tears trailed down her cheeks. "It's my fault. I didn't know where to go or who to call." She looked up at me. "I'm sorry . . ."

I hated it when one of those chills zipped up my back. One of those that meant the train was running hot and you were on the tracks. That what was coming was nowhere near good. That the story I was about to hear would be ugly. I grabbed another napkin and dabbed her cheeks. "Relax. Tell me what happened."

Miranda Richardson had always been the prettiest girl at the dance. My freshman college crush. Lasted a few months as those things do, and then at the end of the year she transferred to Randolph-Macon in Virginia and a year later married Richard.

"You probably don't remember, but my married name is Edwards." I didn't. "Richard had a nasty leukemia. Noel took his death hard. Me, too. It was a week after Noel's sixteenth birthday." She took a deep breath and let it out slowly. Stress lines edged her eyes and mouth.

"I'm sorry," I said. Weak but it was the best I could come up with.

"Noel began to act out. Grades went south. Drugs, mostly marijuana, but I suspect other things too. Ran away several times. Filed for emancipation, saying I was a bad mother. Had one of Richard's former partners file the papers." Miranda gazed out toward the city. "The jerk did it because I wouldn't sleep with him. Hit on me at Richard's funeral. Can you believe it?"

I said nothing, figuring the question was purely rhetorical. The answer obvious. The guy was an attorney, trained to screw people.

"Fortunately, the judge sided with me, and I took her home. She ranted and raved for a couple of weeks and then ran away again. New Orleans this time. Took me three months to track her down. She was living with some thirty-year-old drug addict who threatened to have me killed." Her knuckles whitened as she crushed the napkin in her hand. "Until I reminded him that she was sixteen and I'd have his ass fried for statutory."

"You brought her home again?" I asked.

She nodded.

"When was that?"

"Year and a half ago. She was furious. Said I was ruining her life. Called me everything from a Nazi to a whore." She buried her face in her hands, and her shoulders lurched as she sobbed.

"It's okay," I said. "Let it out."

Miranda did for a minute and then straightened, sniffed back tears, and dabbed her eyes with the balled-up napkin. "I'm sorry. I know I'm not making any sense. I shouldn't be dumping this on you."

"Actually, you're making perfect sense," I said. "Take your time. I've got nowhere to go and all night to get there."

She scrunched up her face, holding back more tears. "I love you. That's why I came here. I didn't know what else to do. I somehow thought . . ."

I laid a hand on her arm. "You're exactly where you're supposed to be."

Miranda looked at me, eyes glistening.

"I take it Noel didn't hang around long," I said.

She sighed. "This time to Atlanta. I found out she was turning tricks for some guy. Then about a year ago I found she had moved here and was in school at UAH."

"Really?" That wasn't the turn I expected.

UAH is the University of Alabama at Huntsville. A tough college heavy on high-tech programs as you would expect from a school surrounded by the US Army's Redstone Arsenal, NASA's Marshall Space Flight Center, and the tech-rich Cummings Research Park. If Noel got into UAH, she must have aced her SATs. And probably inherited her mother's smarts.

"I wish it was that good," Miranda said. "I mean, I'm glad she's in school, but apparently she's been dancing at some strip club and prostituting herself to afford it. I offered to pay for everything, but she refused. Said I just wanted to control her."

"Why do you think she's missing?"

"The one thing she was good about was calling. Once, sometimes two or three times a week. We mostly argued, but I always heard from her. But the last two weeks . . . nothing. I called one of her roommates, but she's brain-dead, and I couldn't get anything out of her. I even spoke with two of her professors. She hasn't been to either class for two weeks."

"Police?" I asked.

"That's why I drove up here from Birmingham. I called yesterday, got nowhere, so I thought I'd better show up in person. Didn't help. She's nineteen now. They said she had the right to disappear if she wanted."

"Did she?" I asked. "Take off again?"

"I don't know. The only thing I got from her roommate Sin-Dee Parker—you're going to love this—she made a point of telling me it was spelled S-I-N-hyphen-D-E-E. The *S* and the *D* capitalized. It'd be funny if I wasn't so scared. Anyway, Sin-Dee said that all her stuff was still there. Said the last she saw of Noel was ten days ago, maybe more. Noel and their other roommate, Crystal Robinson, went out on a date. Sin-Dee wouldn't tell me anything else." Again she tightened her face in an attempt to hold it together. "Something's wrong."

Never argue with a mother's intuition. Truth was, I knew something was indeed very wrong. When a young girl got into drugs, stripping, and hooking and then disappeared, it was never good news. I didn't tell Miranda that. Instead I offered a twig. "Let's not travel down that road."

"Do you think I'm overreacting?"

"I think you're doing exactly what any mother would do."

"I hope I'm just being a ninny. She's run away a dozen times. But this feels different."

"Don't let your imagination tie you in knots. Let me sniff around a bit."

Miranda offered a smile. Not her usual infectious one but more a grimace. She looked tired and defeated, the deep sparkle in her eyes now mashed flat.

"Was Noel ever arrested?" I asked.

"Twice. In Birmingham for drug possession."

"Do you have any recent pictures?"

"I brought these." She reached into her purse and handed me half a dozen four-by-six photos. "These were taken last summer. Needless to say, the purple hair isn't her natural color. I have no idea what it is now."

Two were head shots. Noel got her mother's looks. Intense blue eyes and a great smile. Two of the other pictures showed her standing by a pool in a skimpy two-piece bathing suit. One facing the camera. The other turned away, looking back over her shoulder. Her smile seemed sad. She had a tattoo across her lower back. A yellow rose haloed by thorns. "What's this?"

"The tattoo? Something else we fought over." Miranda dropped her head and studied her hands, one nail digging at the cuticle of another. "Seems pretty trivial now."

"You got an address for Sin-Dee?"

"Just a number." She scribbled it on a slip of paper she took from her purse and gave it to me.

"The club where she danced? Any idea where?"

"I think it's called High Rollers, but I'm not sure."

High Rollers was a bump-and-grind club west of the city off University. Run by some low-rent mafia type.

"Do you think she's okay?" Miranda asked. She wiped her eyes again.

"I'd go with that." I smiled. It felt forced, and I'm sure she sensed that. "Maybe she met some rich guy and took a trip. Aspen, New York, Paris, somewhere exotic."

She stared at me. I don't think she bought it. I didn't, either.

"Where're you staying?" I asked.

"The Marriott. Near UAH."

"Okay. Let me see what I can find out."

Miranda seemed to relax. Somewhat.

"I'm going to call Claire McBride," I said. "Get her involved."

"The TV reporter? Your ex?"

I nodded. Claire was the top reporter of *Channel 8 News*. She and I had had a brief marriage a decade ago. Didn't work. Mostly her fault, I swear. Now we were friends. With benefits from time to time. Long story. "I'll bring Claire up to speed and see if she'll do a spot on her broadcast. If we can get Noel's name and picture out there, maybe something will shake loose."

Tears formed in her eyes. "What would I do without you?"

I walked Miranda to her car and gave her a long hug. I told her not to worry, everything would be okay, I'd find Noel, and yada, yada, yada. Clichés I wasn't sure I believed. But she needed some good news, some hope, to sleep on. Wouldn't hurt me, either.

CHAPTER 4

THE BITCH HAD A BODY. ALEJANDRO HAD TO GIVE HER THAT. LEAN, mean, flat-bellied, and tits that jumped right out there, no questions asked. Everything a lovesick boy like Eddie wanted. Alejandro sat at a four-top, sipping a bottle of Corona, while across the table Carmelita played Eddie. From behind a curtain of dark, curly hair, her bright eyes peeked at the young man. Her full lips parted in an obviously practiced smile designed to convince Eddie that he was her entire world.

She damn sure knew how to use what she had. Same could be said for any of the dancers at High Rollers. Hardened pros, even those who worked under false IDs, saying they were of legal age when that was a year or two down the road.

Alejandro watched Carmelita slither and gyrate and dry hump Eddie in time with the music. Eddie couldn't stuff bills into her G-string fast enough. *Fool.* Alejandro headed to the men's room to off-load the beers he had downed. He'd seen this movie before. Every time Eddie got a wad of cash.

As he exited the restroom, a topless blonde, maybe twenty-one, probably less, grabbed his arm. "Want to buy a dance?"

Alejandro shook his head and started to walk away, but she held on. Even moved closer, one warm breast sliding against his arm. Felt good. Down deep good.

"Come on," she said. "You'll like it."

What the hell. He led her to his table, turned his chair, and sat down. ZZ Top's bluesy "I Need You Tonight" thumped from the sound system. Multicolored swords of light cut swaths through the smoke-filled room. The girl told him her name was Madison and began to grind to the music.

Across the table, Carmelita had apparently decided to sit one out. She and Eddie huddled close. Alejandro caught only scraps of their conversation, but it was enough to put the story together: Eddie telling Carmelita he was a hit man, she asking if he'd ever killed anyone, him saying sure, lots of times. *Jesus.* Eddie, the idiot, always running on about things that shouldn't be talked about. *Cierre la boca.*

The song wound down, and Alejandro extended a twenty toward Madison. She tugged at the waist of her G-string, and he tucked the bill beneath. She giggled and bounced up and down when Bob Seger's "Night Moves" came on.

"I love this song. Another?" She cocked her head.

Alejandro nodded, and Madison began her routine again. Good

cover while he watched Eddie.

Eddie was getting into it, sliding his hand along Carmelita's thigh. She didn't seem to mind. She had him hooked and was reeling him in. Eddie reached into his pocket and pulled out the ring, its blue stone catching the swirling lights. She took it, slid it on a finger. He let her examine it for a minute, then held out his hand. She slipped it off her finger and gave it to him, a practiced pout on her face. He pressed close and whispered something in her ear. Alejandro couldn't hear what he said, but Carmelita shook her head and gave him a playful swat on the shoulder.

Madison now straddled one of Alejandro's legs. She leaned into him, her body falling into the music's rhythm, her breath on his neck.

The song hit its soft area, and Alejandro could hear Eddie and Carmelita again.

"I don't believe you." Carmelita laughed. "You're just messing with me."

Eddie grinned. "I'd like to."

Again she laughed. "I'm not that kind of girl." She flattened a hand over her bare chest and gave him a look of mock surprise.

"Not even for the ring," Eddie said.

"Yeah, right."

Madison's hand slid across Alejandro's chest, and her lips brushed against his cheek. "Hmmm," she moaned as she ground against his leg.

He turned his head toward the conversation across the table.

Eddie's hand traveled high on Carmelita's thigh, near the tiny triangle of her G-string. "For a little taste." He squeezed.

"Why should I go with you? You're lying to me. Pretending to be a big, bad hit man. That ring's probably a ten-dollar fake."

"Come with me," Eddie said. "I'll show you."

"Show me what? Your pistol?" She raised an eyebrow.

"Two dead bodies."

Carmelita grinned. "Two of your victims?"

"That's right. Where do you think the ring came from?"

Her smile collapsed. "You're serious, aren't you?"

"Try me. You'll see who I am."

Alejandro's senses ramped up, Madison now a distraction. He ignored her cooing and writhing.

Carmelita edged her chair closer to Eddie. "I've never seen a dead person before. Is it gross?"

"Not to me," Eddie said, his chest noticeably expanding.

"You'll give me the ring?"

"And another two hundred if you stay the night."

Alejandro pushed Madison's hands away and stood. Her look of shock evaporated when he stuffed two twenties into her hand. He wound through the tables toward the back corner, up the stairs, and approached the big man standing beside a door with a sign that said No Dancers Allowed.

"I need to see Rocco," Alejandro said.

He couldn't remember the goon's name, Tony or something like that. He stared at Alejandro as if he hadn't heard. Maybe didn't understand. More likely simply flexing his gatekeeper muscle, making Alejandro wait. He grunted, pushed open the door, and stuck his head inside. "Alejandro wants to see you."

"Sure," Rocco said.

Alejandro moved through the door. It closed behind him.

Rocco Scarcella leaned back in his chair, cigar in his mouth, two stacks of cash on his desk. "What is it?"

"We got a problem," Alejandro said. Eddie had been a pain in the ass for the past two months. Always the big shot, always overplaying his abilities. Now he had advanced from a headache to a liability. Threatened Alejandro's position.

"Tell me." Rocco snapped a rubber band around each stack of bills.

"Eddie. Running his mouth."

"I see."

"About tonight's job." Alejandro told him what he had overheard.

Rocco chewed on his cigar. "What do you propose?"

"Take care of it."

"When and where?"

"Tonight when I take him home."

"The girl?"

"Looks like she'll be going with us. Makes it clean."

"Need backup?"

Alejandro knew Rocco hated messes. Wanted his people to take care of their own business. "I'll fix it."

Rocco nodded and waved toward the door. "Don't fuck it up."

After Alejandro left, Rocco picked up the phone, dialed, waited for Lefty Bruno to answer.

"Yo," Lefty said.

"Got a problem. Need you and Austin."

"We're rolling. See you in ten."

CHAPTER 5

THIS WAS GOING TO BE TOTALLY COOL. DEAD BODIES. CARMELITA had never seen one, much less two. Would they be gross? Smell bad? She'd heard that they smelled like rotting eggs. What if she threw up? How embarrassing. Still, she'd have a great story to tell. And a ring to show off.

She had been scheduled to work until 1:00 a.m., but this was definitely worth dumping a couple of hours. Besides, it wasn't that busy, and the tips had been lousy. Some nights were just that way. Maybe if this had been a payday Friday, she'd have stayed, but a dead Wednesday? No contest.

Before leaving the club, she changed into jeans and a red T-shirt with a yellow Ferrari logo on the front and told her friend Madison where she was going. Tried to recruit her to come along. Do a double. Both make some cash. But, as usual, Madison balked. She never joined Carmelita on her escapades. Madison called them "sexcapades." Whatever. Of course, she always wanted to hear all the dirty details the next day.

Now Carmelita sat in the cab of a pickup between Eddie and his friend Alejandro, who drove. She had seen Alejandro at the club before. Usually with Eddie. Where Eddie was young and soft, Alejandro looked hard and tough. Didn't smile, didn't say a word when Eddie introduced them. Just looked at her with contempt in his eyes.

She wished Madison was here. Maybe she could've warmed the dude up.

First stop, a liquor store. She and Eddie picked up two six-packs of beer and a pint of Jack Daniel's. In the well-lit store, she saw Eddie clearly for the first time. He was even more handsome than he had seemed in the dark club. Dirty blond hair, blue eyes, and a pleasant smile. She'd screwed worse. A lot worse. For a lot less. Best of all, he was naïve, and if she worked it right, she could double the two hundred he had promised.

Back in the truck, Carmelita swigged her beer and giggled as Eddie ran his hand up her thigh, squeezing firmly. "How far is it?" she asked.

"Just a few miles to my place." He dropped an empty beer bottle in the bag and pulled out a fresh one, twisting off the cap.

"Your place? What about the bodies?" She pushed his hand away. "You promised."

Eddie smiled. "We're going. After Alejandro drops us off, we'll take my truck."

She stared at Alejandro. His dark eyes and set jaw made her uncomfortable. He gripped the steering wheel. "You're not coming with us?"

"No." He gulped a shot from the whiskey bottle.

Eddie laughed. "Alejandro's seen enough bodies, haven't you?"

Alejandro didn't respond. He pulled a Marlboro from the pack in his shirt pocket and lit it with a Zippo. He clicked the lighter closed and tossed it on the dash as he turned off University on to Jeff Road and headed north. They quickly left civilization behind and were now on a country road, passing only an occasional farmhouse.

She looked at Alejandro. "You a hit man, too?"

Alejandro's eyes narrowed, but his gaze never left the road. "You ask too many questions."

Carmelita inched toward Eddie, breaking the contact of her leg with Alejandro's. "I'm sorry. I was just trying to be friendly."

"Don't worry about him," Eddie said. "Alejandro don't talk much."

Alejandro offered a faint grunt and took another swig of whiskey. He wedged the open pint between his legs and flicked ashes out the window. They swirled like fireflies before fading into the darkness.

She glanced out the window and then over her shoulder. Nothing. Not a single car light. No sign of anyone.

They turned onto a rutted road, the truck's headlamps gyrating wildly as they bounced along. They passed a faded sign that read Sunnyvale Trailer Park and wound through a collection of thirty to forty weather-beaten mobile homes that were arrayed along the dusty, serpentine loop. She saw that most had been permanently embedded in the soil while others balanced on dry-rotted tires.

Televisions flickered through the windows of a couple of the trailers near the entrance, but near the rear of the park everything was dark and quiet. As if no one lived back here. Beyond the park? Nothing.

Carmelita had been so busy drinking beer and talking with Eddie that she hadn't noticed just how far into the country they had driven. Or what roads they had taken. She began to feel alone and vulnerable. Her heart thumped harder, and her palms moistened.

"Doesn't look like anyone lives here," she said.

"I do," Eddie said. "Just ahead."

What have I gotten myself into? These men were killers. Eddie told her so. What was to stop them from raping her, killing her, dumping her out where no one would ever find her? Her throat felt dry. She tried to swallow, couldn't, and took a drink of beer. It seemed bitter now. "I should go back."

"What are you talking about?" Eddie asked.

"I'm tired. I don't feel well."

She noticed Alejandro cock his head toward her before she looked into Eddie's face. He smiled. Seemed so innocent. Was he?

"Relax. We'll have some fun, you'll see the bodies, and then I'll take you back." Eddie squeezed her thigh. "You'll see."

CHAPTER 6

THIS WAS A BIG NIGHT FOR TOMMY AUSTIN. HE AND HIS MENTOR, Sal "Lefty" Bruno, were mechanics. They fixed things. Things that Rocco Scarcella needed fixed. Lefty, ten years older and a hundred years more experienced, had been teaching him the art for a year now. Ever since Rocco brought Lefty in from Jersey. Tonight, Austin, a local boy from Decatur, just across the river, would call the shots.

Half an hour earlier Rocco had summoned them to High Rollers. Said he had a job for them. Austin knew it was something important if the big man wanted to see them on such short notice. They came in the back way as always and went straight up to Rocco's office, got the details, and in ten minutes, tops, were back in the SUV.

Now they sat in the vehicle on a low rise, sheltered by two hickory trees. The position offered a view of the decaying trailer park where Eddie lived. They settled in and waited. Wouldn't be long.

Dressed in jeans and a black T-shirt that stretched tightly over his muscular chest and shoulders, Austin aimed the night-vision binoculars at the scattering of mobile homes. They looked like black rectangles, only two punctuated by the green glow from an interior light. He focused on the last and most remote trailer, maybe two hundred feet from where he sat. Dark.

Lefty nudged him. "Here they come."

The truck stopped, nose aimed at the front door of Eddie's stubby, round-top trailer. Eddie climbed out.

Carmelita hesitated. In the circle of light created by the truck's headlamps she could see that the trailer was old, probably white at one time but now a sickly yellow, and listed to one side. A screen door hung askew as if losing its grip. What the hell was she doing?

"Come on," Eddie said. He reached for her.

What choice did she have? Stay with Alejandro? Not a chance. Her only option was to go with Eddie. The lesser of two evils. She hoped that Eddie was as benign as he appeared. She slid out of the truck. The warm night air seemed cooler.

Eddie told Alejandro he'd see him tomorrow. Alejandro didn't respond but simply sat, staring ahead.

Carmelita noticed a rusted-out Chevy pickup parked to the side of the trailer. She thought it might be dark blue. "Yours?"

"Yeah." Eddie opened the door and motioned her inside.

She looked back. Alejandro hadn't moved. *Relax*, she told herself. Everything was going to work out.

Austin watched Eddie lead the girl inside the shit box he called home. Alejandro killed the truck's engine and flicked off the headlamps, everything now dark and quiet. Austin lifted the night-vision binocs.

Alejandro sat behind the wheel, unmoving, his cigarette flaring bright green as he sucked down another drag. For a second Austin couldn't figure out why Alejandro hadn't gone in with them, and then he said to Lefty, "Looks like he's going to let them get comfy before he does them."

"That's what I'd do."

"We take Alejandro out here, and it'll make going in easier."

Lefty nodded. "I hate walking into a situation where I don't know who's a shooter and who isn't."

"I'd bet only Alejandro's carrying," Austin said. "Once he's down, the rest should be a piece of cake."

Lefty screwed a fresh CO_2 cartridge into the air pistol and settled the dart into the chamber. He handed the weapon to Austin.

Alejandro saw the lights in the trailer click on. The shadows cast by Eddie and Carmelita fell against the curtains. He heard Eddie's muffled voice and Carmelita's occasional giggle. The silhouettes came together, moved apart, came back together, and finally went through the motions of undressing. More giggles. Then he heard the hiss of the shower springing to life. Perfect. Good cover for his entry. He'd give them a few minutes. Let them get busy. He lit another cigarette.

Using the sleeping trailers for cover, Austin and Lefty eased up behind Alejandro's truck and crouched by the tailgate.

Alejandro took another drag from his cig. Its glow pushed against the cab's rear window.

Come on, asshole. Get out of the truck.

Alejandro didn't move. Took his own sweet time, casually working on the cig. Like he had all night.

Austin glanced at Lefty.

Lefty raised a palm, telling Austin to stay calm. Be patient.

Sure enough, Alejandro climbed from the truck. He took a final long pull from the cig, flicked the butt to the ground, and crushed it with his boot.

Austin stepped from behind the truck. Alejandro turned, surprise in his eyes. Austin leveled the air gun and fired. The fentanyl-soaked dart struck Alejandro's chest.

Alejandro froze, looked down, then back up. He wavered,

grabbed at the truck door for balance, and spiraled to the ground.

To keep from falling, Carmelita grasped the showerhead. With one foot braced against the corner of the claustrophobic stall, she wrapped her other leg around Eddie. Her back bounced against the wall, the stained plastic creaking, as Eddie increased the intensity of his movements. His frantic probing caused more than a little discomfort. *Not much longer*, she thought. *He's nearly there.* She could tolerate it, especially since she had talked him into an extra hundred if she did him in the shower.

She whispered in his ear, "God, you are so good. You make me crazy."

He moaned and continued his hammering.

"That's it. Come on. You're going to make me—"

The shower curtain flew open.

She recoiled, but Eddie didn't seem to notice, his motions unchecked.

A hand and a long metallic gun barrel extended toward them. A soft spitting sound and a misty puff from the muzzle. A dart appeared in Eddie's neck. He jerked around, then wobbled, released his grip on her, and collapsed.

The man who had fired the dart was muscular inside a black T-shirt. He smiled as he settled another dart into the gun and snapped it closed.

Carmelita pressed her back against the far wall of the shower.

Another spit from the gun. A sharp pain in her shoulder. Her body sagged, and her legs, suddenly heavy, gave way. She felt as if she were floating. Then nothing.

Using a latex-gloved hand, Lefty twisted off the spray of water. Austin pulled Carmelita from the shower. Lefty handed him his 9 mm, sound suppressor attached. Austin snapped a round into the back of Eddie's head and returned the weapon to Lefty.

Lefty gathered the girl's clothes and purse, scattered several bags of crystal meth on the kitchen table, and dug the ring from the pocket of Eddie's jeans. They loaded Carmelita and Alejandro into the back of the SUV. Austin climbed into Alejandro's truck and followed Lefty from the trailer park.

CHAPTER 7

I PARKED IN THE OAK-SHADED CIRCULAR DRIVE OF PATRICE NOMBERG'S antebellum mansion. It belonged in *Architectural Digest*. Two stories, white with black shutters and trim, and six large Corinthian columns that stretched across the front and supported a pedimented portico.

I had known Patrice since we sat next to each other in sixth grade. She had worn many hats in the years that followed: high school wild child, coed madam, real madam, criminal defendant, probationer, businesswoman, quasi-social worker, to name a few. She got tapped by the Huntsville PD a couple of times and with real prison time, not just a day or two here and there, on the horizon, she went legit. Two very successful boutiques, one downtown, one at the Parkway Place Mall. Bought this mansion on Echols Hill, an old money, tree-shaded bump just east of downtown.

Patrice used her home as a sort of halfway house for stray girls.

Girls who had followed Patrice's path and needed help. She wouldn't take in anyone who wasn't drug free and committed to work or school. None under eighteen or over twenty-five. After that, according to Patrice, they were too set in their ways for her to really help. She funded their education, got them jobs, some at her boutiques, gave them room and board, and set up personal savings accounts for them. Everything they needed to get out of the life.

Too bad Noel hadn't found her way here.

Why was I here? If anyone understood the world of strippers and prostitutes, it was Patrice. Even though she was no longer in the business, just dealing with the aftermath, she knew the players.

A young woman with sleep-tousled, blonde hair opened the door and invited me inside. She wore jeans and an oversized sweatshirt, feet bare. She led me to the kitchen.

Patrice greeted me with a hug and introduced me to Nicolette and then to Lola, another young blonde with penetrating green eyes who was placing plates on the table. She wore a lime T-shirt over faded jeans, her feet bare, too.

"Breakfast is almost ready," Lola said. "You joining us?"

"The girls take turns cooking," Patrice said. "You got lucky. Lola's the best cook in the bunch."

Lola gave a mock curtsey. "Bacon, eggs, and biscuits. Homemade. My mom's recipe."

I declined but took a cup of coffee and sat at the counter.

Patrice sat across from me. "I just read your last book. The one about serial killers. Dark stuff."

"Goes with the territory," I said.

"I followed the Brian Kurtz case. You and T-Tommy did a good job there."

"Mostly him."

"Right."

"What have you got for me?" I had called her last night after Miranda left, asking what she knew about Sin-Dee Parker and Noel Edwards.

She cradled her coffee cup in both hands and spoke over it. "Sin-Dee Parker turns tricks for Rosalee Kennedy. An old competitor. I talked with her last night. Sin-Dee's been with her awhile and brought her Noel. Rosalee sent Noel and a girl named Crystal Robinson out for a twofer a week or so ago, and they never came back. Says that's not unusual for Crystal and that she'll turn up soon. Always does."

"Rosalee call the police?"

Patrice frowned. "She's not running the Girl Scouts."

Stupid question. "Who's the guy? The one they went to see?"

She took a sip of coffee and set the cup on the counter. "Attorney named Ben Weiss. Lives near here on Adams. Has an office down on the square across from the Schiffman Building."

The Schiffman Building, a city landmark, was the 1902 birthplace of the legendary Tallulah Bankhead.

"I called him, too," Patrice continued. "Says he's never heard of Noel and has never hired a hooker."

"You believe him?"

She smiled. "I never trust guys. Particularly the lawyer ones. You think something's happened to this girl?"

"Possible. Her mom's an old friend. Says Noel has problems, but calling home isn't one of them. Hasn't heard from her for nearly two weeks."

"That's unusual?"

"Recently, anyway."

"But she's disappeared before?"

I nodded.

"Then she'll probably turn up."

"Let's hope."

The new Noel, the back-to-school Noel, might've turned up by now. At least she would have called. But had the old Noel taken over? The one that ran off to New Orleans with an older guy? I'd seen that all too often. People who had beat their demons, seemed to be getting back on the right track, only to fall in a ditch along the way. Why? Old habits, lack of character, fear, and self-loathing. Clichés I wasn't sure I believed. People do what people do. Sometimes rational explanations didn't fit. That was why AA was forever, no cure, one day at a time.

"You got this guy's info?" I asked.

"Right here." Patrice slid a piece of paper across the counter toward me. "I added addresses for Rosalee and Sin-Dee. I told Rosalee you might drop by."

"Thanks. I owe you."

"I'll remember that." Her smile faded. "There's more. Sin-Dee and Crystal dance at a strip club called High Rollers. Out off University. Owned by the ever-charming Rocco Scarcella."

I had heard the name but couldn't quite grab why out of my memory bank.

"What you need to know is that he's got his hand in every dirty deal in the state. Drugs, girls, you name it. Remember that health insurance scandal a year or so ago? Took down a couple of the docs over at Memorial Medical Center?"

That was where I had heard the name. The story had painted the above-the-fold front page of the *Huntsville Times* for months. "Who doesn't?"

"Rocco walked, but he was in it." Patrice caught my gaze. "A word of advice. Rocco's dangerous. If any of this leads his way, give him a wide berth."

CHAPTER 8

THURSDAY 8:43 A.M.

ALEJANDRO AWOKE WITH A QUICK INTAKE OF AIR, RELIEF FROM THE smothering sensation that gripped him. As if he had forgotten to breathe or had been holding his breath to avoid . . . what? Something or someone? An image began to form in his mind but then slipped away.

His head throbbed. Mouth dry and sticky. Complete darkness except for a faint glow that slid beneath what appeared to be a door. He lay in a fetal curl on a cold, hard floor, back against an equally cold wall. His breathing the only sound. As his eyes adjusted, the darkness softened. The vague image of a square, high-ceilinged room formed. It appeared empty until his gaze settled on someone huddled in a corner. He could make out no details.

"You awake?" The voice was female, Hispanic. *Carmelita.*

"Yeah." He began a mental inventory of his body. Everything hurt. The stiffness in his neck, shoulders, and legs resisted movement, but he pushed himself to a sitting position. His back now rested against the wall. His bare feet flattened against the floor. He patted his pockets, empty, wallet gone. He felt for his watch, also missing. Where was he? How did he get here? He remembered standing outside Eddie's trailer and then . . . Austin. *Shit.*

Alejandro touched his chest, locating an area of tenderness, things now coming together. They had darted him. When? How long had he been here? Why did Rocco sic his dogs on him?

He knew the answer to that one. He had fucked up. Or Eddie had, and he was being taken down with that *boca ruidosa.* The real question was: why was he still alive? Rocco didn't take prisoners, which meant that Alejandro and Carmelita were alive because Rocco needed something.

"What's going—?" she began.

"Sssh."

"But—"

"Quiet."

He started to get up, but as he shifted his weight, he felt another tender spot. Left butt cheek. He pressed his fingers over the area. Small, circular. An injection site. He knew the deal now. Had heard Austin and Lefty talking about it once. A dart with fentanyl would take anyone down, and an injection of a sedative would keep them down. Hours, even days, if need be.

Alejandro stood, legs wobbly. He shuffled toward the door, sliding a hand along the wall. Felt like painted cinder block. Recently painted. He could still detect a faint odor. He continued until he reached the door, where he pressed his ear, but heard nothing. The door was metal, solid, absolutely no play when he leaned into it. He traced its outline. No knob or handle, no hinges, no gaps along the jamb except the quarter inch near the floor. A bitch to crack. Where the hell was he?

He moved to where Carmelita sat and dropped to his knees in front of her. He reached up and curled one hand behind her head.

"Get away from me." She tried to pull away.

He grasped a handful of her hair and yanked her toward him, his cheek against hers. She struggled against him. He held her tightly, lips near her ear. "Don't move. Don't talk."

Carmelita pressed her palm against his chest firmly but didn't push him away.

"The room might be bugged."

"By who?" she whispered, her lips now close to his ear.

Good. She understood. He released his grip on her hair but kept his face against hers. "Whoever put us here. Assume they can hear everything."

She nodded. "Who are they?"

"Tell me what you remember."

Carmelita said things were spotty, only bits and pieces coming to her. She had been in the shower with Eddie. A man had ripped back the curtain and shot Eddie with a dart. Then did the same to her. That was all she remembered until she woke up here. Maybe a couple of hours ago. She couldn't be sure. She crawled around the room and discovered Alejandro sleeping. She tried to wake him but got nothing. So she waited.

"Where'd they shoot you?"

She pressed her fingers against her left shoulder. "Here."

"Any other sore spots?"

"Everywhere hurts. But, yeah. A spot on my right hip."

Alejandro nodded. "They darted us and then injected us with a sedative."

"Why?"

"Don't know."

"The same guy who fired the dart at me came in here," Carmelita said. "Maybe an hour ago."

"What'd he do?"

"Tossed me my clothes, shook you—but you were out—and left."

"He say anything?"

"Yeah. I asked him who he was, and he said, 'Shut the fuck up.'"

"What'd he look like?"

"Big guy. Muscles. Huge arms."

Austin.

"You know him?" she asked.

Alejandro spun around and sat next to her, back against the wall. "Maybe." He wasn't ready to tell her what was what yet. She might freak.

"What the hell does *maybe* mean?"

"It means maybe."

"You don't have to be an asshole."

"Just give me a minute to sort this out."

"I'm cold, I'm hungry, and I've got to pee," she said.

"Join the club."

They sat silently for a while, and then she whispered, "Why are they doing this?"

"Don't know."

"Where are we?"

"Don't know that, either."

"What do we do?"

"Wait."

CHAPTER 9

I DROPPED DOWN OFF ECHOLS HILL INTO DOWNTOWN HUNTSVILLE, parked on Franklin, and walked the half block to Weiss's office. When I reached the corner where Weiss's building stood, I settled beneath the canopy of a maple tree and tried Sin-Dee's number. Got the answering machine. Didn't leave a message. I then called Miranda. Told her I had talked to Claire last night and that Claire would call her this morning to set up an on-air interview. Get the story out there. Miranda cried. I said that wouldn't help, and besides, she didn't want to have puffy eyes on TV. She laughed. She needed to laugh.

Weiss's office occupied the entire top floor of a three-story, gray brick building on the southeast corner of the courthouse square. Gold lettering on the double glass entry doors indicated that Benjamin Weiss, Esq. was a senior partner of Weiss, Wolinsky, and Wolff, who were esquires, too. *What the hell is an esquire?*

The reception area was tasteful and expensive. Overstuffed maroon sofas, black marble-topped coffee tables, and light gray walls dotted with signed and numbered serigraphs. I recognized a Chagall and a Dalí. A single client sat on one of the sofas, clutching a briefcase to his midsection as if it were a life preserver. The fingers of his other hand fidgeted with the latch. He had that caught-in-headlights look. Probably looking at jail time or maybe a ball-crushing divorce.

At the reception desk, a stern-looking, middle-aged woman in a fitted navy blue suit, a white blouse buttoned to her neck, and thick-rimmed glasses chained around her neck greeted me with a forced smile. A nameplate indicated she was Ms. Rachel Brodsky.

After I requested to see her boss, she looked me up and down, a frown developing. I guessed she didn't like my jeans and black T-shirt. Probably really hated the jogging shoes. She most likely expected anyone who entered her world to have the decency to wear a suit. I did have on a sports coat. A nice one, I thought.

Ms. Brodsky asked, "Do you have an appointment?"

"I'm sure he'll want to talk with me. Only need a couple of minutes."

The annoyed wrinkle in her brow deepened. "Today's impossible. His schedule is quite full. I can make an appointment for another day." She flipped open a leather-bound appointment book.

"Today's better for me," I said, glancing at my watch. Nine fifteen. "Nine fifteen will be just fine."

"Listen, Mister . . . uh . . ."

"Walker, Dub Walker." I smiled.

Ms. Brodsky didn't. "You still need an appointment."

"Why don't you ask him?"

"What's this about?"

I detected a sliver of concern in her voice. "It's personal."

"I'm sorry. I can't interrupt him unless I know why. If you feel the need for such secrecy, you'll just have to make an appointment."

Time for a little dive-bombing. "It's about the hooker he hired last weekend. She's missing."

Ms. Brodsky's cool evaporated. She paled and for a second looked as if her brain had vapor locked. If nothing else, she was a pro and recovered quickly. "Just one moment." She stood and headed down a hallway to her right.

Two minutes later, I was before Benjamin Weiss, Esq. He wore a tan suit, a blue shirt with a white collar and cuffs, a red tie, a solid gold Rolex, and what appeared to be diamond-studded gold cuff links. His cologne was on the heavy side. Mr. Weiss obviously did well for himself. He was gracious, even though a smidge of apprehension lined his face.

"What can I do for you?" he asked, offering me a seat.

I sat. "I'm looking for a missing girl. A prostitute. Her last client was you."

"I'm afraid not."

I said nothing, letting him wonder what I knew, feeling the pressure rise.

Finally Weiss said, "This would be the girl I received a call about a little while ago? Some woman looking for her? Patrice something?"

"Nomberg," I said.

"That's it. I told her and I'll tell you, I don't know anything about this. And I'd never hire a whore."

I studied his face. No stress, no anxiety, no pursed lips, no forehead wrinkle. His gaze never wavered. Could be a good liar—he was a lawyer, after all—but he was clean and I knew it. Intuition? Experience? Either way, Weiss wasn't hiding anything. He was just confused.

"Who are you?" he asked.

"A friend of her mother's," I said.

Weiss seemed to relax. "I'm afraid I can't help you." He started to stand, but I waved him back down.

"Just a couple of questions if you don't mind."

He consulted the Rolex. "I have a client waiting."

"Do you know of anyone who would use your name? Your address?"

"What do you mean?"

"You live over on Adams, don't you?"

"Yes."

"The girl in question and a friend were sent to your house. Then disappeared."

I could almost see his mental wheels turning. Nothing's worse for an attorney than to become a criminal suspect. They, more than anyone, know the system can chew you up, and innocence or guilt makes little difference. "When was this?"

"Saturday before last. Appointment was around 11:00 p.m., I believe."

Weiss shook his head. "I was away that weekend. In Nashville for a meeting."

"Who knew that?"

"Lots of people. Everyone here in the office. My friends. My girlfriend. She was with me."

"She'll vouch for you?" I asked.

"She and about two hundred other people. I was speaking at a national ABA meeting." He rested his elbows on his desk. "I know where this is going. Yes, I was around people all the time. Either with my colleagues or my girlfriend." His eyes narrowed. "All the time."

"Anyone staying at your house while you were gone?" I asked.

"No. And it was locked and alarmed."

"No one has a key? The alarm code? Maid? Family?"

"No one."

I pulled Noel's photo from the envelope and handed it to Weiss. "Ever seen her before?"

"No. Never." His gaze lingered on the photo. "She's very pretty. And young."

"Nineteen," I said.

Weiss passed the photo back to me. "Too young for the work she does."

Ain't it so.

CHAPTER 10

THURSDAY 9:21 A.M.

ALEJANDRO SAT QUIETLY, THINKING THINGS THROUGH. CARMELITA paced around the room, saying that if someone didn't hurry she'd piss her pants. He suggested she squat in the corner. She told him to fuck off.

A bank of overhead fluorescent lights sprang to life, causing him to flinch. He could now see the room. Maybe twenty-feet square, cinderblock walls that were indeed painted a light tan, ten-foot ceiling, no windows. He stood as he heard the sound of approaching footsteps. Someone keyed the door and it swung open, revealing three men and two guns. Lefty and Austin had the guns. The other guy Alejandro didn't recognize.

Austin had that smirk. The same arrogant half grin he had every time he and Lefty delivered the wrapped bodies. Dragged them right out of the SUV, dumped them at Alejandro's feet, gave that smirk, and drove away. No "How you doing?" No "Can I help you load them in the pickup?" Like he and Eddie were scum, not worthy of their time.

"Step back," Austin said. "Against the wall."

Alejandro didn't move.

He waved the pistol at him. "You want to play hero, go ahead. I'd as soon shoot your sorry ass as stand here. Now, against the wall."

Not the time, not the place. Alejandro stepped back, propped a shoulder against the wall, and folded his arms over his chest.

Austin turned to Carmelita. "Come here."

She hesitated.

"Want me to drag you out?"

Alejandro nodded to her, then tilted his head toward the door. She took a step that way.

Austin grabbed her arm, tugged her through the door, and then closed and locked it. They brought her back in ten minutes and led him down a dimly lit hallway to a bathroom. Lefty watched, gun in hand, as Alejandro pissed and washed his hands and face.

When they returned him to the room, Alejandro saw two paper bags and two bottles of water on the floor.

Lefty said, "Eat up. Lights out in fifteen minutes."

"Who are you?" Carmelita asked. "Why are you doing this?"

The door slammed shut, and the lock engaged.

Ham and cheese on wheat and a package of chips were inside each bag. They ate in silence until Carmelita scooted close to him and whispered, "You figured this out yet?"

"Almost."

"Want to tell me?"

No, Alejandro didn't want to tell her, risk her going all hysterical, blowing his only hope of getting out of this. The truth was he would need her to pull off the plan that was roaming around in his head. Not a good plan, not one that was likely to work, but the only thing he could come up with. "Let me think on it."

They finished their sandwiches and half of the water, saving the rest for later, not sure when the men might return. As promised, the lights went out.

Alejandro moved close to her and spoke in a soft whisper. "Now, listen. Don't say a word. Don't react in any way."

She nodded.

"Are you strong?" he asked.

"What do you mean?"

"You aren't going to like this. Fact is, it's going to scare the hell out of you. Can you handle it? Do what's necessary?"

"Do I have a choice?"

Good answer. Just maybe this could work. "I know them. You know their boss."

"What?"

"Tommy Austin and Lefty Bruno. Very bad guys. Work for Rocco Scarcella." The dim light from beneath the door reflected off her eyes, now wide and moist. "They're going to kill us."

Carmelita tensed but didn't scream or panic but rather simply said, "Why do you think that?"

"It's what they do. Besides, I know them, and now you've seen their faces."

She let out a soft sound somewhere between a sigh and a moan. "Which means we can identify them."

"Only reason they haven't done us already is that they want something. Something we can provide."

"What? I don't know anything. I don't know who these people are or what . . ." Carmelita pulled back, and he could tell she was looking at him through the darkness. "Is it the bodies? The two Eddie was talking about?"

"That was his bullshit."

"Playing the big guy, huh? Trying to get my panties off? Like every other hard dick that comes in?"

But it worked this time, he wanted to say. She had swallowed it. Had shucked those panties right off and humped Eddie in the shower. Of course she didn't know that Eddie had told her the truth and that it was this truth that put them right here.

Alejandro knew what was coming. Rocco needed to know who else knew about the bodies. Did either of them talk? Rocco would do what was necessary, and it wouldn't be pretty. Then they would both die. Rocco was tidy that way.

Alejandro knew something else. This was his fault. He should have done Eddie himself, never mentioned a word to Rocco. Tell him

Eddie went back to Atlanta, back to his petty drug deals. *Fuck.*

"I don't think so," Carmelita said. "He wasn't lying."

"He lies all the time."

"Don't fuck with me. I saw truth in his eyes. And if he did it, you did it. He couldn't by himself. Doesn't have the *cojones*. You do."

The girl wasn't dumb. She knew people. Men, anyway. Came with the territory. Alejandro figured that listening to testosterone-stoked truths, half-truths, and outright lies night after night gave her a fairly accurate radar.

"It doesn't matter now," he said.

"The hell it doesn't. I'll tell them I had nothing to do with it. *Nada.* That I won't say a word."

"I'm sure they'll be thrilled to hear that. Right up until they gang rape you and stick a gun in your mouth."

Carmelita pulled completely away from him, crawled to a corner, and sat, locking her arms around her knees. "Fuck you."

He moved close to her. "I'm not the one you have to worry about. I'm your only hope."

"Right."

"You want to be a bitch, or you want out of this?"

CHAPTER 11

THE HEADQUARTERS OF THE HUNTSVILLE POLICE DEPARTMENT WAS housed in the North Precinct, a tan and brick building on Mastin Lake Road north of downtown. It sat across from the Lakewood Shopping Center and next to Lakewood Baptist Church. I walked beneath the pyramid-shaped roof that shaded the entry alcove and pushed through the glass doors.

Two uniformed officers stood just inside, talking, one sipping coffee from a paper cup. They nodded as I walked past.

Directly ahead, the duty officer sat behind a high counter. Metal detectors flanked him and guarded the two hallways into the building. He was forty or so, balding with a gut barely restrained by his wide duty belt, and a face devoid of expression. Bored was the look.

I told him the story and showed him Noel's photos.

Not overly enthusiastic about a missing hooker, he said, "They come in, turn a few tricks, and go back to whatever small town they escaped from. Find that life here ain't much different than where they were. Or they fall in love, fly off to la-la land. When she runs out of money, she'll be back." He gave me the standard form. "They always do."

He was a real poet. A philosopher. His concern was touching.

"This one might be a little different," I said.

He smirked. "Right." He scanned the photos. "How old?"

"Nineteen."

He handed the photos back. "Then she has the right to disappear."

"I believe she might have been kidnapped." That sounded lame, even to me.

"Why?"

I couldn't tell him I was running with a hunch. "Look. She's a responsible kid." I hoped this lie rolled out convincingly. "Wouldn't just take off. College kid. Hasn't been to class. Hasn't contacted her mother." I slid the pictures toward him. "Just put out a flyer on her. Maybe one of the patrol guys will see something. Couldn't hurt. Might save her life."

He nodded and scooped up the photos.

I filled out the form, while he made photocopies. The entire process took fifteen minutes and inspired zero confidence.

CHAPTER 12

ALEJANDRO SAT IN A METAL, STRAIGHT-BACKED CHAIR, TWO BRIGHT lights aimed at his face. Rocco stood near the far wall, hands stuffed into his pockets, Lefty beside him. Austin leaned on the opposite edge of the table, triceps all roped out, and stared at Alejandro.

"Let's have it," Austin said.

"Have what?" Alejandro tried to appear passive, unconcerned, while inside he wanted to run. Or fight.

"Who else knows?"

"Eddie."

"Besides him and the girl."

"No one." Alejandro looked toward Rocco. "You know that. How long I worked for you?"

Rocco shrugged.

"Three years. I ever done anything but what I was told? Ever opened my mouth about anything? Any of the shit I did? Any of the bodies I stuffed in the ground no questions asked?"

"That's all real nice." Austin leaned forward, so close that Alejandro felt his breath against his face. "We're talking about now. Right here, today. You're only as good as your last at bat, and yours don't look so good."

Alejandro smiled. "And yours does?"

Austin recoiled a bit, his chin coming up, head cocked. "What the hell does that mean?"

Good. Put him on the defense. "I had Eddie and the girl. Clean. In and out." He rubbed his neck. "Then you two clowns waltzed in and fucked it up."

"We didn't—"

"Rocco, tell these assholes I'm not as dumb as I look." Alejandro slid to the front of the chair, forearms on the table, bringing his face even closer to Austin's, staring directly into his eyes. "You guys act tough. Truth is, you could fuck up a one-car funeral. You turned a simple hit into all this." He waved a hand across the table.

Austin glared at him, working his jaw muscles.

"Without you guys," Alejandro continued, "Eddie and the girl would be gone. End of story. End of problem. Now?" He leaned back in the chair and opened his hands, palms up.

Austin moved away from the table and said, "Boss?"

Rocco sighed. "You see, Alejandro, this is much bigger than you think. I can't afford any loose ends." He came closer and turned off one of the lights. Alejandro could now see his face. No anger, just resignation. Not good news. "You brought Eddie into this, and he involved the girl. I have to assume that one of you told someone else. I have to know who that someone is."

"I didn't and you know it. Eddie and the girl didn't have time."

"Dancers talk. All the time and about everything."

"She didn't."

"Problem is, you don't know for sure. There's a difference."

"Ask Eddie. He'll tell you the same thing."

"I did," Austin said. He winked at Lefty. "He didn't have much to say."

Rocco glanced at Austin, irritation on his face, as if Austin had stepped out of line. He brought his gaze back to Alejandro as he retrieved a quarter from his pocket. Rocco flipped the coin above the table and when it landed slammed his open hand over it. "Heads or tails?"

Alejandro hesitated and then asked, "What's the bet?"

"Your life. Your freedom. Whatever. The point being . . . do you like those odds? Are you willing to bet your life on a fifty-fifty chance?"

"I'd rather not."

Rocco picked up the coin and returned it to his pocket. "Yet you're asking me to do exactly that. Either one of you talked or you didn't. Fifty-fifty."

Alejandro felt his stomach wind into a knot. He was a dead man unless he did something. He glanced at Austin and Lefty and then the door, gauging the distance. Could he take them both before one of them could get to his gun? Not likely.

Alejandro had known from the beginning that Rocco couldn't be trusted. Neither could Austin or Lefty. Knew that this could end badly for him. *That's life. La vida.* But if he went down, they would follow. *La venganza dulce.* Sweet revenge. Pain he could handle. Knowing that Rocco would pay for his sins was all he needed to get through what was coming.

Should he show his hole card now? Buy his way out of this? Not possible. To play that card he needed to be out. Free. He never planned on being trapped this way. Always thought he'd see trouble long before it arrived. Instead of exposing his play, he simply said, "Let me talk to Carmelita. See what she knows."

"I'll handle her," Rocco said. "She'll talk."

"But—"

"I'm sorry," Rocco said.

Austin and Lefty moved to each side of the room, guns in hand. They weren't that stupid. Maintaining a separation meant that Alejandro couldn't surprise them both, one always having the luxury of distance and line of sight. Able to snap off a round or two.

"Let's go," Lefty said.

Back at the room, Lefty unlocked the door and Austin shoved him inside. Carmelita looked up from where she sat, fear in her eyes.

"Come on," Lefty said to Carmelita.

Austin grabbed her arm and pulled her into the hallway.

After they left, Alejandro picked up his half-full water bottle and drained it, tossing the empty into one corner. He was fucked. Any doubts about whether Rocco intended to kill them or not were now gone. The question was: why hadn't he already done it? Didn't make sense. Keeping them alive was risky. Rocco didn't take risks. Always hedged his bets. Rocco liked ninety-nine to one, not fifty-fifty.

Rocco knew Alejandro hadn't told anyone. If he thought otherwise, Alejandro wouldn't have left that room with his face intact. Probably not his ribs or spleen, either. Rocco liked to dole out pain, and no pain meant that Rocco knew he was clean on this one. But Rocco needed something, and he would do what was necessary to get it. Meant things could still get ugly. The when, where, and how might be in question, but the end game wasn't. Unless Alejandro pulled off a miracle.

He looked around the room. Concrete walls, thick metal door, and a twelve-by-four inch A/C vent didn't offer much hope of escape. That left a surprise attack as his only option. He'd need Carmelita for that. Could she do it? Was she strong enough? Didn't matter. He'd make her help. Scare her into it. If she came back, that is.

CHAPTER 13

I PULLED INTO THE LOT AT SAMMY'S BLUES 'N' Q, BUT BEFORE I went inside I tried Sin-Dee's number again and again got her answering machine. This time I left a message with my cell number. I didn't tell her what I wanted, figuring she'd think I was a john, which meant she'd probably call back. I called Miranda and brought her up to date. I told her I'd call later but for her to plan on dinner at my place.

When I pushed through the screen door and went inside, T-Tommy was sitting at the bar, beer in hand. I'd called him when I left the HPD office and asked him to meet for lunch. We'd known each other since fourth grade. Played football at Huntsville High where T-Tommy was an all-state linebacker. Still acted like one most of the time. A sort of in-your-face kind of guy. Made him HPD's top homicide investigator.

I sat on a stool next to him. "How's it going?"

"Slow. Seems like lately people just don't want to kill one another."

"How you doing, Dub?" Sammy, the owner of the joint, asked as he slid a cold Corona toward me and then wiped the already clean bar with the towel he always kept draped over one shoulder.

"Mighty fine," I said. "You?"

Maybe seventy, Sammy was mostly bald and as tough as seasoned leather. Brian Kurtz had found out just how tough when he attacked Sammy in the alley behind the restaurant. He had knocked Sammy unconscious but not before Sammy bit a chunk out of his arm.

Today Sammy wore a crimson sweatshirt, sleeves removed at the shoulder hem, *Bama Football* in white letters across the front. Behind and above him his favorite picture of the Bear looked down as if giving us his blessing. Taken at Legion Field in Birmingham. Houndstooth hat on his head, rolled-up pages of lineups and plays in one fist, and a scowl on his face as he watched his boys get ready to massacre Tennessee again. Bear had signed it, *To Sammy Lange, the best BBQ man I know. Warm personal regards, Paul "Bear" Bryant.*

"Business's been good so I can't complain." Another swipe at the bar. "A pair of pulled-pork sandwiches?"

"That'll do," I said.

T-Tommy nodded.

I told T-Tommy about my visit from Miranda. About Noel and Crystal Robinson disappearing. About my visits to Weiss and the HPD.

"I know that Weiss guy. Nice fella. You don't think he had anything to do with these girls' disappearing, do you?"

I shook my head.

"You're thinking someone used his name and address to lure the girls there?"

"That's assuming the girls are really missing. Maybe they just took off."

T-Tommy grunted. He didn't believe that, either. Someone used Weiss's name. Someone got the girls into a quiet neighborhood where people turn in early. And no one had seen them since then. Didn't bode well. When things felt bad, they usually were.

"My money's on an abduction," T-Tommy said.

"For her mother's sake, I hope you're wrong," I said.

Sammy's head cook, Willie Tucker, a huge black man, shorter and a good fifty pounds heavier than T-Tommy, came from the kitchen with two plates, each with a sandwich and a mound of Sammy's famous peanut coleslaw.

"The pork cooked up real nice today," Willie said.

I took a bite. "Great, Willie. As usual."

He flashed his big grin. "Told you."

"Only needs one thing." I reached into my jacket pocket and pulled out the small bottle of Tabasco I always carried. I shook a generous amount on my sandwich. Another bite. "Perfect."

Willie laughed. "It's your chitlins." He headed back toward the kitchen, whistling.

"So how you going to handle this?" T-Tommy asked. "Finding

the girls?"

"I've been trying to reach this Sin-Dee Parker. Doesn't answer her phone. Thought I'd drop by and knock on her door. Then visit Rosalee Kennedy."

T-Tommy nodded. "Mind if I tag along?"

"Sure. So long as the taxpayers don't mind you goofing off."

"Got nothing else to do." He shook his head. "Must be the economy. Nobody can afford alcohol. No alcohol, no murder."

"Sorry you're bored."

T-Tommy spoke through a mouthful of food. "You say these girls danced out at Rocco Scarcella's place?"

"That's right. I might give him a visit, too."

"Hmmm."

"What is it?"

"I take it you don't know Rocco."

"Just what I read in the paper about that insurance fraud case."

"Tip of the iceberg. A real scumbag. Dirty to his DNA." He gulped some beer. "Better watch your six if he's in this."

"Think he could be?"

"Girls danced there. Girls disappeared. That's not very many dots to connect."

CHAPTER 14

THURSDAY 12:18 P.M.

CARMELITA WAS GONE FOR AN HOUR. THE DOOR OPENED, AND SOMEONE shoved her into the room. She stumbled and fell to her knees. Completely naked. Her wadded clothing came through the door, followed by her shoes, and the door closed with a clang.

Carmelita buried her face in her hands and sobbed, making no attempt to cover herself.

Alejandro dug through her clothing, found her shirt, and draped it around her shoulders. He sat next to her. "You okay? Did they . . . ?"

"Did they what?" She jerked upright onto her haunches and looked at him, her eyes flashing black. She pulled her shirt across her breasts. "Did they touch me?"

Alejandro brushed a strand of hair from her face. She pulled away.

"Tell me," he said.

She swallowed hard. "They made me strip and stand in front of them while they asked questions." She stood, stepped into her panties, and then her jeans.

"Nothing else?"

"Yeah, there was something else." Carmelita buttoned her shirt. "But standing there naked like some *puta* was enough."

Alejandro looked up at her. "You do that every night."

She glared at him. "Fuck you."

"You do."

Carmelita kicked him in the ribs. Hard. He grunted, and when she launched another kick, he grabbed her ankle, toppling her to the floor. She kicked at him with her other foot, but he blocked it, rolled on top of her, and pinned her.

"Get off me, you asshole."

"Quit kicking."

She grabbed a handful of his hair and tried to bite his ear, but he turned his head away. Her fist landed against his jaw.

Alejandro grabbed her throat and squeezed tightly. "Don't do that."

Carmelita hit him again, high on the side of his head, and tried to wiggle from beneath him, but he held her with his legs on either side. He increased the pressure on her throat. Her face purpled, and she clutched at his fingers, attempting to pry them from her neck.

"Quit fighting and I'll let go."

She relaxed, so he released his grip and rolled off her. She sat up, gasping for air, and moved away from him, massaging her throat.

"What was that all about?" Alejandro asked.

"Fuck you, you arrogant asshole. You're like all of them. Think because I'm a dancer I'm just a piece of meat. I take my clothes off when I want to. On my terms. Not because some fat prick with a couple of thugs says so."

"Look, I'm sorry. I didn't—"

"Didn't what?" Even in the dim light he could see tears flowing down her cheeks. "Didn't look at me as a person? Didn't think my feelings mattered?" Carmelita wiped her nose with the back of one hand.

It was true. Alejandro hadn't considered her as anything more than a stripper. A tramp who'd fuck a worm like Eddie for a few bucks. But now, here she sat, angry tears staining her face, defending herself with a couple of pretty good shots. He rubbed his ribs, then scooted toward her. She backed into the corner, but he moved near her, touching her arm.

"I'm sorry. I didn't think . . . I didn't mean to . . ." His voice trailed off. He couldn't find the words, was never very good at apologies.

They sat quietly for a moment, the only sounds a sniff or two from Carmelita, until she said, "There's more." When he didn't say anything, she continued. "They made me touch myself. Made me sit in a chair right there in front of them."

"What?"

"I refused until the muscle-headed one stuck a gun in my ear."

"What'd you do?"

"What they wanted. I gave them a show. That's one thing I'm good at." She whimpered, and Alejandro pulled her to him. "They laughed. Called me names." She placed her cheek against his chest and let it out. He could feel her tears soaking through his shirt.

He stroked her hair. "I'm sorry."

They moved against each other and stretched out on the floor. He held her tightly as she cried. They lay entwined for several minutes, her sobs finally subsiding.

"Thank you," she whispered.

Alejandro kissed the top of her head and then rolled away from her. They both swung around and sat against the wall, her head lolled against his shoulder.

"I'm scared," she said.

"Me, too."

Carmelita laughed. "Great. We're truly screwed."

"Not yet."

"Sure feels that way."

"What did you tell them? In the other room?"

"That I don't know anything. That I didn't tell anyone what Eddie told me. That I didn't believe a goddamn thing he said. That he was just some punk, trying to get laid."

Good answers. "Did they believe you?"

She sighed. "Does it matter? They're going to kill us, anyway."

"Unless we do something drastic."

"Like what? Jackhammer through a wall?" Her voice carried fatigue and resignation.

"There are other ways. Won't be easy. *Muy peligroso.* Not good odds. But what I have in mind could work."

Carmelita looked him in the eye. "The motherfuckers made me strip naked, made me finger myself. I'll do whatever I have to."

The pain in his ribs told him she just might be able to do her part. This could work after all.

CHAPTER 15

THURSDAY 1:08 P.M.

By the time we reached Quail Ridge, a cluster of upscale condos a couple of miles from downtown, the sun was bright and the day warm. Rumor had it that more rain was on the way, but you wouldn't suspect that from the few billowy clouds that splotched the clear blue sky.

I wheeled my Porsche up the twisting drive, which was flanked by prefab waterfalls that tumbled over prefab boulders, islands of bright flowers, and sprinklers that hissed rainbows into the air. Runoff water striped the asphalt.

"Sin-Dee seems to be doing okay for herself," I said.

"A Grover or so a night pays a bunch of rent," T-Tommy said.

Quail Ridge consisted of a dozen gray clapboard two-story eight-plexes, four units up and four down. A dyslexic numbering system led to a couple of laps through the development before we finally stumbled on number 25, a lower left corner unit. Sin-Dee's little slice of the American Dream.

I pulled into a parking slot. Her condo appeared quiet, curtains drawn, no signs of life. Leaning on the buzzer and rapping on the dark green door didn't stir up anything inside.

"Can I help you?" The voice carried the deep rasp of alcohol and cigarettes.

I turned to see a woman standing on the porch of the next-door unit. Middle-aged, with a sun-leathered face that carried a hard demeanor, she held a drink in one hand and clasped the lapels of a silk Japanese kimono to her neck with the other. A smoldering cigarette dangled from her mouth.

"We're looking for Sin-Dee Parker," I said.

"Who are you?"

"I'm Dub Walker." I nodded toward T-Tommy. "This is Investigator Tortelli."

She smirked and looked T-Tommy up and down. "Well, I just bet your parents are real proud."

I couldn't prevent the smile that followed. "Look, Miss . . . uh . . ."

The woman stared at me for a moment. "Name's Martha. Martha Godwyn. What do you want with Sin-Dee?"

"Need to ask her a couple of questions about her roommate."

An ash tumbled down the front of her kimono, but she ignored it. "Which one? Crystal or the new one?"

"Noel Edwards."

"Yeah. The new one. Only lived here a couple of months."

"I take it you know her, then?" I asked.

Martha shrugged. "Seen her around."

"When was the last time?" T-Tommy asked.

She eyed him through the smoke that swirled around her face. "Can't say. They come; they go. All hours."

"You know where Sin-Dee might be?" I asked.

"In there." Martha nodded toward Sin-Dee's door. "She just don't answer at this hour. Works nights. Heard her partying until about four this morning. She'll be up and around soon."

T-Tommy stepped off the porch. The gravel around the flanking shrubs crunched beneath his weight. He moved close to the window, cupped one hand around his eyes, and peered through a narrow gap in the curtain. "She's there. On the sofa." He rapped on the window. "She ain't moving."

I turned to Martha. "Where's the manager's office?"

Another ash fell. "Atlanta. Absentee owners. That's why we can't get a goddamn thing fixed around here."

From what I'd seen, this place was spotless. I suspected that Martha had pretty high standards. For everything but herself. Drinkers tend to complain a lot. "How well do you know Sin-Dee?"

"Me and Clark know her a little."

"Clark?"

"My husband. Works over at the Cadillac dealer."

"I see."

"She gave me this robe, though." Martha flicked an ash from one sleeve. "I think maybe one of her johns gave it to her."

"It's very pretty." I glanced at Sin-Dee's door. "You wouldn't happen to have a key to her place, would you?"

She shook her head and blew a stream of smoke up and to her left.

"We should check on her," I said.

T-Tommy slipped a credit card from his wallet, wedged it into the gap between the door and the jamb, and began working the lock.

Martha tugged a pack of Kools from the kimono's pocket, shook one up, and clinched it between her teeth. She lit it with the remnant of the one she had been smoking, then dropped the dead soldier to her porch and crushed it beneath a sandal. "Think that's a good idea? Breaking in?"

"Not breaking in if she could be ill," T-Tommy said. "Or dead."

"You can come in with us if you want," I said.

Martha took another long pull from her smoke but didn't move.

In less than a minute T-Tommy had the door open.

Sin-Dee lay on her stomach, one arm dangling to the floor, face turned toward me. Her mouth hung slack, and her eyes were cracked a bit, showing a thin strip of white. An empty wine bottle and a mirror with a hefty mound of white powder sat on a glass coffee table. As I approached, I could see she was breathing. No signs of trauma. She was probably attractive on normal days. Not today. Then again, maybe this was a normal day for her.

I nudged her but got no response. I gave her shoulder a shake.

She grunted and released a stuttering sigh.

"Sin-Dee?" I shook her again.

Her eyes fluttered open. She looked up, confusion on her face.

"It's okay," I said. "We're friends."

A deep cough racked her as she struggled to a sitting position, wiping drool from her mouth. "Who are you?" Her voice was thick.

"I'm Dub. This is Investigator Tortelli."

Sin-Dee blinked and looked around. "How did you get in here?" She tried to focus on Martha, who stood in the doorway.

"We didn't damage anything," I said. "We thought you might be sick."

She massaged her temples. "What time is it?"

"Nearly one thirty."

"Morning?"

I smiled. "Afternoon."

"You got any coffee?" T-Tommy asked.

Sin-Dee pointed toward the kitchen, and he headed that way.

She sank back on the sofa. "What do you want?"

I sat down next to her. "We're looking for Noel."

"Haven't seen her or Crystal for . . . I don't know . . . a couple of weeks or so."

"Don't you think that's a little unusual?"

She shrugged.

T-Tommy reappeared with a cup of coffee and passed it to Sin-Dee. "It's instant. Not exactly steaming. I made it with hot tap water."

Sin-Dee took several sips. "Who are you guys?"

I gave her our names again.

She looked at T-Tommy. "You a cop?"

"HPD."

"I didn't do anything." Then she seemed to notice the pile of cocaine on the table for the first time. Her eyes widened.

"It's okay," I said. "We won't roll on you. We're only looking for Noel."

"Why?"

"Her mother's worried about her. Asked if I'd try to find her. Apparently no one's seen her for a couple of weeks."

Sin-Dee took another sip of coffee. "Look, Crystal does this all the time. Girl's got a knack for picking a guy that'll pay her thousands and take her away for a week or two. Hawaii, Europe. Greece for a month once. She has a gift."

"You think she and Noel are on one of these trips?"

"I did. Except her mother kept calling, looking for her. Then I thought maybe she might be in trouble or something."

"You didn't call the police?"

"Like they would help." She glanced at T-Tommy. "Sorry."

"No problem," he said.

"They went to meet some guy. A double." Sin-Dee drank some more coffee. "I think some place over on Adams. A hot-shit attorney. Was going to pay them double the usual. That's all I know."

"They drive themselves?"

She nodded.

"What kind of car?"

"They took Crystal's. A white Lexus."

"You know where her car is now?"

"I'm not her garage attendant." Sin-Dee set down her coffee cup, then pushed her blonde hair back. I waited her out. "Maybe they took off in it."

"How old are you?" I asked.

"I'm legal. The rest don't count."

Maybe twenty, I thought. Already with a hard-on for the world. Don't fight it; go with it. "Did they have any other dates set up for that night?"

"Not that I know."

I stood and walked around the room, noticing that Martha was no longer at the door. Probably needed to refresh her drink.

The condo was tasteful, with expensive furnishings, a stone fireplace, plush white carpeting, and, like Weiss's office, numbered and signed serigraphs on the wall. All forms of prostitution paid well, I guessed. At least Noel had had a nice place to hang. Not Patrice's place nice but nice.

"Where'd Noel stay?" I asked.

Sin-Dee gave me a sideways look, sniffed, and dragged the back of her hand across her nose. "Upstairs."

I glanced at the oak stairway. "Mind if I take a look?"

"Why?"

"Maybe find something that'll lead us to her." I attempted a benign smile.

Sin-Dee picked up the coffee cup and started to take a sip, then realized it was empty. She handed it to T-Tommy as if she expected more. "Sure. Go ahead. Second room on the left."

T-Tommy mixed another cup of instant and passed it to Sin-Dee before he and I climbed the stairs.

The room was clean, nothing out of place, bed made, no clothes lying around. A jewelry box and two perfume bottles sat on top of a three-drawer chest. A gold necklace and two brightly colored scarves hung from the corner of a framed mirror.

T-Tommy rummaged through the drawers, while I slid back the mirrored closet door. Noel had few clothes, but they were neatly hung. Several pairs of shoes were arranged on the floor. A New York Yankees baseball cap perched on the upper shelf.

"Nothing here," T-Tommy said as he closed the last drawer.

I stood in the middle of the room and looked around. *Where are you, Noel?* I got no answer. "Let's go."

As I followed T-Tommy down the stairs, I saw Sin-Dee leaning over the coffee table and heard the sound of her snorting the coke. *Hair of the dog.*

She looked up. "You guys want some?"

"Not my drug of choice," I said.

Sin-Dee nodded toward the mirror. "I get it for practically nothing. " She massaged her nose with the heel of her hand. "I blow a couple of guys once a week, and they give me the blow." She laughed. "That's funny. Get it? A blow for some blow."

We left.

CHAPTER 16

ROSALEE KENNEDY LIVED IN THE HIGH-DOLLAR ENCLAVE OF Promontory Point that draped over the rolling hills along the eastern edge of Jones Valley just south of Monte Sano Mountain. Most of the seven-figure homes bore an antebellum feel with front columns, shutter-flanked windows, and perfectly manicured lawns. A broad circular drive led us to Rosalee's abode, a columned, two-story affair with views across the valley.

Heavy wooden double doors parted as we got out of the car. A slab of beef stepped out. Black. Shaved head. No neck. Barrel chest. Single gold earring. No smile.

"Miss Rosalee don't see no one without an appointment," he said after we asked for her. I told him it'd only take a couple of minutes, but he didn't budge, saying no appointment meant no way.

T-Tommy flipped open his badge.

The slab didn't flinch, but his brow furrowed. "Miss Rosalee won't see no cops."

"Just a few questions."

"About what?"

"We're looking for a girl," T-Tommy said. "Works for Rosalee. Name's Noel."

"What about her?"

"Seen her lately?"

"Not since she skipped. A couple of weeks ago."

"Skipped?" I asked.

"She and Crystal. That girl's a real flake. Crystal, not Noel. Fact is, I like Noel."

"So, you know Noel?"

He nodded. "Seen her a couple of times. When she and Crystal drop by."

"Chat with her?"

"Yeah. Seems to be in a good place. Know what I mean? Got it screwed on real tight."

I didn't mention that her mother saw it differently. "Any idea where they might have run off to?"

"No. Crystal does this shit all the time. Why you looking?"

I explained that Noel's mother was concerned.

The block of muscle grunted but didn't comment.

"What's your name?" T-Tommy asked.

"Max."

"Well, Max, we don't want to cause Rosalee any trouble. We're just looking for a missing girl."

He rotated his neck as if working out a kink.

"Maybe ask her if she'll talk to us?"

"Hang here. I'll see if Rosalee's in the mood." Max walked inside and returned in a couple of minutes. He led us into a comfortable, wood-paneled room with a stone fireplace and big sofas. He offered us a drink. We declined.

"Welcome," Rosalee said as she came into the room.

Not what I expected. Maybe forty tops, curly red hair piled on her head, pale skin, and a diamond nose stud. She wore designer jeans and a dark green open-collar silk shirt. A pear-shaped diamond hung from a gold chain and nestled in generous cleavage. We introduced ourselves and sat down.

"Max tells me you're looking for Noel," she said, getting right to it.

"That's correct. We hoped you could help us."

"Don't know what I can tell you."

"Crystal and Noel work for you, don't they?"

She eyed T-Tommy. "Can't say."

"We know you run girls. Everyone knows. Not a big secret." I nodded toward T-Tommy. "He ain't vice, and we ain't overly concerned about how you make a living. We do care about finding Noel."

Rosalee hesitated and then said, "Yeah, they do. And when you find Noel give her a kick in the ass for me. I expect this crap from Crystal, but I thought Noel was different."

"We hear Crystal's done this before."

"All the goddamn time. She makes a ton of money. Can up sell better than anyone. Has a knack for squeezing the lemon. Otherwise I'd have fired her ass a long time ago."

"Any idea where they might be?"

"Timbuktu or Kalamazoo. Take your pick. I'd bet she hauled Noel off on one of her adventures."

I nodded.

"Don't worry. They'll be back. Dude'll get tired of them or run out of money."

"Crystal work for anyone else or just you?"

"Just me. She does dance at High Rollers from time to time."

"I take it you know Rocco Scarcella?" I asked.

Her gaze darted away, back again. "Everybody knows Rocco."

"You have any kind of arrangement with him?"

"No."

"Just that some of your girls work there?" I said.

"Only Crystal. As I said, she has a mind of her own."

"I understand Noel dances there, too."

"Maybe once or twice. Not a regular, though."

"You and Rocco friends?" T-Tommy asked.

Rosalee laughed. "Rocco doesn't have friends."

"Why's that?"

"He likes to put his fat fingers into everything."

"Like your business?" I said.

"I don't have any partners, if that's what you mean."

"So none of your money finds its way into his pocket?" I asked.

"That's not how my business works." Her pale blue eyes seemed to dance and deepen in color, and a smile lifted a corner of her mouth. "Men usually give me the money." She laughed again. "I supply the pussy, and they pay for all this." She waved a hand.

I liked her. Didn't yet know why, but I did. "Rocco doesn't get a cut?"

She shook her head. "Not a chance."

I stood. "If you hear from Noel or Crystal, could you give us a call?"

"Absolutely."

I wrote down my numbers, home and cell. We thanked her and made our exit. As I twisted the car back down the hill, I said, "Bet she buys protection from Rocco."

T-Tommy grunted. "And Rosalee gets his political muscle in the deal. Which is a lot of rhythm."

"At HPD?"

"Rumor has it."

I accelerated the Porsche through its gears as we climbed over the hill and out of Jones Valley. "Wonder who."

"Someone up the food chain a bit. That's usually how it works, ain't it?"

CHAPTER 17

MIRANDA, CLAIRE, T-TOMMY, AND I SAT IN MY LIVING ROOM AND watched the prerecorded broadcast of the interview Claire and Miranda had filmed this afternoon. A tearjerker. Miranda pleaded for Noel to call if she could and if she couldn't, or wouldn't, for someone, anyone, to call and tell her where she could find her daughter. It was punctuated with several photos of Noel. Powerful stuff.

It was obvious that watching herself on TV, begging for her daughter's return, tweaked Miranda. She said she needed to lie down, so I took her to the spare bedroom and closed the door, leaving her to her thoughts.

Claire and I then settled on the deck with glasses of wine, while T-Tommy made a pot of his famous Bolognese sauce. We asked if we could help, knowing the answer. He shooed us outside.

Kramden and Norton, my two pet crows, showed up, begging for a handout. Not really pets. I had rescued them from a nest after their mother disappeared and nursed them to health. Once they could fly, I turned them loose. Now they roamed all over the city but still showed up on a daily basis. Often bringing me shiny presents—bits of metal, rings, pens, anything they could steal or scavenge. Mostly they came for food. And to annoy me. I dumped a handful of corn from the bag of kernels I kept in the kitchen into a bowl, took it out into the yard, and let them fight over it.

"What do you think?" Claire asked when I sat down across from her. "About Noel?"

"I think it won't be pretty." I took a sip of wine and looked out over the valley. The setting sun painted the streaky clouds near the horizon a deep orange. They looked like torn streamers. A squadron of chimney swifts performed aerobatic maneuvers as they fed on an invisible cloud of bugs, their wings catching the fading rays of the sun. "Seems like it's always that way."

We sat quietly, each of us inside our own thoughts. That was one of the many things I loved about Claire. We didn't need to talk or entertain each other. We just couldn't share the same roof. We learned that, survived it, and moved on. Right now I liked where we were. I knew she did, too.

I thought about Noel. Maybe she did simply run off. Atlanta. New Orleans. The West Coast. Without taking her stuff? Didn't settle well. I pictured her raped, tortured, murdered, and stuffed into a car trunk or tossed into a ditch. Or being held in a secluded dungeon by some drooling psychopath. Sometimes I hated how I knew so much about the bad guys. About what they could do. The thought that we might never find her did a couple of laps in my head, too. Like my sister, Jill.

We never found her. I pictured the parking lot where a single shoe and her purse, the flotsam of her abduction, laid on the rain-slicked asphalt. I pictured my parents slowly dying before a drunk slammed into their car, taking them both. I pictured Miranda descending into that same desperate spiral that nearly choked the life out of me. The only thing worse than knowing was not knowing.

T-Tommy gave us a five-minute warning, so I woke up Miranda and opened two bottles of Biale Black Chicken Zin. When we gathered at the deck table, T-Tommy served up plates, and I poured wine. The food was great, and the wine helped lighten the mood. Soon even Miranda was laughing. But the black cloud of Noel was never far away, and inevitably the talk turned to her.

I gave Miranda the details of our visits to Sin-Dee and Rosalee Kennedy. She took it as progress, but I felt like the day had been a waste. I didn't tell her that, leaving her this sliver of comfort. Truth was, we had nothing that would lead us to Noel. T-Tommy offered that at least we knew where she wasn't, and that was something. I couldn't argue with that logic, but I still felt like we were buried to our hubcaps in mud.

"What does your gut tell you?" Miranda asked. "Is Noel okay?"

Should I lie? Give her the usual clichés? Should I tell her the truth? What I truly felt? What my experience told me the end game would be? I did neither. I said, "I don't know."

Miranda sighed. Her fingers trembled as she cupped her wineglass close to her chest. "When I went to lie down earlier, all the ugly images rose up in my head. She's hurt. She's sick. She's captured and locked away somewhere. I never thought I'd pray for her to relapse." She looked at me. Pain radiated from her face like an open flame. "That's what we're hoping for, isn't it? That she's strung out and shacked up?"

There it was. Her pain and fear had driven her right to the heart of it. Better that Noel stumbled and fell and ended up humping another drug addict than something worse.

"Maybe that's exactly where she is," I said. "Wouldn't be the first time, and history does repeat."

Miranda nodded and sniffed back tears. "What now?"

"Later tonight T-Tommy and I are going to visit High Rollers and see what Rocco Scarcella knows."

"Later?" Miranda asked. "It's already late."

"For you," T-Tommy said. "Rocco's a night crawler. His midnight is your noon."

"You guys just want the lap dances," Claire said.

"I like yours better."

She rolled her eyes. "You wish."

Yes, I did.

CHAPTER 18

T-TOMMY AND I ARRIVED AT HIGH ROLLERS A SHADE PAST MIDNIGHT. The twenty-foot-high windowless metal building sat near the county line just off West University. Flanked by a liquor store and a fireworks stand, it looked more like a warehouse than a den of sin. Except for the age-faded neon High Rollers sign, that is. The *G* was dead, and the *O* flickered as if taking its final breaths. Ten-foot-high painted images of nearly nude women, one blonde, one brunette, each snaking around a stripper's pole, bracketed the neon lettering. Not exactly works of art, but you couldn't miss them, so I guessed it worked.

Beneath the sign, a black canvas awning shaded the entry door. Two twentysomething guys, each familiar with the gym and sporting permanent flexes beneath black High Rollers T-shirts, guarded the entrance. One of them held the door open for us and mumbled something I couldn't hear over the music that spilled out.

Just inside, a young woman sat behind a counter. Her halter top hid little, and there was a lot to hide. She stopped texting on her cell phone long enough to extend a palm toward us. We paid the twenty-dollar cover charge and entered the main room, where the music thumped and the girls humped and gyrated as bills were stuffed beneath G-strings. A drunk with an erection was easily separated from his cash.

While some strip joints were classier with centerfold girls, comfy banquets, gourmet food, and higher dollar liquor and others were skanky, even downright skin-crawling filthy, they were mostly the same. Girls twisted around poles for lonely, horny dudes and collected cash by the fistful.

High Rollers leaned toward the skanky end of the spectrum. The air smelled of booze and testosterone. Though some of the girls were attractive, most had been beaten down by the stripper life.

High Rollers hadn't burned much cash in the decorating department. It looked as much like a warehouse on the inside as it did on the outside: high ceilings crisscrossed with exposed metal beams and conduits; neon beer signs slapped on the walls; ceiling lights that swiveled, slicing red, green, and yellow beams across the crowd; a single long bar to our left; and a main stage straight ahead where two girls, G-strings only, performed a mock lesbian act. Four-tops filled the remainder of the room, most with lap dances under way.

God bless America.

A single flight of stairs led to a small balcony and a square room that seemed to hover near the ceiling above and to the left of the main stage. Probably Rocco's office. Bands of light slipped through the blinds that blocked a large picture window, which, if open, would allow a view over the entire floor. Sort of like God looking down on his people.

T-Tommy and I hung at the bar, while Sean, one of the bartenders, went to see if Rocco was "available." His word.

I took an inventory of the room. Maybe two hundred customers, twenty or so dancers, and a dozen waitresses. Across the way were the private rooms. I knew this because there was a sign above the door that read, VIP Lounges—Private. I was observant that way. I suspected that for the VIPs anything in the realm of sex, drugs, and rock and roll was available. For a price. Looked like Rocco did all right for himself.

Sean returned and led us upstairs to Rocco's office. A man, all neck and chest, dark hair, darker eyes, no smile, stood next to the entrance and swung the door open for us.

Rocco was short, round, combed-over, and wore a white shirt with a pulled down brown tie, thin end two inches longer than the wide one. Rosalee was right. He did have fat fingers.

The office was large as was Rocco's desk. The top was clean, no papers, no photos, only a phone and a lamp. The wall behind him held framed photos of two topless women. I doubted they were his family, probably his favorite dancers, but you just never knew about things like that in this world of sin and sleaze. Still, I saw little family resemblance.

Smoke from the cigar Rocco crushed between his teeth circled his head as he motioned for us to sit, not bothering to get up himself.

"Thanks for seeing us, Mr. Scarcella. I'm Dub Walker, and this is Tommy Tortelli."

"What can I do for the law this evening, Investigator Tortelli?" He smirked.

"Just a couple of questions," T-Tommy said.

"We're looking for a girl," I said. "Noel Edwards. You know her?"

Rocco's gaze settled on me. "Maybe."

"What about Crystal Robinson?"

His eyes narrowed, and he clamped down on his cigar. "What's this about?"

"I understand they dance here. We're looking for Noel."

"Why?"

"Her mother hasn't heard from her. Couple of weeks. She's worried."

"She hire you to find her?"

"She asked if I'd look into it."

He shifted the cigar to the other side of his mouth. "You think I can help you?"

"Word is you're the man that knows everyone and everything, and since Crystal and Noel dance here, we thought you might know where they are."

"They're both missing," T-Tommy said.

Rocco hesitated as if working on what to say. "Yeah. Crystal dances here. No regular schedule. Not very reliable but with a body like hers . . ." He turned his palms up.

"Write her own ticket?" I asked.

"You bet. She calls when she wants to work, and I make room for her. My customers love her."

"And Noel?"

"Been here a couple of times. With Crystal. Definitely not a regular dancer."

"When's the last time they were here?" I asked.

"Three, four weeks ago."

"Any idea where they might be?"

"None. Might try their roommate. Sin-Dee Parker. Lives at—"

"We talked to her," I said.

He smiled and spread his hands on the desk. "Not much help, was she?"

I shook my head.

"Coke whore. Brain-dead for years."

"She ever dance here?"

"Year ago. Talk about unreliable. She'd show up, just couldn't stand up most of the time. Can't run a business that way."

I handed him a card with my cell number on it. "If you hear from Crystal or Noel, I'd appreciate a call."

Rocco took the card. "You can count on it."

I stood and looked down at him. "Any other of your girls missing?"

"They come; they go." He offered a fleshy smile. One of those inside-joke-man-to-man deals. "They're dancers and whores."

Translation: meat. Furniture. Consumable commodity. I wanted to hit him square in his fat lips.

"Sorry I couldn't help," Rocco said. He pulled open a desk drawer, came out with a couple of business cards, and gave them to me. "Lap dances. On the house."

We left.

Rocco picked up the phone and punched in a number.

Lefty answered after one ring.

"I just had a couple of guys in here. Investigator Tortelli. HPD. Him I know. The other guy's Dub Walker. See what you can find out."

CHAPTER 19

THE SEVERELY CHEWED ARM WAS MOSTLY BONE, THE FLESH STRIPPED away by predators. The barely attached hand had fared a little better, two fingers missing, the others gnawed and cracked, remnants of bright red nail polish still visible. No sign of any other remains.

T-Tommy stood in a small clearing near the edge of a heavily wooded area, which was sandwiched between an old cemetery and a rarely used county road. He watched as two coroner's technicians prepared to wrap the arm in plastic sheeting for transport to the Department of Forensic Sciences. He hated bodies, especially those that were damaged, decayed, hacked, or chewed on. And to think that just yesterday he had lamented the fact that he had no murders to investigate. Should've kept his mouth shut.

"Anything else?" T-Tommy asked.

Head criminalist Sidau Yamaguchi looked up, shading his eyes from the morning sun that stabbed through the trees. "This is all so far. I'd suspect the rest of the corpse isn't far away."

"Who found it?"

Sidau spun on his haunches and pointed through the trees to where a man and a boy stood at the edge of the cemetery next to an off-kilter tombstone. The boy looked about ten. They were talking with Derrick Stone, one of HPD's uniformed officers. T-Tommy headed their way.

Stone introduced him to Bill Jenkins and his son Robbie. The older Jenkins told him what had happened. As he spoke, Robbie leaned against his father, who clasped a protective hand on the boy's shoulder. They had been out hiking. Nothing unusual, a beautiful day, and then Robbie spotted the arm.

"You hike here often?" T-Tommy asked.

"Sometimes," Jenkins replied. "We have several trails we follow. Really like a couple over near Paint Rock, don't we, sport?" He ruffled the boy's hair.

Robbie gave a slight nod but kept his gaze on the ground.

"We live near here and decided to stay close to home today since Robbie has a birthday party to go to at noon. We were headed home when we found this."

T-Tommy looked at the boy. Tear trails marked his cheeks. *I don't like this, either, son.* "And the guns?" He motioned toward two shotguns that leaned against a nearby tree. Looked like a double-barreled 12-gauge and a smaller pump. Probably a 20-gauge.

"We always take them. Find some old stumps, things like that, for target practice. Teaching Robbie how to handle his new gun. Get ready for next hunting season." Jenkins squeezed the boy's shoulder. "It'll be his first."

"You a good shot?" T-Tommy asked Robbie.

Robbie rolled a sneakered foot up on one side, shrugged, and looked at T-Tommy. "Pretty good."

T-Tommy smiled and then faced the father. "See anyone else out here this morning?"

"Not a soul," Jenkins said.

"You didn't move or touch anything, did you?"

"No. We watch *CSI*. We know what to do, don't we?"

This time the boy managed a weak smile.

"Investigator Tortelli?"

The shout came from his left. He turned and saw a uniformed officer emerge from the trees and motion to him.

"You better take a look at this," the officer said.

T-Tommy excused himself, telling Jenkins that he'd contact him later if he had any more questions. Then he and Stone followed the officer through the forest.

After about fifty yards, the uniform said, "Just a bit more." He pushed aside a cedar limb and held it as they moved past him.

T-Tommy picked up the odor of freshly turned soil, a smell that he knew well from his farm-raised childhood. The scent was laced with something else he recognized—the faint odor of decay.

They reached a clearing where three other uniforms stood near a rectangle of gouged away earth. The first thing T-Tommy saw was the gnawed remains of a shoulder, bone and gristle exposed, flesh shredded. It was framed by torn plastic sheeting. As he moved closer, he saw a leg protruding through another rip in the plastic. Like the shoulder, large chunks of flesh were missing, the bones clearly visible. Attached to the damaged leg was a bare foot, nails painted purple, not the bright red polish he had seen minutes earlier. *Two bodies or a fashion statement?*

The decay odor was weak, and though flies buzzed around the shredded flesh, he saw no maggots. The victim hadn't been dead long. He backed away and watched as the evidence team went to work.

Forty-five minutes later, Sidau and his crime lab crew had photographed the site, completed a grid walk of the immediate area for other evidence, and collected what they could find. The coroner's techs then excavated the grave, finding two nude bodies. Young girls. Early twenties, give or take. Each had been wrapped in plastic. They removed them from the grave and sliced open the wrapping, careful to keep each corpse cupped within its sheeting, preserving any trace evidence. One of the bodies belonged to the arm, the other to the leg.

"Pigs," the tech said.

"You sure?" T-Tommy asked.

He nodded. "Seen it before. Drummond and Cooksey can tell us more, but that's what it'll be."

"There was a pack near here a couple of months ago," Stone said.

"Wiped out a chicken coop and killed a few calves. The local farmers put together a hunting party. Killed six of them. Must have been more."

"How'd you know that?"

"My uncle was one of the hunters."

T-Tommy knelt next to the bodies. He scanned them for strangulation bruises and evidence of gunshot wounds but saw none. What he did see was not what he expected. Each corpse had several small wounds over the abdomen. Not open gashes as in a stabbing, but rather each wound was closed by a neat row of little metal clips.

"What the hell is all this?"

Stone leaned closer. "Looks like when my dad had his gallbladder taken out."

"He had these metal things?"

"Yeah. They sometimes use them instead of sewing things up."

"These girls must have had a bunch of shit wrong, then," T-Tommy said. "Maybe they were in an accident of some kind."

Stone squatted beside him. "Or a knife fight."

"With each other?" T-Tommy shook his head. "Then they went to the hospital and got fixed up?"

"You don't think this could be some kind of torture deal, do you?"

At first T-Tommy thought Stone must be kidding, but when he looked into the younger officer's eyes, he saw that he was dead serious.

"What kind of sick fuck would do that?" T-Tommy asked. "Hack up these girls, patch them up, and then kill them?"

"The world's full of candidates," Stone said.

"Maybe some surgeon decided to dump his bad cases," one of the techs said.

Stone offered a grim laugh. "Probably an HMO."

T-Tommy returned his attention to the bodies. Cause of death? No way he could tell. He'd leave that to the MEs.

He stood and circled the corpses. He noticed the edge of a tattoo peeking around the side of one of the bodies. It was low, near the base of the spine. He tugged on a pair of latex gloves, dropped to one knee, and rolled the body on one side. The stiffness told him that death had been at least twenty-four hours or so earlier and not more than forty-eight. Fit the level of decay and the lack of visible maggots. Sometime Wednesday most likely. He could now see that the tattoo, a yellow rose wrapped in thorns, extended across the victim's lower back. "Shit."

"That's her," Stone said. "In report this morning we got a BOLO on a missing girl. Blonde, nineteen, rose tattoo on her back. I've got it in my car. I'll see who filed it."

T-Tommy stood. "Dub Walker."

"What?"

"Dub Walker filed it. He's looking for her." T-Tommy sighed and looked up. The sun approached its noonday zenith in the cloudless sky, and the temperature had begun its daily rise. "Nothing like a double homicide to screw up a perfect spring day."

CHAPTER 20

ROCCO SCARCELLA PICKED UP THE FAT ENVELOPE LEFTY TOSSED ON his desk. He rolled off the rubber band, removed a stack of one hundred dollar bills, and thumbed through them. Twenty grand always felt good. He counted out four grand for Austin, the same for Lefty, and slipped the remainder into his desk drawer.

Austin stuffed his cut into his jeans' pocket and sat facing Rocco. Lefty carefully folded his money, slid it into the inside pocket of his jacket, and then leaned against the wall, working on a cuticle with a small red Swiss Army knife.

Rocco fired up a fresh cigar, leaned back in his chair, and propped one foot on his desk. "Good work."

"Alejandro didn't talk to anyone," Austin said. "And the girl don't know shit."

Rocco nodded. "Knew that from minute one. The girl was fun, though."

Austin laughed. "And knew her stuff." He massaged his crotch. "Wouldn't mind having a go at that."

"You got that right," Lefty said.

"Our friend would have a coronary if he found out," Rocco said.

"Fuck him," Austin said.

"I thought it was the girl you wanted." Rocco wheezed out a laugh, followed by a fit of coughing. Once he composed himself, he looked at Austin. "But since he pays the bills, leave her alone."

"Anything we do isn't going to interfere with what he's got planned for her," Austin said.

Rocco scratched one ear. "Don't fuck with his merchandise."

Austin glanced at Lefty, who said, "He calling the shots here?"

"It's his show. He's paying the freight."

Austin grunted. "Any chick that'd fuck Eddie must be a head case, anyway."

"When will he go to work on them?" Rocco asked.

Lefty closed his knife and put it into his pocket. "Tomorrow night."

"Not before?"

"That's what he said. Has some work to do on that gadget of his first. Or some such shit."

Rocco let out a long sigh. "So we have to keep them on ice for a couple more days." He puffed on his cigar, creating a fresh cloud of smoke. "What'd you find out about that Walker dude?"

"He and Tortelli are buddies," Lefty said. "Go way back. Grammar school. Walker filed the report on the girl. Tortelli's probably just helping him with that. My guy says Tortelli isn't working any new cases right now, just a couple of old ones, so he's got the time. Dub Walker's some sort of forensics hotshot. Worked over at the crime lab for a few years. Writes a bunch of books. Lectures, consults, that sort of thing. Owns a lumber company. Rakes in good bucks."

"Walker Lumber?"

"That's the one."

"That's why his name's familiar." Rocco puffed the cigar to a cherry glow. "Doesn't sound like paying him to go away will work." He dumped a long ash in the ashtray near his elbow. "Maybe we can scare them off."

"Maybe," Lefty said. "My guy at HPD says Tortelli doesn't fuck around. *Relentless* was the word he used. An in-your-face attitude."

Rocco nodded. "Seemed that way to me."

"Want us to make them go away?" Lefty asked. "Permanently?"

"That might complicate things. Right now they're looking for two runaways. The bodies won't be found, and the trail's been scrubbed. No Eddie, and Alejandro won't be with us much longer. Everything'll go cold and they'll give up. Tell the mother that her daughter disappeared. Maybe ran away somewhere."

"And if they don't?" Austin asked.

Rocco shoved the cigar into his mouth. It bobbed when he spoke. "We'll sell them to our friend."

CHAPTER 21

NORTON AND KRAMDEN HOPPED AROUND THE YARD, PULLING UP grubs here and there, while I watered the plants on my deck. The day was hot so I had on shorts, no shirt, bare feet. I was nearly done when T-Tommy showed up. His expression said it all.

I turned off the water and dropped the hose on the deck. "You found her."

He shoved his hands into his pockets and rocked back on his heels a bit. "A couple of hikers found an arm."

I didn't want to hear this.

"Called us. We found two bodies wrapped in plastic. Buried in the woods up north. Near Jeff Road."

"Dismembered?"

"Pigs. Looks that way."

Jesus. This will kill Miranda.

"The farmers there've had problems with a feral pack," T-Tommy continued. "Organized a hunt. Killed half a dozen. Apparently not all of them."

Pigs are not Disney characters. They're big, strong, fast, smart, and extremely aggressive. Ask anyone who has ever been around them. When domestic pigs escape their pens, melt into the woods, pack up, and become feral, they are a bitch to track and kill. They tend to hunt at night and being omnivores can live off anything— roots, grubs, small animals, calves, sheep, and chickens. And corpses. If cornered, they've been known to kill humans.

T-Tommy went on. "I saw the tattoo on her back. The one in the picture."

"Where is she?"

"Over at Forensic Sciences."

"Not at Dreyer's?"

Edwin Dreyer, owner and operator of Dreyer's Funeral Home, was the county coroner, which in Madison County was an elected position with no medical requirements. He was a funeral director and as coroner handled all things death. Except the medical stuff. Though he received any and all corpses, those that required autopsies were shipped to the nearby Alabama Department of Forensic Sciences where Lou Drummond and Becka Cooksey, the two full-time medical examiners, did the work.

"These went straight over to Drummond and Cooksey."

I raised an eyebrow.

"You'll understand when you see the bodies. They're doing the posts today."

"What is it?"

"You'll see."

There was that feeling up my back and across my scalp again. The one I hated. "The other girl. Crystal Robinson?"

"Don't know. Drummond is running the prints on both."

"Noel's will be on file in Birmingham. Couple of drug busts. I'd bet Crystal's in the local system. Prostitution and possession raps most likely. I'm heading over to see the bodies."

"I need to swing by the South Precinct first. I'll meet you there."

CHAPTER 22

I TURNED INTO THE FRONT PARKING LOT OF THE ALABAMA Department of Forensic Sciences, which sat northwest of downtown on Arcadia Circle in the shadow and hum of Memorial Parkway. It shared space in a low, tan brick building with the Department of Public Safety and a branch of the Madison County Sheriff's Department. After leaving med school, fighting off depression, marrying and divorcing Claire, and doing two years as a Marine MP, I had worked there for nearly six years, during which I learned everything I now know about forensic science. Mostly from head criminalist Sidau Yamaguchi.

People sometimes asked me exactly what I did. The simple answer was that I owned a lumber company and goofed off, but that wasn't what they were usually asking about. The other stuff was hard to label. I'm not a doctor. Missed that by three months. Quit when someone abducted Jill, a blow that knocked my career path into a ditch. I'm not a criminalist. Not like Sidau. I'm not a psychiatrist or a profiler. Not trained in either. I usually said I was a criminal consultant. Not sure what that was, but it seemed closest to what I did.

During my nearly six years in this building and my eighteen months with the FBI Behavioral Analysis Unit guys, I found that I had a knack for understanding evidence, seeing how it all stuck together, and for unraveling what the bad guys were likely thinking. Didn't know where that came from. Probably the healthy dose of common sense I got from my parents. Particularly my dad. His approach to life was to look at something square on, let it rattle around in his brain a little, and then decide if it seemed reasonable. That approach made sense to me.

Soon, law enforcement agencies, DAs, attorneys from both sides of the courtroom, coroners, and various government officials began asking me to review cases and get involved with their investigations. So, one of the things I do is consult all over the country on difficult and odd cases.

My gut told me that this case would be both difficult and odd. I hated that feeling. I never ignored it, but I hated it.

As I climbed from my Porsche, T-Tommy pulled into the lot. Inside we hooked up with Dr. Lou Drummond. He wore his usual gray surgical scrubs beneath a white knee-length lab coat. We followed him down the hall and into the autopsy suite.

"You'll know why we rushed the autopsies when you see the

corpses," Drummond said.

I wished people would quit saying that. First T-Tommy and now Drummond. I wasn't very good at prayer, not much practice, but I tossed out a silent one, anyway. *Don't let it be weird.* Actually, I first asked that it not be Noel and then not weird. I figured two prayers might be pushing my luck given my shaky relationship with the big guy, but what the hell.

The room smelled like every other autopsy suite I'd ever visited, the odors of death and formalin being universal. Six banks of overhead fluorescent lights cast a shadowless glow, and the brick-red tile floor returned each of our footsteps as flat echoes. Two metal dissection tables butted against a central stainless steel sink, one on each side in a head-to-head arrangement. The far one held a covered corpse, the shape suggesting a small female. The one nearest us held the body of a young woman, chest and abdomen open, autopsy in progress.

We approached Dr. Becka Cooksey, a slight woman with straight shoulders and delicate hands. She wore gray surgical scrubs and moist latex gloves and held what looked like a liver in her hands. Handshakes could come later. She peered at me through a plastic face shield. "How are you?"

"Been better. What've you got?" I glanced at the girl on the table. "That's not Noel."

Cooksey peeled off her gloves, tossed them into a bucket near her feet, and removed her face shield. She walked to the draped form and lifted the sheet. Noel appeared. No doubt. She looked exactly like her photos. Except that now she was pale, waxy, and very dead.

I swallowed hard. "That's her."

Cooksey rolled her on one side, exposing the rose tattoo. I nodded, and she settled Noel's corpse back on the table.

Bodies almost never bothered me. Even the mushy, bloated ones I had pulled from lakes and swamps. Even those that had been ripped open by shotgun pellets. Not even the ones that had been charred a crispy black by an accelerant-enhanced fire. But Noel's corpse did. She seemed small and innocent. And damaged. Severely damaged. The pigs had taken huge chunks from her arms, legs, and one shoulder. I swallowed acid back into my stomach.

"What we have here is an enigma wrapped in a conundrum," Cooksey said.

I hadn't noticed it on the other girl, her chest and abdomen still open, but when I was finally able to pull my gaze away from Noel's face, I saw that several one- to two-inch long wounds dotted her abdomen. Metallic clips, which I recognized as surgical staples, held each of them closed. I knew these weren't part of the autopsy procedure. The ugly Y incision, now sutured closed, yes, these other wounds, no.

I pointed to them. "What's the story with the staples?"

"These wounds on both girls aren't traumatic," Cooksey said. I knew that. "They're surgical. Carefully and skillfully done. By someone with experience, expertise, and the latest tools."

"Want to explain?" T-Tommy asked.

"The other girl" —she gestured toward the table behind me—

"had three procedures. An appendectomy, a gallbladder removal, and a nephrectomy . . . kidney removal. This one had the same three procedures plus a colon resection."

"All that through these little openings?" T-Tommy asked.

Cooksey shrugged and nodded to me.

"It's a minimally invasive technique," I told T-Tommy. "That means using a small incision. Cannulas—hollow metal tubes—are passed through the openings, and then instruments are passed through the cannuli and the surgery is done. Popular technique."

"And all these surgeries can be done that way?" he asked.

"Sure can. Even open-heart surgery."

T-Tommy's brow furrowed. "I thought they opened the chest right down the middle for that." He glanced at me. "Like Mike Savage had."

"They usually do," Cooksey said. "But this minimally invasive, or buttonhole as it's also called, approach is less traumatic."

"Can just any surgeon do this?" T-Tommy asked.

"Nowadays most surgeons do at least some procedures this way." Cooksey gestured at Noel's corpse. "Whoever did this is good."

"Were any of these surgeries necessary?" I asked. "I can't imagine a couple of teenage girls needed all this."

"Obviously, I don't have the removed organs. The gallbladders, the appendices, the others . . . so I can't be 100 percent sure that disease wasn't present in them. But this number of illnesses in women of this age would be very unlikely." Cooksey sighed. "That's not the weird part."

Here it comes.

Cooksey massaged the back of her neck, rotating her head slightly as if working out a kink. "These didn't all happen at once but over several days. This nephrectomy is at least five or six days old, and the gallbladder removal is more like two."

This was beyond weird, bordering on surreal. "You're telling us that someone did a handful of unnecessary surgeries on two healthy girls over several days?"

"Afraid so."

"Why?" I asked.

"Maybe stealing organs?" T-Tommy said. "Black market stuff?"

"All that organ stealing that was supposed to go on in hotel rooms is urban legend," I said. "Never happened. Besides, not much of a market for an appendix or a gallbladder." I looked at Cooksey. "What was the cause of death?"

"Good question. Don't know the answer yet. Definitely not bleeding or a botched surgery. Not a heart attack or a pulmonary embolus. The procedures were perfect. Every cut exact. Toxicology stuff will go down to the lab in Birmingham."

"Time of death?" I asked.

"Based on the rigor and the lack of any real putrefaction, I'd guess around thirty-six hours ago."

"Both of them?"

She nodded. "The bodies were moved two to four hours, maybe more, after death. The lividity pattern indicates that they were on their backs for a few hours, then dumped in the position they were in at the burial site."

T-Tommy's cell phone buzzed, and he answered, spoke to some-one for a minute, and slipped it back into his pocket. "Prints gave up positive IDs on both." He faced me. "The other girl is Crystal Robinson."

CHAPTER 23

T-Tommy and I stood in the parking lot, trying to make sense out of what we had just seen and heard.

"This is insane," I said.

T-Tommy grunted, his way of saying I had stated the obvious.

"It would take more than just a skilled surgeon. Had to be done in a hospital."

"Why?"

"The cutter would need anesthesia, ventilators, drugs, an operating room, an ICU, post-op care. That takes special equipment and trained people."

"Makes sense."

"I think I'll pay a visit to Liz," I said. "Get her take on it."

Dr. Liz Mackey was a CV surgeon at Huntsville Memorial Medical Center. The only one who did pediatric heart cases. T-Tommy and I had gone to high school with her. She was a year behind me in med school. Unlike me, she finished. In fact, Liz climbed all the way to the top of the medical food chain.

"I'll go with you." T-Tommy started to say something else, but he focused on something over my shoulder. "Shit," he murmured.

I turned to see Sergeant Wayne Furyk heading our way. Short, square, solid, buzz cut. A cross between Napoleon and Schwarzenegger. A permanent scowl cut into his face. Head of the HPD Major Crimes Unit and T-Tommy's boss. I had met him once. More like butted heads with him a couple of years ago when he ran with the Narc guys out of the West Precinct. I was brought in to consult on a multiple murder. Drug related. He took exception to my reading of the crime scene. He was wrong; I was right. Really, I was. His move up to head of Major Crimes was controversial. Jumped over a few guys who probably deserved it more.

"Sergeant," T-Tommy said.

Furyk ignored him and looked at me. "What are you doing here?" He didn't offer to shake hands but rather stood with his fists balled on his hips, chest pushed out, confrontation written all over him.

"Came to identify the body," I said.

"We know who they are." His square chin jutted directly at me.

"I had to see her."

"She family?"

"Sort of," I said.

"Sorry," he said, but it didn't seem to me that he meant it. "Chief didn't call you, did he? Ask you to come in on this one?"

Turf. Always got to protect your turf. "No," I said.

"So you'll stay out of this investigation?"

"Didn't say that."

"You're not going to give me trouble, are you?" He hooked his thumbs on his belt and widened his stance.

Furious Furyk. His behind-the-back nickname. With good reason. Had a legendary temper. Right now he seemed to be looking for a fight.

"Wouldn't dream of it," I said.

"I'll make it clear for you. We don't want or need you rooting around this case."

Fuck him. "Can't make that promise."

"You get in the way or fuck anything up, I'll put my boot on your neck."

"Sounds like fun."

Furyk stared at me for a minute. I hoped he wasn't armed. He turned to T-Tommy. "Cooksey called. Said the bodies had some unusual injuries. Something about surgeries."

"That's right," T-Tommy said. "Want to take a look?"

"That's why I'm here." He turned and headed toward the door. "See you inside," he shot over his shoulder.

"I see he's mellowed," I said.

T-Tommy shook his head. "So why do you want to bang heads with him?"

"He started it." I smiled. "Besides, I need something fun about now."

"Pissing on Furyk is it?"

"It's a start."

T-Tommy sighed.

"You want me to stay out of the way?"

"Yeah, right. Like you'd listen."

"Just being polite."

T-Tommy grunted. Meant that wasn't one of my strongest qualities. He scratched an ear. "Just try to stay off his radar."

"Will do."

T-Tommy scowled. I didn't think he believed me.

"Any similar cases on the books lately?" I asked. "Girls going to fake setups and disappearing?"

"I heard of one. Wasn't directly involved in the case. Grapevine talk. Couple of months back. Supposed to meet a john at his house. Out toward Gurley. Poof. Gone. Guy denied everything and it checked out. Out of town, if I remember it right." He kicked a small stone, sending it skittering across the parking lot. "Like Weiss."

Was this a pattern? A killer luring hookers out on fake out calls and nabbing them? "What was her name? The other girl?"

"Bambi. Working name. Don't remember her real name. Black chick."

"Who'd she work for?"

"Sally Workman. Goes by Miss Sally. Operates out of the Bel Aire Motel. Out off the Ardmore Highway. Rents a room for her office. Been there for years."

"Maybe I'll stop by and see her," I said.

"We'll both go. Of course, if Furyk finds out, he'll string me up by the balls."

"You going to tell him?"

"Not likely."

"Then there you go," I said.

T-Tommy nodded. "Better get in there so I can hold his hand through this."

"I'll go see Miranda." I gazed out across the lot. "Not looking forward to this."

"I know."

"I'll give Liz a call and see when we can hook up with her."

CHAPTER 24

FRIDAY 3:39 P.M.

MIRANDA'S SOBS RIPPED A HOLE IN MY GUT. I KNEW I COULDN'T FACE this alone, so I'd taken the chicken way out. I'd called Claire, thinking having a woman here might soften things a bit. Miranda sat on the bed in her hotel room, Claire next to her, one arm around Miranda's shoulders.

"I have to see her," Miranda said.

I pulled the chair away from the desk and sat, getting down to her level so I could look her in the eye. "No, you don't."

"But . . ."

"But nothing." The image of Noel's mutilated corpse flashed in my head. "I told you what happened. Remember her as she was."

I had told Miranda everything. The surgeries. The burial. The pigs. I blurred the details but left nothing out, knowing she'd discover the details soon enough. This was a story the media would devour. That was another reason I wanted Claire here. If she broke the story, she could round off the sharp edges.

Miranda buried her face in her hands, and her shoulders convulsed.

"I'll handle everything," I said. "Arrange to have her taken back home."

"No," Miranda said, the tissue she held wound tightly around a finger. "I can't let you do that."

"Consider it done. You have enough to deal with right now."

She sighed and began sobbing again. After a minute or so, she sniffed back her tears and said, "When?"

"As soon as Coroner Dreyer gives the go-ahead. Should only be a day or so." I motioned to Claire, signaling her to follow me.

She stood, and we stepped out into the hallway and moved away from the door.

"This is going to be your story, right?"

"What do you think?"

It was a stupid question.

"Me doing the story isn't what I'm worried about," Claire said. "It's you. Don't make it personal."

"It is."

"I know. Just don't let that muddy the water."

"That's how you drive the snakes out of the swimming hole. Churn things up. Make them nervous. A slug like this will leave a slime trail. It's just a matter of finding it."

"Be careful. I've got a bad feeling about this one."

Me, too. "I'm meeting T-Tommy over at the medical center. We're going to chat with Liz Mackey. She has an hour between cases."

"About what?"

"You want to go? I'll tell you on the way."

"Okay."

We returned to the room. Miranda seemed to have pulled herself together. Sort of. After she assured me she didn't need anything, I told her that T-Tommy and I were going to begin turning over rocks to see what crawled out.

"We'll find whoever did this," I said.

Miranda stood and hugged me. "I don't know what I'd do without you." She sat down on the bed again. "I have so many calls to make. My boss. My attorney. Funeral arrangements." She glanced around the room as if searching for something. "I don't even know where to begin."

"I'll help you," Claire said. "I have to do a quick interview, but I should be back in an hour, maybe less."

CHAPTER 25

CLAIRE AND I CLIMBED INTO MY PORSCHE, AND I FIRED UP THE ENGINE. I called T-Tommy and told him we were on the way over to the medical center. I then dialed Rosalee Kennedy's number and was surprised when she herself answered. I told her about Crystal and Noel. Not the details, just that they were both dead. She seemed neither surprised nor saddened. She did mumble condolences of sorts.

I asked, "You know Sally Workman?"

"Everybody knows Miss Sally."

"Tell me."

"Runs a string of low class girls out of a cheap motel. That about says it all."

"The Bel Aire?"

"If you know, why're you asking?"

"She a competitor?"

"Hardly. She picks up the rejects."

"Girl named Bambi?" I asked. "Would she be one of the rejects?"

"You do get around, don't you?" Rosalee laughed, and when I didn't respond, she went on. "Yeah, she worked for me. Maybe a year ago. Black girl. Beautiful. Got a habit and waltzed off with four grand of my money. You know where she is?"

"That's what I'm trying to find out. What's her real name?"

"The one given to her by her alcoholic asshole father and her whore mother?"

"I take it you've tried to find her?"

"Four large is four large," she said. "Name's Marlene Johnson. From Phoenix. Don't waste your time on her family. She'd never go back there, and they don't give a rat's ass. She's probably off to the big city. Atlanta. Miami. New York. Who knows?"

"Thanks, Rosalee."

"You find her, tell her to bring me my money."

"They found the fucking bodies," Rocco said to Lefty and Austin. "Alejandro and Eddie fucked up."

"Shit," Lefty said.

"Our friend isn't going to do Alejandro until when?" Rocco asked. His knuckles whitened as he gripped the edge of his desk.

"Tomorrow night. Preparations are under way."

"Why not now?"

"I told you. He's got to work on that gadget of his. I don't understand all that shit. Anyway, he said Saturday night at the earliest."

"So it could be even longer?" Rocco asked.

Lefty shrugged.

Rocco swiped a hand over his balding pate. "This could screw everything up."

"Maybe not," Lefty said. "We're heading over there now. Make sure things are moving along."

"Don't let this lead back here," Rocco said.

Lefty stood. "It won't. There's no Eddie. Soon there'll be no Alejandro. After that, we're clean."

"Unless they find the others," Rocco said. "That could blow this thing up."

"What are the odds of that?" Austin asked.

"Odds are for fools. What if Alejandro and Eddie fucked up all of them?"

"We'll have a chat with Alejandro," Lefty said.

"And what? Move them all? To where? Better to let things lie." Rocco sighed and picked up a cold cigar from his ashtray, clamping it between his teeth.

"Alejandro is the only one who knows where the others are," Austin said. "Might be better to know that before he goes down. Just in case."

"Maybe crank up the cover plan?" Lefty asked.

Rocco shook his head. "Only as a last resort."

CHAPTER 26

T-Tommy met us inside the main entrance of the Huntsville Memorial Medical Center. The eight-story, nine-hundred-bed, tertiary care facility had a strong association with the massive University of Alabama at Birmingham's School of Medicine, where I had labored for nearly four years.

A receptionist sat behind a desk along one wall of the spacious lobby. She smiled as we approached.

After I told her we had an appointment with Dr. Liz Mackey, she called for an escort and motioned that we should sit in a bank of chairs across from her desk. We did.

While we waited, I gave Claire the details of our visit with Drummond and Cooksey. She took notes in her special shorthand, scratches that only she could decipher, and shook her head more than once. She also said, "You're shitting me," a couple of times. I wasn't.

Wished I was, but bizarre was bizarre no matter how you packaged it.

As I finished, a friendly young woman appeared, introduced herself as Monica Walters, and led us to the elevators. On the third floor, we followed her into the doctors' lounge near the entrance to the hospital's surgical suites.

"Coffee and donuts," Monica said, indicating a corner table with a coffeepot and two boxes of Krispy Kremes. "Help yourself. We have soft drinks, too."

"That's okay," I said.

"I'll let Dr. Mackey know you're here." She left the room.

T-Tommy poured a cup of coffee and grabbed a donut.

A minute later, Liz came in. She wore blue surgical scrubs beneath a white coat, short blonde hair peeking from the edges of her surgical cap. A mask dangled around her neck. We hugged and said all the hellos and how-are-yous, and then Liz said she had only a few minutes. Crazy day. Her third open-heart surgery coming up.

"We'll make this short," I said. "We need to know about this new minimally invasive surgery."

She nodded and waited for me to go on.

"What we say here isn't for public consumption," I said. "Not yet, anyway. Okay?"

"I understand," Liz said.

"The corpses of two nineteen-year-old women were found this morning. Buried in a rural wooded area. The autopsies showed that both had had several procedures. All done by this method. Appendix, gallbladder, a kidney removed. They apparently didn't need any of them." I spread my hands on the table. "The procedures were done a few days apart. Over about a week."

"Did they die from surgical complications?" Liz asked.

I shook my head. "Dr. Cooksey said all the procedures were perfect. Her word. Doesn't know the cause of death yet."

Liz stared at me, apparently trying to take it all in. "I'm not sure I understand. Are you telling me that over a few days, two young women had several buttonhole procedures, all done correctly, yet they died and were buried out in the boonies?"

"Exactly."

"Why? Who?" she asked.

"That's what we want to know. Maybe some crazy doctor. Maybe some hospital trying to dump its mistakes."

"Patients don't just disappear. Too many people involved. And a surgeon couldn't do a bunch of unnecessary procedures on a nine-teen-year-old without making some waves."

"So," Claire said, "that brings us to who's capable of doing this stuff, and why is it done?" She flipped her notepad open.

"Let me answer the why first," Liz said. "Dub already knows all this, but you might not. It's called minimally invasive since we make small incisions instead of the long ones of the past. If we can do the procedure through a small incision, the patient suffers less pain, fewer complications, and heals much faster."

"What surgeries are done this way?" Claire asked as she scribbled.

"Everything from coronary bypass surgery to gallbladders to appendectomies."

"What's the actual procedure?"

"We make three or four incisions, an inch or two long, and insert cannulas through each opening and into the body. Through the abdominal wall and into the abdominal cavity for an appendectomy or gallbladder or any of the other abdominal procedures we do. We then pass fiber-optic lights and cameras and specially designed instruments through these tubes and work that way."

T-Tommy wiped donut sugar from his hands with a napkin. "How big are these tubes?"

Liz held up her thumb. "About this size."

"How do you get a gallbladder or a kidney out through something that small?"

Liz smiled. "A gallbladder, once you remove the bile juice and any stones that might be inside, collapses into nothing. Like a deflated balloon. Kidneys we simply cut into smaller pieces and remove them a chunk at a time."

"Sounds tricky," Claire said.

"Can be."

"Can any surgeon do this?" T-Tommy asked.

Liz laughed. "Only the good ones."

I smiled. "Most of this is after my time. What's the training program for this?"

"It's part of virtually every surgical training program now. Surgeons who have been out in the real world for several years can go back for a two- to three-week training session, then work with a surgeon who already has the skills and get up to speed fairly quickly."

I nodded. "Besides you, do any other surgeons on staff here do this stuff?"

"I think a dozen at last count. Two of our older surgeons went down to Birmingham for training. A couple of the other guys and I have been working with them. They'll be credentialed soon."

"Anyone at any other hospitals in the area?"

"A few."

"Other than the tools you use, does it require any other special equipment?" Claire asked. "I mean, do patients undergoing this type of surgery need any special stuff afterward?"

"Fact is, they need less. The hospital stay is typically much shorter."

"Can it be done at any hospital?" T-Tommy asked. "Or maybe at one of those small surgical centers?"

"If the procedure can be done by any technique at the facility, then it can be done this way. For example, any hospital could do an appendectomy this way, but only a hospital equipped to do open-heart procedures could do those regardless of the technique."

"This may sound odd," I said, "but could you do it in a basement or a garage?"

"Not a very sterile environment," Liz said.

"If you want the victim to survive," I said. "Maybe death was the real purpose."

Liz raised an eyebrow. "You mean like some psycho killer?"

"Perhaps. But if so, this guy isn't just some off-the-shelf psycho. The skill and equipment used on these young ladies aren't found in some back alley or crack house."

"So you're thinking this is some doctor gone awry?"

"Awry is being a shade on the kind side," I said. "Whoever did this split from the family tree a long time ago."

"Amen," T-Tommy added.

"The world's full of psychos who thrill kill. We've hunted down a couple ourselves." I looked in T-Tommy's direction.

"I ain't never seen anything quite like this," T-Tommy said. "Only good thing is that the skill needed here shrinks the suspect list more than a little."

"Besides an MD or a med student, who else might be able to do this?" I asked. "A nurse? Medic? Vet?"

Liz drained her coffee cup, walked to the coffeemaker, and refilled her cup. She leaned against the counter. "Not likely. If these surgeries were indeed perfect, then the person who performed them has surgical skill and experience. Can't pick that up from a book. Or TV."

"What if it isn't a doctor or a med student," Claire said. "What if he's in another area of the medical industry?"

Everyone looked at her, waiting for her to continue.

Claire laid down her pad and pen and laced her fingers, resting them on the table. "I have a friend who's a technical rep for a pacemaker company. When the doctor puts in a pacemaker, she goes into the operating room and helps with testing the pacer. She told me that she had seen so many pacers done she could do one herself by now."

Liz nodded. "So the question is, could someone learn to do this type of surgery simply by watching?"

"Exactly," Claire said. "I assume you have manufacturers' reps in the OR when you're using their equipment."

"Sometimes. When it's something new and we need to learn the nuances of a particular piece of equipment. Once we get comfortable, the reps disappear until they have another product to sell."

"Do you think a rep could learn to use this equipment while watching you and other surgeons?" Claire asked.

Liz paused, stared into the cup of coffee she held, and then said, "I don't see how. The real work goes on inside. The rep couldn't see that."

"Just a thought," Claire said.

"I mean, it's possible. But if the surgeries on these two girls were as skillful as you described, he'd have to practice on animals or cadavers beforehand. Couldn't just up and do it."

I hadn't thought of that before. Of course, whoever did this would have to practice. Doctor or not. "Let's say he did. Where would he get cadavers?"

"There are several companies that supply them. When people donate their bodies for medical research, this is where they go. They then sell them to equipment manufacturers and medical schools where they are used in research and teaching."

"Easy to get?" T-Tommy asked.

Liz shook her head. "Very tightly regulated. You have to show why you need the corpses, what you are going to do with them, and account for each and every one."

"They could be stolen," T-Tommy said.

"Anything can be stolen," Liz said. "Including bodies, I'd suspect."

"Or bought," Claire said. "Remember the stolen body parts ring at UCLA a few years ago?"

"That shook up the entire industry," Liz said.

T-Tommy finished his coffee, crushed the cup, and tossed it into a nearby trash can. "Working through these hollow tubes sounds tedious."

"And backbreaking. Standing there, hunched over, both arms working." Liz smiled. "If I can ever convince the administration to buy one of the new robotic machines, I can sit down on the job."

"Robotic?" Claire asked. "You mean like 'Danger, Will Robinson'?"

Liz laughed. "Not exactly. Robotic is actually a misnomer. A surgeon still does the work; he just doesn't stand over the patient or use his hands. At least not for the actual surgery. Let's say he wants to take out a gallbladder. Just as with the buttonhole technique, he'll first make a few small incisions in the abdomen, slip in the cannulas, and pass through the lights, cameras, and instruments he'll need. The difference is that he then sits across the room at a console, which has a monitor that displays the images. He uses handles to operate. His assistants will change out instruments as needed. A scalpel, a cautery, a staple. Whatever the procedure calls for. Sure saves the back."

"Why go through all that?" T-Tommy said. "Why not just stand there and do it?"

"With the right equipment and a few trained assistants, you could have the best surgeon in the world even if you were on safari in Africa. Or on the space station."

"Clever," T-Tommy said.

"Have you done any of those?" I asked. "The robotic stuff?"

"I'd love to, but the equipment would break the bank. A couple of million and up to get the right setup. And that's just the basics. Maybe after the price comes down, I can get the hospital board to sign off on it."

"Where do you get your equipment?" T-Tommy asked. "For these buttonhole deals?"

"There are several places. Most people buy from the three or four big manufacturers. One's here in Huntsville."

"Really?" I asked.

"Talbert Biomedical. They make all kinds of surgical equipment, including the tools for minimally invasive surgeries. Since they're local we buy a lot from them."

"Dr. Mackey?" The voice came through the wall-mounted two-way intercom.

She turned toward the voice. "Yes?"

"We're ready to rock. Hot lights, cold steel."

"I'm on the way." Liz stood. "Time to get to work." She seemed to notice the quizzical look on Claire's face and laughed. "Hot lights and cold steel. Surgery. The hot overhead lights and the cold steel scalpel." She shrugged. "Got to find humor where you can."

CHAPTER 27

WE STOPPED BY THE MARRIOTT. WHEN MIRANDA OPENED THE door, she appeared tired and worn. I saw her packed bags on the bed.

"I was just getting ready to call you," she said, stepping back and letting us enter.

"You leaving?"

"I have so much to do. Plan the funeral." Miranda swallowed hard. "Deal with the trust we set up for her." She looked around the room. "I have a list here somewhere."

"You in any condition to drive?" T-Tommy asked. "We can take you."

She shook her head. "I'm fine."

"You have people down in Birmingham to help you?" Claire asked.

"I have great friends, and they're all pitching in."

"When are you leaving?" I asked.

"Now."

T-Tommy and I grabbed her luggage and carried it out to her car. We put it in the trunk, and then I opened the car door for her. She hugged T-Tommy, Claire, and me before sliding behind the wheel.

"You sure you're okay?"

"No. But I have to get home." Miranda gripped the steering wheel and stared straight ahead. "I thought Richard's death was hard. But this? How do you get past this?"

"Time," I said. "It takes time."

"Are you over your sister? It's been . . . what? Ten years? More?"

"No. But it's better. Not nearly as acute as it once was."

"I hope you're right, but I don't see how."

"It will get better. I promise."

"Thanks for that. And for everything you've done."

"I'll call you tomorrow." I closed the door and then watched as she drove from the parking lot and turned left. Wrong way. That led to a dead end at the adjacent U.S. Space & Rocket Center. A minute later, her car came back headed toward the freeway entrance. Maybe we should have insisted on driving her the one hundred miles to Birmingham. Probably wouldn't have worked. One of the many words I always connected with Miranda was *stubborn*. Like Claire. Maybe there was a pattern there.

After arranging to meet later at Sammy's, Claire went to the station, and T-Tommy and I set out to chat with Miss Sally. The Bel Aire Motel squatted a few miles northwest of town off the Ardmore Highway, near where State 255 crossed. It wasn't the Marriott. Not even close. A dozen units facing a gravel parking area. Dirty white stucco with faded turquoise trim. A tiled roof, once red, now a sun-bleached, anemic orange.

Miss Sally sat behind a cluttered desk in unit 1, the door standing open. A cloud of cigarette smoke greeted us. We introduced ourselves. She offered a weak, moist handshake.

Sally stubbed a cigarette into an ashtray, half-filled with butts, lit another, and took a heavy drag. She sipped what appeared to be Scotch, neat. I knew that from the nearly empty bottle of Johnnie Walker Red next to the glass. I told you I was observant.

She looked midsixties, probably midfifties, booze and cigarettes adding the decade. Her light blue cotton dress appeared a couple of sizes too large. Several ash burns spotted the front. She didn't invite us to sit in the folding lawn chairs that faced her desk. She asked what we wanted.

"Just a couple of questions."

She stared at me and blew a large, slow-moving smoke ring down and to her left. Then with a series of slight jerks of her jaw, she fired three smaller ones through it before it disintegrated against the floor. "About what?"

"We're looking for a girl who goes by Bambi. Worked for you."

"Maybe she did. Maybe I don't know her." Sally blew another

smoke ring that twisted into a figure eight before falling apart.

"Neat trick," I said.

"Got a million of them." As if to prove her point, she shot out another one that seemed to spin as it skidded across her desk and off one end.

I gave her mock applause.

"I don't talk about my business. Especially to no cop."

"I'm not a cop," I said.

"He is." Sally jabbed the cig toward T-Tommy. "Seen him in the paper."

"We ain't here to lean on you," T-Tommy said. "Unless you want us to. We're investigating something else."

Smoke drifted out of her nose as she looked at him. Finally she said, "Name's Marlene Johnson. Why're you looking for her?"

"I understand she's missing. Went to meet a guy who'd never heard of her. We had a friend who disappeared under similar circumstances."

"She black? Your missing friend."

I shook my head.

"You think your friend and Marlene went off somewhere together?"

Again I shook my head. "We found our friend. Along with another girl. On a slab at the coroner's office."

Sally's shoulders straightened.

I went on. "We're looking for a connection. A pattern. A lead of any kind."

She flicked an ash toward the ashtray on the corner of her desk.

Missed. "So you're thinking your friend might've been set up? Marlene, too?"

"Possible."

Sally studied me for a moment. Smoke drifted from her mouth and was captured by her nose. "Why?"

"That's what we want to know."

"Your friend. Shot? Stabbed? Raped? What happened?"

"Can't really say," T-Tommy said. "It's an ongoing investigation. I'm sure you understand."

"Gee. Cops keeping secrets. I'm shocked." She stubbed out her cigarette, stood, and walked to the open door. Leaning against the jamb, she stared out over the front lot, then turned her head back toward us and spoke over her shoulder. "Marlene, Bambi, whatever, took a hike about six months ago. Had about twenty-five hundred of my money. I filed a report with the police, for what that's worth. Haven't seen or heard from her since."

"Did you set up her date that night?"

Sally returned to her chair, sat down, and fired up another cigarette. "No. Marlene did some freelance work."

"You didn't mind? The freelancing?"

"Of course I minded. Money's money." She blew another figure eight. "But what are you going to do? Whores act like whores. About everything."

"So she set up her own date that night?"

"Far as I know. Unless she went back to Rosalee Kennedy. Used to work for her."

I shook my head. "She didn't. Rosalee said she took off with her money, too."

"Like I said, whores are whores." Sally took a gulp from her drink. "I'd bet she headed for the coast. South, east, west. Take your pick."

I didn't believe it. Not for a minute. I had no evidence, no real reason to believe otherwise, but deep down I knew Marlene had never left the city. Not alive, anyway. I also knew that Miss Sally couldn't help us. Unless we wanted to learn smoke ring tricks, that is.

CHAPTER 28

THE PLAN WAS SIMPLE, DANGEROUS, AND NOT LIKELY TO SUCCEED, BUT Alejandro could see no other way out of this. Even now as he ran his hands over the rough cinder blocks for what seemed the twentieth time, pressing a fingernail into the cement that separated them, searching for a weakness, he knew he'd find none. Whoever designed this room had covered all the angles. That left the open door as their only escape route. The trick was getting through it alive. They would be outnumbered three to two and outgunned two to zip. Not a pretty prospect.

What choice did he have? No doubt Rocco had something nasty planned. Why else had they not pounded on him? If they really believed he or Carmelita had talked, they would do anything to get a name. But other than humiliating Carmelita, they had done no damage to either of them.

That brought up another question: if they were going to kill them, why hadn't they done it? Keeping them here was risky. What could Rocco need so badly that he would take the chance? Alejandro came up with no answers that even remotely made sense. Whatever it was, escape seemed a better option than waiting for Rocco to play his hand.

They had made their conditions a bit more comfortable. Air mattresses and blankets. Leaving the overhead lights on. Dim but better than the darkness they had endured the first day. Earlier they were allowed to shower. Lefty and Austin watched Carmelita and again made her do things to herself. To her credit, when she told Alejandro what had happened, she didn't cry but rather stood in the center of the room, fists balled at her sides, anger dripping off her. That anger would be useful.

Alejandro now had a handle on their captors' routine. Breakfast, lunch, dinner, always the same. Each time the door opened, the three men performed a little dance. Austin would enter the room, gun in hand, expand his chest, and start giving orders. Always the tough guy. Lefty would linger just outside the door to one side, clear line of fire toward Alejandro, not giving much thought to Carmelita, obviously feeling she was no risk. The third man hung in the hallway.

Taking down Austin and Lefty would be the trick. The other guy was smaller and appeared less threatening. Of course, he could be armed, but Alejandro would have to go with the hope that he wasn't.

Only a blitz attack would work. Take on Austin straight up, surprise on his side. A quick hit to the throat, go for the gun. Carmelita would wait just inside the door until Lefty stepped into the room, looking for a clear line of fire. She would then throw herself at him, using that anger, scratching and biting and kicking. She needed to occupy him for only a few seconds. If Alejandro couldn't take Austin down and out quickly, they were done, anyway.

He had gone over it with her a dozen times. They had practiced all the necessary moves. Carmelita learned quickly.

Alejandro decided that tonight when the men brought food was the time. If they could pull off the attack, get down the hall to the restroom he had used, and smash through the window, they just might make it out of here.

The problem was that the men had broken their routine. Should have been here already.

"You ready?" Alejandro whispered. He sat next to her on one of the mattresses, back against the wall.

Carmelita shrugged.

He could sense fear replacing her anger. An hour earlier she had been pumped up, ready to go. But time killed emotion. Now she just appeared tired, almost resigned to a bad ending.

"Go for his eyes," Alejandro said. "Get your fingers in there. Anywhere. Like I showed you. Then tear his face up."

"You make it sound like I'm an animal."

Alejandro turned toward her. "You want to live? Then you become a complete animal. Go crazy. *Loco en la cabeza.*" He grabbed her arm. "If you hesitate or hold back, we'll lose. They'll kill us right here."

She nodded.

"Just remember what they made you do. Hold that anger tightly."

"I will. I promise." Carmelita didn't sound very convincing.

He couldn't lose her now, couldn't pull this off without her. "If you don't, he'll kill you. Understand?"

She sighed. "I just want to get it over with."

CHAPTER 29

I SAT IN A FOLDING CHAIR ON THE SMALL CORNER STAGE AT SAMMY'S Blues 'n' Q next to local bluesman Colin Dogget. I fingered Colin's blond spruce Gibson J-50 through several riffs as he walked through Robert Johnson's "Terraplane Blues" on his Vintage Sunburst L-7C Archtop. I loved playing with Colin and sat in with him every time I had a chance. The best way to close the week, particularly after a day like this one had been.

The after-work crowd had gathered and were well into their third or fourth round. The men in suits or jeans and blue work shirts, some even in overalls. The women wore everything from business attire to jeans to cutoffs. Sammy's attracted all types.

We settled into "Stormy Monday," followed that with "Crossroads," "Five Long Years," and finally "Third Degree." Halfway through that one, Claire showed up.

Fresh off the set, she wore a navy blue blouse beneath a gray suit, and her thick red mane was pulled back and tied with one of those deals that looked like silk panties. Loved those things. She joined T-Tommy at the bar where Sammy poured her a glass of red wine.

I thanked Colin, acknowledged the applause from the crowd, and headed toward the bar. Colin eased into "Little Red Rooster."

Sammy came from the back, wiped down the bar, and asked, "Get you guys anything to eat?"

A BBQ chicken salad for Claire, sliced BBQ brisket for me, and a full rack of ribs for T-Tommy. With a side of hot links. We moved to a table in the corner.

"Thanks for your help with Miranda," I said.

Claire shrugged. "No problem. She's a tough lady. She'll get through this okay."

"I hope so." I took a big slug of Blanton's. "It's not every day that you learn your daughter was not only tortured and murdered but also chewed on by wild pigs."

Silence settled for a beat, and then Claire said, "How do you figure this?"

"Hard for me to believe these were done at a hospital," I said. "You can't simply dump your bad outcomes in the trash. Or out in the woods."

"I spoke with a friend of mine," Claire said. "A surgical nurse over at Crestwood. She said there was no way anyone could be oper-ated on and then simply disappear. Too many regulations, watchdogs, people involved. Not to mention families, hospital staff, other patients. Even insurance companies. Someone would know. Or at least ask questions."

"What about one of those surgicenter deals?" T-Tommy asked. "They're small. Maybe below the radar."

"Not likely." Claire sipped her wine. "My friend said that they have to bow to the same regulations as hospitals. In some ways they're even more closely watched. To hide something like this would require quite a conspiracy. Involve a ton of people."

"And to do all this over several days?" I said. "Hell of a trick to hide it."

"Then where?"

Our food arrived and we began to eat.

"A house or motel might work," I said.

"Or a mobile unit like a motor home," T-Tommy said.

I looked at him. "If you're not concerned about the patient's survival, it could be done almost anywhere."

No one said anything for a moment, letting that concept seep in. Hospitals were clean, well staffed with professionals, and had the latest equipment for one reason: to make people better. They actually wanted their patients to survive. But with Noel and Crystal, survival didn't seem to be an issue.

"So the where could be anywhere," Claire said. "What about the who and the why?"

"The who is someone with training and tools," I said. "Maybe some psycho surgeon with an OR in his basement."

As soon as I said that, I thought it was a crazy idea. But was it? Could the killer be some rogue doc, doing illegal surgeries? Or some psycho with a doctor fetish who captured and practiced on prostitutes? Was this his method of torture? Some sick fuck getting his jollies? If so, it was pretty damned complex.

That opened up other questions. What had it been like for Noel? Was she asleep for the procedures? Jesus, I didn't want to think about that.

"Maybe this is some elaborate form of piquerism," I said.

"What's that?" Claire asked.

"It's a type of torture. A piquerist is someone who tortures his victim with small cuts and pricks. I saw a case when I was with the FBI behavioral science guys."

Claire pulled a notepad from her purse. "How do you spell it?"

"Seen it two ways," I said. "P-i-q-u-e-r-i-s-t and p-i-c-a-r-i-s-t. Either way a bad deal."

"Is this for real? People actually do that?"

"It's rare but it's out there. Death by a thousand cuts."

Claire turned to me. "You don't think that's it, do you?"

"No. This is something else." I twisted away the knot that was gathering in my neck. "Something worse."

"What?" Claire asked. "And why?"

"That's the question," I said. "The key. If we uncover the why, we'll find the who. That's the way it works. People always have a reason for doing things. Even these kinds of things."

"Well, it's not for money," Claire said. "If that were the case, survival would be paramount. Hard to collect from a dead person."

"Unless they paid up front," T-Tommy said.

"These girls didn't need surgery," I said. "Why would they pay for them?"

"Maybe they thought they were getting something else. Boobs, noses, whatever. Once they were asleep, anything could happen."

True. But it still didn't answer the why question. "I don't see this as a money deal. If that was his motive, why not take the money and simply kill them? Why go through all this surgery?"

No one had a comment.

"This would be a risky setup. Both girls were operated on over and over again. Means they were held somewhere between the surgeries. Means that the surgery itself is the real payoff or why take the chance." None of this made much sense. Even as I spoke I wasn't sure I believed or even understood any of it. "I also can't buy this being some guy with a head full of bad wiring, playing doctor in his basement. All this would require more than just the cutter. A nurse, someone to give anesthesia, some kind of ICU arrangement."

"Not to mention monitors, drugs, IVs, ventilators, all that scary shit you see in hospitals," T-Tommy added.

I stared into my bourbon, trying to pull something rational from a pile of craziness. Two healthy young women, subjected to multiple surgeries they didn't need, using some new, high-tech procedure, and, after the killer was finished with them, buried in the woods.

Why? What was the payoff? There was always a payoff. Sometimes it wasn't obvious, but it was there. I just couldn't get my mind around it.

When something didn't make sense, either there were things you didn't know yet, or you were looking at the things you knew all wrong. Or both. Not sure which was the case here, but I hated it.

CHAPTER 30

ALEJANDRO HEARD THEM COMING. HE SETTLED CARMELITA INTO position, reminding her to follow his cue. If he sensed something was wrong, he'd hold back, but if he attacked Austin, she had to be ready. He retreated to the far wall, a few steps from the door.

He heard the key settle into place and the lock click open. The door swung inward. Austin stood there, filling the space, but instead of entering the room, he waved his gun at Alejandro. "Let's go."

Alejandro moved toward him. Austin stepped back, clearing the doorway. Alejandro looked at Carmelita and then walked into the hallway. Austin and Lefty took him to the same room he had been in before and sat him in the same chair. This time there were no bright lights in his face. Austin stood behind him, pressing the muzzle of his gun against the base of Alejandro's skull. Lefty sat across from him.

"You fucked up," Lefty said.

Alejandro stared at him. Waited him out.

"They found the girls' bodies. The ones from the other night." He set his jaw. "You didn't bury them deep enough. Some goddamn pigs dug them up."

Fucking Eddie, Alejandro thought. He should have dumped that little prick long ago. But he didn't and so here he sat. "Not much I can do about that."

Lefty's jaw muscles pulsed. Austin ground the muzzle against Alejandro's skull. It hurt.

"We want to know where all the others are," Lefty said.

Alejandro laughed. "You're kidding."

"No. I'm not."

"They're in the woods. Here and there. I don't remember where. We just drove out to a dark place and stuck them in the ground."

Lefty leaned back. "You don't remember where?"

"I couldn't even tell you exactly where the last ones were. I didn't know I was supposed to keep a goddamn diary."

Austin rapped the barrel of his gun against Alejandro's head. Lefty tossed a scowl to Austin.

Why weren't they beating on him? Why was Lefty calling Austin off? This was the second time they'd held back. Could only mean that they still needed something. And he had it. His get-out-of-jail card. Giving it up wasn't an option. Not until he was free. Not until he had leverage.

"Ask Eddie," Alejandro said. "Maybe he'll remember."

"We'll do that," Austin said.

"Where's Eddie?"

"He's around."

"I want to see him."

Austin rapped the barrel against the side of his head again. "Ain't going to happen."

He rubbed his head and said, "We might be able to find some of them. We could take a drive and see if it stirs my memory."

"You'd like that, wouldn't you?" Lefty said. "Give you a chance to try an escape."

"You could keep Carmelita here. As insurance."

Lefty snorted. "Like you give a shit what happens to that whore. Too late for that, anyway."

"What does that mean?"

"It means they've already found the bodies. You should have done it right the first time."

"Then why are we sitting here? If it's too late, what do you want?"

Lefty said nothing. Apparently he didn't have an answer to that one. Must have thought that Alejandro would just roll over and do tricks. Maybe draw them a map. No way. As long as they needed him they'd keep him alive. That gave him time, and time gave him a chance.

CHAPTER 31

THEY LET ALEJANDRO RELIEVE HIMSELF BEFORE THEY TOOK HIM back to the room where Carmelita sat against one wall. A woman knelt next to her. Carmelita held one arm folded against her chest, while the woman placed three tubes of blood into slots in a wire basket.

"What the hell is this?" Alejandro asked.

Austin pushed him toward the opposite wall. "Just shut your mouth, sit down, and stick your arm out."

Alejandro sat.

The woman now knelt next to him. He extended his arm. She secured a tourniquet around it, made a swipe with an alcohol swab, cool against his skin, and deftly punctured the thick purple vein in the soft recess inside his elbow. She filled three tubes with blood, removed the tourniquet and the needle, and folded his arm on a cotton ball. She then stood and left the room. Not a single word.

Austin used his shoe to slide two bags and two bottles of water into the room, his gun never leaving Alejandro's chest. "Time to visit the john." He waved Carmelita toward the door. "You know the drill." He stepped aside, allowing her to pass into the hallway.

After the door closed, Alejandro settled back against the wall, deep in thought. What the hell was that? Some woman came in and drew blood. Didn't say a word. Then food and trips to the john as if nothing was different. He jumped when he heard a key click against the lock. The door opened.

A man entered the room. He wore a tailored suit and carried a Glock. "Hello, Alejandro."

"Who are you?"

"Karl Reinhardt."

Reinhardt. Alejandro had never met the man, only talked with him on the phone. "What are you doing here?"

"Just wanted to let you know that I had nothing to do with this. I wasn't consulted."

"Get me out of here."

"Can't do that. Not just yet, anyway." Reinhardt pursed his lips. "Have you said anything? About us?"

"Of course not."

"Good. Don't. I can only help you if they trust me."

"Are you here to help me or cover your own ass?"

"Don't you think those two go hand in hand?"

Alejandro started to get up, but Reinhardt waved the gun,

indicating that it wasn't a good idea. Alejandro hesitated, considering whether he should take a chance, try to overpower the man. Better one than three. Square head, close-cropped hair, chiseled features, Reinhardt looked like he could handle himself. Even though Reinhardt wore a suit, Alejandro could see that he was hard, fit. "So, why're you here?"

"To let you know that this will all work out. Just relax and don't do anything stupid."

"How do I know I can trust you?"

"Didn't I come to you? Haven't I paid you regularly?"

That was true. Ten months ago Reinhardt had contacted him, waved a proposition under his nose. A grand a month and all Alejandro had to do was report in once a week. Let Reinhardt know what Rocco was up to. He didn't know who Reinhardt was or who he worked for, but he knew that Reinhardt resented Rocco and his goons and more than once had called Rocco "that fat wop." No love lost. Maybe he could use that.

"Who do you work for?" Alejandro asked.

"That's not important. What's important is that you have to trust me."

"I'm just brimming with trust about now."

Reinhardt glanced over his shoulder.

"Who are you afraid of?" Alejandro asked. "Who's in charge? You? Rocco?"

Reinhardt's face stiffened. "This is my domain."

"Exactly where is here?"

He ignored the question. "Rocco and his people are invited guests."

"Doesn't look that way to me."

"Trust me. This'll all be over soon."

"This what?"

Reinhardt's gaze dropped to the floor and then back up to Alejandro. "This detention."

"Then what? You take care of Rocco and just let us go? Have a nice day. All that shit? Why do I find that hard to believe?"

"I can't explain everything now." Reinhardt glanced over his shoulder again. "I've got to go. Sit tight, and everything will work out." He slipped back through the door and locked it.

Lying motherfucker. Reinhardt came here to find out if he had talked. Just like Rocco, he didn't give a good goddamn what happened so long as it didn't get any shit on his shoes. Alejandro had to get out of here. Then he could bring the whole thing down.

Carmelita didn't return for nearly half an hour. As soon as the door closed, she curled on the mattress and pulled the blanket over her head. Alejandro could see her shoulders shaking and hear her crying. He knelt next to her as the door behind him snapped shut and the men retreated down the hallway.

"What's wrong?" he asked.

She said nothing, sliding deeper beneath the blanket.

Alejandro peeled the cover back and looked at her tear-streaked face. He then pulled her into a sitting position, bringing her face against his chest. She cried even harder. He waited, letting her get it all out before he spoke. "Are you okay?"

"I can't stand it." Carmelita sobbed against him. "I'm tired of being their *puta*. Why don't they just go ahead and kill us?"

"Because they need something."

She moved away from him and tugged the blanket around her, tucking it beneath her chin. "Not from me. From you. What is it?"

"I don't know."

"Fuck you, you asshole. You and that loser Eddie got me into this. I don't know anything. I'm not part of your bullshit."

"Keep your voice down."

"Oh, I forgot. They might be listening." She threw the blanket aside, stood, and walked to the door. "Fuck you. You motherfuckers want to kill me, come ahead. I'll rip your goddamn eyes out."

"This isn't helping," he said.

Carmelita whirled on him, fire in her eyes. "You arrogant prick."

"We have to stick to the plan."

"Oh yeah. Your great escape plan."

His jaw tightened involuntarily, and he balled his fists. "You got a better idea?"

She paced back and forth, breathing heavily, but said nothing. He let her steam for a minute until she finally stopped and looked at him. "I'm scared."

"I know." Alejandro patted the mattress. "Sit down. Eat your food."

She hesitated but then sat next to him. He opened a bottle of water and gave it to her. She took several gulps and wiped her eyes with the back of her hand.

"I'm sorry," she said. "I just can't stand the waiting."

"That's because this is a war, and that's what war is. Hours of boredom and moments of terror. Boredom saps your will, makes it harder to prepare for the battle." He unwrapped the sandwiches, handing one to her.

Carmelita took a bite. "Were you in the military?"

"Marines."

"Any idea what that was about?" she asked. "The blood?"

He washed a bite of sandwich down with water. "None."

"Do you think they might use it to frame us for something?"

Alejandro considered that but rejected it. Didn't make sense. "The last thing they want is for us to talk to the police. Frame or no frame."

"Then what?"

"No clue."

CHAPTER 32

I STOOD NEXT TO T-TOMMY, BOTH OF US WEDGED IN THE TRAILER'S tiny bathroom, and looked at the body that lay crumpled on the shower floor. Thirty minutes earlier I had been stretched out on my sofa reading the latest James Lee Burke novel when T-Tommy called.

"We got the guy that buried the girls," he said.

"Where?"

"In his trailer. Dead."

So here I stood. The air was warm and sticky and laced with death. I breathed through my mouth to knock down the odor, but it still tweaked my stomach. Nothing in the world smelled like a rotting corpse. I guessed this one had gone down a few days ago, and, with daily temperatures in the eighties, the putrefaction process was well under way. Most of Mother Nature's odors were pleasant. Flowers and honey and fresh mowed grass and things like that. This wasn't one of those. This hung at the other end of the spectrum.

Cause of death here no mystery. Single entry wound in the back of the head just above the right ear and an ugly, gaping exit wound through the left orbit. Took the eye with it.

"Boy's gettin' a bit ripe," T-Tommy said.

"You got that right," I said.

"Bathroom's the most dangerous place in the house. Falls, 'lectrical shit, Norman Bates. Bad news all the way around."

"How'd you find him?"

T-Tommy nodded toward the door. I turned and saw a uniformed officer peering past T-Tommy. T-Tommy introduced me to Derrick Stone.

Stone gave me the story. "The lab guys pulled a handful of prints off the plastic the girls were wrapped in, a couple of others off an empty whiskey bottle, and a partial from the glass lens cover of a flashlight found near the dump site. They believe they're from at least two people. Maybe more. Problem is that only a couple of the prints were usable. Others were smeared. Ran the good ones through IAFIS and got a hit. Eddie Elliott. Has a pending armed robbery trial in Georgia and a sister who lives here."

"Here?" I asked.

Stone shook his head. "Not here as in this trailer. Here in Huntsville."

"Where'd you get that?"

"Arrest report in Atlanta. She posted the bail. Gave her a call. Said she didn't know where her brother was. I figured, yeah, right.

She makes his bail. She'd know he was in town, where he was hanging. Maybe with her. So I went over to her place, gave her the accessory-after-the-fact BS, and she told us about this place."

"Where is she?" I asked.

"Out in the car, giving a statement to one of the guys. She ID'd the body." Stone motioned to the corpse. "So, meet Eddie Elliott, the guy who dumped the two girls. Maybe killed them, too."

I leaned into the shower and inspected the body more closely. "Any estimate of the time of death?"

"Coroner's tech guessed forty-eight to seventy-two hours. Maybe a little longer." T-Tommy took a step back, wrinkled his nose, and waved a hand in front of his face. "I hate this shit."

The blood spatters on the wall and floor of the shower stall were the typical high-velocity spatters of a gunshot wound. Their pattern indicated that Eddie had been shot more or less where he lay. Had he been knocked unconscious first? I didn't see any evidence of head trauma. Other than the entrance and exit wounds. Could have been cowering, turning away from the muzzle, not wanting to see it coming. Maybe he'd been drugged. Drummond would do the tox stuff as part of the autopsy, so we'd find out what turned up there. Right now, I'd seen enough of the late Eddie Elliott.

T-Tommy led the way into the living room and stopped near the table. He pointed out several bags of white powder on its surface.

"Crystal meth?" I asked.

"Probably. Lab boys haven't arrived yet."

"What's this guy's story?" I jerked my head toward the bathroom. "Other than armed robbery and burying dead girls. Any indication that he dealt?"

"A minor player, according to his sheet," Stone said. "Mostly crystal. Ellie—that's his sister—said he doesn't use. Never did. That he wasn't dealing anymore. Not since he left Atlanta and came here."

"I'm sure I believe that." I looked around the trailer. No damage, no signs of a struggle. Either Eddie knew the killer, or the killer caught him in the shower. I indicated the drug packets on the table. "I'd bet those are plants. Disguise the hit."

"Could be," T-Tommy said.

"Maybe Eddie's past caught up with him?" Stone said.

I noticed a couple of bags on the floor beneath a chair. Probably slid off when the shooter tossed them on the table. Hit probably happened at night. In the dark the hitter didn't see the bags tumble to the floor. "Except dealers and strung out junkies don't usually leave product behind. User wants to get it up inside him. To the dealer it's cash."

T-Tommy shoved his hands into his pockets and rocked back slightly on his heels. "I guess it's possible Eddie owed somebody and they decided to send a message. Word gets out; next guy won't screw around."

"Hope this isn't the start of another drug war," Stone said. "Remember the last one?"

"All too well," T-Tommy said.

Drug wars. I'd seen a few of those. The weaponry involved was downright military. Some of these jerk weeds would use RPGs if they had them. Which would be fine if they just killed each other. Unfortunately citizens often caught the collateral flak.

"Maybe we can find the cook," Stone said. "Maybe the lab can match this batch to him. Build a trail from there. Round up the usual suspects."

I refrained from launching into my favorite tirade on why the usual suspects weren't behind bars, why defense attorneys were allowed to live, why the system was fucked up and on its way to extinction. Instead I said, "That's what whoever dumped these bags is hoping you'll do. Spin your wheels in the wrong direction." I turned to T-Tommy. "The real question is why Eddie buried two bodies in the woods. Two bodies that had undergone an entire textbook's worth of surgical procedures. Eddie doesn't look like he had a medical degree, which means he isn't the cutter. He's simply the garbageman."

"And now somebody took out the garbageman."

"Exactly."

CHAPTER 33

SATURDAY 6:29 P.M.

WHERE THE HELL ARE THEY?

Alejandro paced the room, stopping near the door occasionally to see if he could hear anything. Something was wrong. They should have been here by now.

"Sit," Carmelita said. "Save your energy."

"Got to keep moving."

"Come here." She motioned him toward her.

He knelt in front of her. "What?"

"You think they know?" Carmelita whispered.

"I don't know."

"Should we call it off?"

Alejandro sensed doubt creeping into her voice. He had beaten back those fears, instilled a degree of confidence in her, showing her several ways to go for the face and eyes. She bought into it, steeled her nerves, ready to go. But now? The wait had sapped that confidence. "No. Last night didn't work but tonight will. I feel it."

"*Adivino.*" She laughed. "You a fortune-teller now?"

"All I know is the longer we're here, the weaker we get. We do it tonight."

She sighed. "I just wish they would hurry up. Something must be—"

"Shhh." He heard voices and footsteps. "Here they come." He looked her in the eye. "You ready?"

Carmelita stood. "Let's do it." She moved to the left of the door, out of the line of sight, and crouched.

Alejandro took his position facing the door.

The lock clicked, the door swung open, and Austin walked through. His arms hung loosely at his sides, gun stuffed beneath his belt, not in his hand as usual. *Good.*

Alejandro stepped toward him, fists tightly balled, preparing his attack. Austin's right hand snapped up. A whispering puff. A sharp pain in his gut. He looked down. A metal barb penetrated his shirt. A small halo of blood. His arms felt heavy and weak. His vision dimmed as he saw Lefty enter the room. Carmelita launched herself at him. Alejandro's world faded, his legs folded, and he seemed to float to the floor.

CHAPTER 34

"So how do you read this?" T-Tommy asked.

We stood outside Eddie's trailer. The sun had made its retreat, leaving behind a Dreamsicle western sky. A wad of blue-black thunderheads crouched near the horizon and pushed a cool breeze, heavy with the smell of rain, in our direction.

"I'd like to think Eddie was popped for doing sloppy work. Screwed up the burial, bodies were found, and someone took him out. But the timing's out of whack. Eddie was done two or three days ago. The corpses weren't found until yesterday."

"He was somebody's liability," T-Tommy said. "This ain't no robbery, and it ain't no drug hit."

"Which means he became a problem before the bodies were found."

"Maybe with other corpses," T-Tommy said. "Maybe this guy's a serial killer."

I saw lightning pulse against the distant clouds, gilding their edges and lighting a fire in their bellies. Too far for the thunder to reach us. "If so, he's not the run-of-the-mill type."

T-Tommy stared at me.

"A serial could do all this stuff. The surgeries. If he had the skills. They can do some sick shit. But I've never heard of one getting someone else to dump the bodies. Then executing that someone. Doesn't fit."

"Even for an organized type?"

"Not saying it isn't possible, only that it isn't likely." I glanced at the door to Eddie's trailer. Stone stood inside talking with a uniform. "I don't see the fantasy here. Most serials, at least the sexually sadistic subtypes, are driven by sexual fantasies. They don't usually share their fantasies with anyone. Like a garbageman."

"Just the victims," T-Tommy said.

How true. "There were none of the sexual assaults or genital mutilations typical of the sexually sadistic types."

"Then what type is this guy?"

"Don't know, but he sure has an elaborate method of torture."

"You think maybe he hired Eddie to grab victims for him," T-Tommy said. "Not share what he's doing or why. Just paid him to pick up hookers."

I thought about that for a beat. "That would expose him, but it could work." Another pulse of lightning caught my eye. Closer. I mentally counted to eight before I heard the faint rumble of thunder. "This is more than just skill and fancy equipment. Couldn't be done by a single person and probably not by two people . . . Eddie and the killer. I'd guess at least three or four. Someone has to capture the victims, someone has to operate on them, someone has to guard them, someone has to care for them after the surgeries, and someone has to dump the bodies. Even if Eddie was hired to do the capturing and dumping, the logistics of doing the surgeries, the aftercare, and the guarding would be a team effort. Serials aren't pack animals."

"Now, there's a visual," T-Tommy said. "A pack of serial killers. What would you call that? A pod? A gaggle?"

"A murder," I said. "Like crows."

"Maybe it's some kind of satanic cult," T-Tommy said.

"Speaking of visuals," I said. "A cult of satanic surgeons. This is just too weird."

"Let's talk to the sister."

CHAPTER 35

SATURDAY 6:47 P.M.

WE FOUND ELLIE ELLIOTT SITTING IN THE BACKSEAT OF A PATROL car, door open, feet on the ground, head bowed. She had twisted a tissue into a frayed knot. Red, puffy eyes looked up. Even through her grief I could see she was an attractive woman. Maybe thirty, blonde hair, blue eyes, white blouse, blue jeans, Rolex knockoff on her left wrist.

T-Tommy rested a hand on top of the cruiser. "Ms. Elliott, I'm Investigator Tortelli. Huntsville PD. This is Dub Walker."

She looked at me.

"Investigating the murder of a friend," I said.

"You were a friend of Eddie's?"

"No. Someone else."

Her gaze moved to T-Tommy and back to me. "What does that have to do with Eddie?"

"Maybe nothing," I said.

"Or maybe something?" Ellie swallowed hard, sniffed, and brought the tissue up to dab one eye.

T-Tommy squatted. "I need to ask you a few questions, if you don't mind."

"Sure." Her hands dropped to her lap. Trembling fingers wadded the tissue into a ball.

"I know your brother has an armed robbery trial coming up over in Georgia. And I know you bailed him out."

"I didn't know about the trial." She sat up straighter and let out a long, uneven breath. "Eddie told me he'd taken care of it. Had some attorney who was going to get the charges dropped. That it was best if he stayed over here until it was done."

"You believed him?"

"Yes," Ellie said, then shook her head. "Not really. I wanted to."

"Any idea who might have done this?"

"No."

T-Tommy shifted his weight. "No threats or problems with anyone?"

"Not that I know."

"What about someone from Atlanta? Maybe came over to settle an old drug dispute?"

"I don't know much about what went on in Atlanta. Eddie rarely talked about it."

"The drugs we found. He selling again?"

"No. He told me he wasn't, anyway."

"What did he do for money?" I asked. "Any kind of job?"

"Nothing steady. I give him a little once in a while."

"Who pays the rent here?" I nodded toward the trailer.

"He does. It's only about a hundred and fifty a month."

"The odd jobs," T-Tommy said. "What are we talking about? Construction? Yard work?"

"I don't know. He never said."

"Who'd he work for?"

"A guy named Alejandro. Alejandro Diaz. He's an old boyfriend of mine. Gives Eddie work sometimes." A wavering roll of thunder caught her attention, and she looked in that direction. "I heard on the news when I was driving over that a storm was coming in. Had some flooding over in Florence."

"Can you give us a description of Mr. Diaz?" T-Tommy asked.

"Mr. Diaz?" Ellie rolled her eyes. "You make him sound like a bank president or something." When neither T-Tommy nor I responded, she went on. "He's tall, Hispanic, maybe thirty-five now. Very hot looking."

"What does he do?" I asked.

"Nothing regular. When we dated, a year or two ago, he bounced at a place called High Rollers. You know it?"

Well, well. Is this a cozy little planet or what? I made the connections in my head. Crystal worked for Rocco. This Alejandro dude worked for Rocco. Eddie worked for Alejandro. Crystal and Noel ended up dead with Eddie's fingerprints all over the place. Now someone whacked Eddie. Makes you wonder, don't it?

"He still work there?" I asked.

"Maybe. I don't know."

"Where does Alejandro live?"

"An apartment. Not far from here."

Ellie picked up her purse from the floor of the cruiser and pulled one of those day planner deals out. After flipping it open, she scribbled the address on a note page and tore it out, handing it to T-Tommy.

"I might have more questions later." He gave Ellie one of his cards. "If you think of anything, give me call."

CHAPTER 36

IT TOOK ONLY FIFTEEN MINUTES TO REACH THE PINE VIEW APARTMENTS, a pale yellow, two-story shit box, chewed around the edges by the years and the weather. A fresh coat of paint and a new roof wouldn't hurt.

T-Tommy and I got out of my Porsche. Four uniformed officers emerged from the two patrol cars that had followed us. One showed us a picture of Alejandro Diaz from his DMV file. He had brought it up on the computer in his cruiser and printed a copy. Dark hair and eyes, Hispanic, handsome, six one, one eighty. Just as Ellie had described.

T-Tommy instructed two of the officers to stay out front, the others to circle each end of the building. "Be ready. This guy could be armed. Watch out for civilians."

Alejandro lived in J, ground floor, back side of the sixteen-unit building, facing a forested area. No answer to T-Tommy's knock. I peered through the gap in the front window drapes. Dark inside. We walked back around to unit A, the manager's apartment, according to the sign on the door.

I knocked on the door. Cracks mapped its chocolate-brown paint, the angled light from the porch lamp causing their curled edges to jump up in stark relief. A pair of moths fluttered around the light and cast giant shadows on the porch. I heard movement inside.

The door eased open until the safety chain pulled taut. An elderly man in a gray terry cloth bathrobe peeked out. "Yes?"

T-Tommy badged him, saying, "Investigator Tortelli. HPD. Mind if I ask you a couple of questions?"

The man released the chain and swung the door open. His white hair was sparse and unruly. Probably caught him napping in front of the TV that I could hear through the open door. Sounded like an old Western, horses' hooves pounding in pursuit mode. I could envision the black hats fleeing from the white hats. Past the same rock formation over and over. Life was much simpler when viewed in black and white. The bad guys were bad, the good guys good. End of story. Technicolor screwed it all up.

We learned that Walter Moxley had been manager for eight years and that he knew Alejandro Diaz. Good tenant, no problems.

"What's this about?" Moxley asked.

T-Tommy offered a benevolent smile. "Just a routine follow-up on a case."

Moxley's age-creased face now creased further. "Is Alejandro in some kind of trouble?"

"Just need to ask him a few questions about a friend of his."

"Who?"

"Can't say. It's an ongoing investigation. I'm sure you understand."

Moxley nodded. "Bet it's that smart-assed kid."

"Which kid?" I asked.

Moxley shook his head. "Eddie something. Don't know his last name. A real asshole. Every time he comes here he has his radio blasting that rap shit, parks all sideways, taking up two, three spaces. I warned him, but he don't care."

T-Tommy tossed me a glance and then looked at Moxley. "When was the last time he was here?"

"Week. Maybe a little longer." Moxley cocked his head. "He the one you investigating?"

"Can't say."

"Wouldn't surprise me none. That boy's trouble with a big *T*."

"Any idea where Alejandro might be?" I asked. "When he'll be back?"

Moxley scratched the gray stubble on his chin. "Heard his truck leave yesterday—no, wait . . . before that." His gaze turned upward. "That's right. Wednesday afternoon. I remember that's the day I had a doctor's appointment. Saw him getting in his truck as I was leaving. Maybe two thirty or so. Haven't seen him since."

I glanced at the parking lot, an asphalt rectangle at the end of the complex right next to Moxley's apartment. Hard for the old man not to know his tenants' comings and goings. "Is that unusual? For him not to come back for a day or two?"

"Not really."

"What kind of vehicle does he drive?"

"Pickup. Red. Don't know the make."

"Besides this Eddie guy, anybody else drop by to see Alejandro?" T-Tommy asked.

"Occasionally a woman, but mostly he's quiet."

"Pay his rent?"

"Always on time." He waved a hand toward the building. "Wish I could get the others to do that."

"Don't mention to Alejandro that we were here," T-Tommy said. "Okay?"

Moxley shrugged.

"Wouldn't want to upset him." T-Tommy handed Moxley a card. "Call me if Alejandro returns."

"Want me to call if Eddie comes by, too?"

"Sure," T-Tommy said. "That'd be helpful."

Eddie won't be coming by, I thought. Eddie was bagged and tagged and on his way to see Drummond and Cooksey.

CHAPTER 37

ALEJANDRO EASED INTO CONSCIOUSNESS, AWARE THAT A BRIGHT light pushed against his closed eyelids. Momentarily confused, he remained still and silent, absorbing sensations. He lay on a firm surface. Cool air with an astringent odor. Faint voices nearby to his left. He cracked open his eyes. A blast of light hit him. Where was he?

He searched his memory and quickly came up with the last scene he remembered. The room, Austin, the dart.

How long had he been out?

Alejandro attempted to raise one arm to block the light but was unable to move. At first he thought he was just too weak, too groggy, but then he realized that something bound his wrists to the table. Ankles, too. He blinked his vision clear. The glare above him became a circular bank of lights. He lifted his head and saw that he wore a pair of blue drawstring pants, no shirt, his feet bare.

The voices captured his attention again, and he turned his head toward them. Three men, one of them Austin, and a woman stood near a computer console.

One of the men looked in his direction and moved to his side. Light brown hair, with a hint of gray, hung beneath a surgical cap, and intense blue eyes peered down at him. "Welcome back."

"Who the fuck are you?" Alejandro asked.

"Your doctor."

"What?"

Austin stepped forward. "What? Is that all you can come up with? Not such hot shit now, are you?"

"Mr. Austin tells me you were a bit of a problem," the so-called doctor said.

"That's why I'm going to enjoy this." Austin laughed. "Almost as much as I'm going to enjoy the four grand me and Lefty got for your sorry ass."

"What the fuck are you talking about?"

"You're such a moron. You think the peanuts me and Lefty tossed your way was a big deal? We were making a fortune selling all those bodies to my friend here." Austin clapped a hand on the doctor's shoulder. "We just didn't want to do the digging. The grunt work. That's why God created Mexicans like you and brainless pricks like Eddie."

Alejandro jerked against the restraints. "Remove the straps, *hijo de puta*. Then we'll see how tough you are."

Austin leaned forward and pressed a thumb into Alejandro's

cheekbone. Pain shot through the entire side of his face. "Be careful, or I'll gouge an eye right out of your face."

The doctor laid a hand on Austin's arm. "That's enough."

"Who are you?" Alejandro asked.

"I told you. I'm your doctor."

Another man appeared and stood next to the doctor. He also wore a cap and had a surgical mask dangling from his neck. He was younger, his skin pale, and his eyes icy blue.

"This is my assistant," the doctor said.

Alejandro felt a chill slide along his back. "What's this about?"

"The future, Mr. Diaz. Medical progress. Your contributions will be well appreciated."

Contribuciones? "What the hell are you talking about?"

"All in good time."

"Carmelita?" Alejandro asked. "Where is she?"

"Don't worry about her. She's nearby."

Austin laughed. "Four grand for her, too. You guys just paid for my trip to Hawaii next month."

Alejandro twisted and pulled against the restraints. "Fuck you."

Austin slammed a fist into his ribs. "No. Fuck you, you Mexican piece of shit."

"Stop it," the doctor said. "Mr. Austin, why don't you go? We can handle everything here."

"Fine. Give me a shout if you need anything." Austin turned and left the room.

"Sorry about all that," the man said. His voice was soft, almost soothing. "Mr. Austin can be a bit rude at times." He touched Alejandro's ribs. "I don't think he broke anything."

The man clapped his hands together. "Let's get to work." He retreated to a corner of the room where he grabbed the handle of a cart. He maneuvered it up next to Alejandro.

"What's that?" Alejandro asked.

The older man looked down at him and smiled.

Alejandro felt panic swell in his chest. "What the fuck is that?"

"Your surgeon."

CHAPTER 38

EARLIER T-TOMMY AND I SWUNG BY SAMMY'S FOR SOME Q AND THEN rolled toward High Rollers. The temperature had dropped a few degrees, and mist peppered the windshield. The storm was on its way in.

"Time for a little carpet bombing," T-Tommy said as we walked toward the entrance. "Give the locals a shake, and see what falls out."

Another twenty-dollar cover charge and we settled at a table near one wall. A thick haze of cigarette smoke and the pulse of rock music filled the room.

Immediately a waitress appeared. Lean, blonde, and wearing the uniform: bikini-like shorts and a skimpy halter top. "I'm Kirsten. What can I get you?"

We ordered a pair of Maker's Marks, neat. I watched as she walked away. Great legs and a practiced strut.

"My, my," T-Tommy said.

"How do you want to play it?" I asked.

"Straight up. Let's ask around, let the word get back to Rocco, and see what he does. I'll hit up the bartender. The one we saw the other night. Believe his name was Sean." He headed toward the bar.

In five minutes, T-Tommy slid back into his chair just as Kirsten returned with our bourbons.

"Anything else?" she asked.

"Not now," T-Tommy said. "Don't be a stranger, though."

I sipped my Maker's and looked around the room. The patrons were almost exclusively male, only a handful of women, probably here for the men but maybe not. Everyone's gaze seemed to be locked on the tight-bodied blonde on the main stage, bumping and writhing to the rhythm of the Stones' "Honky Tonk Women." Three rowdy suits, probably lawyers, stuffed bills beneath the elastic of her G-string. *Fools and their money.*

The song ended, and the blonde stepped down from the stage, slipped into a thin jacket, hiding nothing, and snaked her way through the tables, collecting bills from the guys. She stopped at our table and smiled. "Want a private dance?"

I shook my head. She headed to another table.

Kirsten reappeared. "You guys doing okay?"

"Got a question for you," I said. When she didn't respond, I went on. "We're looking for a guy. Used to bounce here. Maybe a year ago. Name's Alejandro Diaz."

"Don't know him. I've only been here a few months. What's he look like?"

"Hispanic. Tall. Maybe six one."

She thought for a minute. "Not sure, but you could mean this guy that hangs with one of Carmelita's regulars. A guy named Eddie. His buddy's tall. Don't remember his name, though."

"Alejandro, maybe?"

She shrugged. "Could be."

"Where's Carmelita?"

Kirsten scanned the room. "I haven't seen her. I don't think she's working tonight."

"Thanks."

She started to turn away but stopped. "You might ask Madison. She's Carmelita's best friend. I'll send her over when I see her."

"That would be great," I said.

"Another round?"

"Sure."

As T-Tommy and I continued working on our drinks, a striking blonde walked up. She looked young. Maybe too young.

"I'm Madison." She smiled. "Kirsten said you wanted a dance."

"Maybe later," I said. "Buy you a drink?"

"That would be nice." Translation: easy money. "A gin and tonic would be great." Which meant tonic on the rocks for ten bucks. Talk didn't come cheap at High Rollers. Not that anything did. "You guys from out of town? Never seen you in here before."

"We don't get out much," T-Tommy said.

She gave us a knowing nod. "Married."

I laughed. "No. Just heard this place was fun."

"If you want fun, you're definitely at the right place."

"Packed like this every night?" I asked.

"Sometimes more," Madison said.

"How long you worked here?"

"I came on at six."

I smiled. "I meant, how many years?"

She laughed. "Oh. Couple of years. Before that I worked at a bank."

"You like this better?"

Madison looked at me. "That must be it."

I waited.

"It's a money thing," she said. "A girl can do real well here. If you can tolerate the grind."

"We're looking for someone."

She cocked her head but said nothing.

"Guy named Alejandro Diaz. You know him?"

I noticed Madison's posture stiffen. A slight squint to her eyes and a barely noticeable pursing of her lips. She looked at the floor and then back at me. "I remember faces, but I'm not very good with names."

Quick under pressure, her answer nearly perfect. No admission, no denial. Would have been perfect had her gaze not dropped again, avoiding me, giving her away.

"Used to bounce here. Still might sometimes," I said.

She glanced around as if hoping someone would rescue her

before she had to answer. She got lucky. Kirsten walked over.

"I see Madison found you," Kirsten said. She smiled at Madison. "Anything?"

"Gin and tonic."

I noticed Sean the bartender go up the stairs and into Rocco's office. The gorilla beside the office door didn't move. Looked to be half asleep, boredom on his face.

Rocco looked up when he heard a knock on the door. Lefty and Austin, sitting in the chairs across from his desk, didn't move. "Yeah?" Rocco said.

Sean pushed the door open and walked inside. "Those two guys? The cop types? They're back. They asked about Alejandro, and now they're huddled at a table with Madison."

Rocco nodded. "Thanks. I'll handle it."

Sean closed the door when he left.

Rocco retrieved a half-smoked cigar from the ashtray near his left elbow and stared at Lefty and Austin. "These guys are becoming a pain in the ass." He relit the cigar stub and clamped it between his teeth. "Asking about Alejandro. Chatting up Carmelita's friend Madison. Nothing good can come from that. Get down there. See what the hell they're up to."

They stood.

"Make sure Madison keeps her fucking mouth shut."

"How far can we go?"

Rocco blew a cloud of smoke into the air. "As far as it takes."

CHAPTER 39

MADISON TOOK A QUICK SIP OF HER DRINK. "SURE YOU GUYS DON'T WANT a dance?"

I scooted my chair close, leaned forward, elbows on knees. "We're just looking for Alejandro, and I think you know who he is." I scanned the room. "I'd bet most of the girls in here know him, too."

"Then why don't you ask one of them?"

"You're the prettiest."

She gave me a half smile. "You guys cops?"

"Him yes, me no."

"You look like a cop."

"I get that a lot."

Again a half smile lifted the corners of her mouth.

"We know Alejandro works here. Off and on. We know he has a sidekick named Eddie."

Madison glanced at Rocco's office, then the bar. "I don't want any trouble."

"I promise we're not trying to bring any down on you, but you do know Alejandro and Eddie, don't you?"

She nodded.

"When did you see them last?"

"A few nights ago. Wednesday."

"You sure?"

"Yes. They left about eleven."

"Where were they going?"

Her gaze bounced up at Rocco's office again. "I have to go." She pushed her chair back.

Looking up, I saw the gorilla staring at us. So were the two guys who came out of Rocco's office. I grabbed Madison's arm. "Relax. Nobody's going to do anything to you."

Madison jerked her arm away and stood. "Don't touch me. I've already told you too much. Leave me alone." She moved through the tables, ignoring several guys who waved bills at her, before disappearing through a door that I suspected led to the dancers' dressing area.

The two guys came down the stairs, watching us.

"We got company," I said.

They pushed through the crowd, taking the direct route. One was tall, lean, maybe midthirties, the other younger, with iron-pumped muscles. Each had dark, close-cropped hair, and there wasn't a hint of a smile between them. They wore black T-shirts beneath sports coats, one tan, one gray. Probably some unwritten tough guy dress code.

I was wearing the same outfit. Except my jacket was black. Maybe they'd think I was part of their club. Probably not, based on their scowls.

I sensed T-Tommy slide to the front of his chair, ready to react.

"Can we help you guys?" the muscular one asked when they reached our table.

"Maybe two more bourbons," I said.

"Funny. Mind telling me what you're doing here?"

I grinned. "We love naked women. Don't you?"

"Drink up," he said. "That was last call."

Me: "Really? This early?"

T-Tommy: "Does seem early, don't it? Not even midnight yet."

Me: "How do they stay in business closing so early?"

T-Tommy: "Beats me."

Me: "Maybe it's a tax write-off."

The taller man's jaw tightened. "Listen up, assholes. Mr. Scarcella says you go, you go. Now get the fuck out."

Me: "Where'd you guys train for this job?"

T-Tommy: "Must have been a correspondence course."

Me: "They do seem a little short on people skills."

T-Tommy: "Were you guys close to your mothers?"

Me: "Didn't teach them any manners."

T-Tommy: "None at all."

"Are you guys deaf?" Muscles asked.

"You could ask nicely," I said.

He smirked. "Okay. Please. Pretty please with sugar on top. Get the fuck out of here."

"Soon as we finish our drinks."

"And she finishes her act." T-Tommy motioned to the slim redhead on the main stage. "Kinda hate to miss her."

"Want us to drag you outside?" the older guy said.

I shook my head. "Don't see much wisdom in following that path."

The man opened his jacket, exposing the butt of a gun stuffed beneath his belt.

"Would you look at that?" T-Tommy said. "He's got one, too."

"Kind of small, though," I said.

The man's face hardened. "This town's full of clowns. You assholes better take your act somewhere else. Or I might have to use this." He patted the gun.

T-Tommy smiled. "Be hard to use all stuffed down in your pants like that."

"Might shoot your own balls off trying to get it out of there," I said.

The muscular one tugged a handheld stun gun from his jacket pocket. I recognized it as a Raptor 100,000 volt job. He pressed the button, and a blue electrical arc sizzled between the two contact probes.

"My, my," T-Tommy said. "He brought his garage door opener with him."

The man closed in on T-Tommy, the Raptor extended in front of him. Bad idea. T-Tommy clamped his thick fingers around the guy's wrist and cranked his forearm outward. The man went to one knee, and the stun gun dropped to the floor.

T-Tommy leaned forward and dug his fingers into the guy's neck, squeezing his face purple. "Play nice, or I'll fuck you up."

The other man hesitated, apparently unable to believe that T-Tommy could move that quickly.

That gave me time to stand, step to the other man's side, and yank his weapon from beneath his belt. "Be cool," I said. I examined the gun, a SIG P226, 9mm, stainless steel finish. "Nice piece." I slipped the clip out and worked the slide, popping the chambered cartridge out. It spun across the table and fell to the floor. I handed the nine back to him. "Relax. Enjoy the show."

T-Tommy let go of Muscles's neck but maintained control by twisting his wrist into an awkward position. The man held his breath. Sweat popped out on his forehead. T-Tommy jerked the man's gun free and handed it to me.

I removed the clip and ejected the chambered shell from it, too. I laid it on the table. "That's better. Now, who are you guys?"

"None of your fucking business," the smaller guy said.

"Actually it is." T-Tommy pulled his badge from his pocket and flipped it open. "Threatening a police officer is serious stuff. You can answer the questions here or downtown. Your call."

Neither said anything for a moment, and then the man beside me said, "I'm Lefty. This is Austin."

"That wasn't so hard, was it?" T-Tommy released Austin's wrist and stood.

Austin rose and backed up a couple of steps.

"Maybe you guys can help us," I said. "We're looking for someone. Works here so I'm sure you know him. Alejandro Diaz."

Austin smirked. "Never heard of him."

"Me neither," Lefty added.

"Didn't think so." I looked at T-Tommy and nodded toward the door. "Been a real pleasure chatting with you gentlemen, but it's past our bedtime."

The two men glared at us as we pushed past them and headed toward the door.

I stopped and turned around. "When you hear from Alejandro, tell him we're looking for him."

"Didn't get your names," Austin said.

"I'm sure you know," I said.

As we walked out of High Rollers, T-Tommy clapped a hand on my shoulder and said, "That ought to shake the tree."

CHAPTER 40

ALEJANDRO SLIPPED FROM A STRANGE DREAM INTO AN EVEN stranger reality. He felt smothered, as if something had lodged in his throat. He tried to cough, met resistance, and then felt air forcibly rush into his lungs. He bucked and struggled to grab a single breath. Didn't happen. Another rush of air. He opened his eyes. His vision, fuzzy and distorted at first, cleared with a few blinks. A tube protruded from his mouth and joined a coiled hose that fell away to his left.

"Relax." The voice was female.

He turned his head, but the tube tugged at his throat, causing him to cough. Or something like coughing. It was more a spasm. He tried to reach for the tube, but his arms were bound to his sides. Pain ripped through his belly with each cough.

The woman came into view above him, smiling. Her face looked familiar, but he couldn't place her. "Relax. Everything's okay."

Again a coughing spasm hit him, and he gagged against the tube. More belly pain. What the hell was happening to him?

"Don't fight it. Take slow, deep breaths."

Alejandro did, but his lungs fought back. More gagging.

"That's the ventilator tube. Let me check a couple of things, and we'll get it out. Okay?"

He nodded, still unsure what was happening, fighting the impulse to cough, trying to remain calm. Not easy to do. Strapped down, unable to breathe, he felt a wave of panic rise. He took a slow breath. Then two more. That was better. Everything seemed to fall into rhythm once more.

The woman clipped something on his finger, waited a few seconds, and then said, "Perfect. O$_2$ sat's up to ninety-eight." She unclipped the gadget. "I was waiting for you to wake up. Now I can get that tube out." She smiled again.

It was coming back. He was strapped to a bed just as he had been earlier. Those two doctors, or so they said, were there. He remembered the woman looking down at him. Same smile. She had been there, too.

The woman disconnected the coiled hose from the tube in his throat. "Take a couple of deep breaths. Slow and easy." He did. She loosened the tape that wound around the tube and bound it to his cheeks. "This will only take a second. Now, don't breathe."

She held a thin plastic tube that whistled slightly as it sucked in air and quickly threaded it into the larger one in his throat. The suction tube gurgled, and he gagged and sputtered as it snaked into his lungs. Then with one smooth movement, she pulled both tubes from his throat. He coughed and gasped for air.

"That's better," she said. "Take a few breaths, and you'll be fine."

She was right. The smothering feeling evaporated, and he could breathe. After a couple of minutes, he had hacked his lungs clear, each cough sending shots of pain through his belly. The woman wiped his face clean.

Alejandro now noticed that an IV tube fed into his arm. Above his head a monitor emitted a steady beep. Floor-to-ceiling curtains blocked his view to either side. Beyond the one to his right he heard the rhythmic churning of another ventilator. The wall toward the foot of his bed was a bank of windows interrupted by a single door.

"Where am I?" he asked.

"Our little ICU," the woman said. "I'm Darlene. Your nurse."

"What happened?"

"Your surgery went well. Other than being absent a gallbladder and an appendix, you're as good as new."

He looked at the curtain.

Following his gaze, Darlene said, "Your girlfriend had the same procedures. She just got back a half hour ago, so she'll be out for a while yet." She peeled back the sheet that covered him to his waist. "You have a little bleeding from one of your wounds."

Alejandro looked down and saw two bandages, one high, one low, both on the right side of his belly. A patch of red stained the upper one.

He watched as she loosened the bandage. "Not bad." She rolled a metallic stand piled with gauze and instruments to the side of his bed. "I'll put on a new dressing."

While Darlene worked, removing the tape and gauze, swabbing on an astringent-smelling red liquid, and taping a new bandage into place, Alejandro put together bits and pieces of his memory. Slowly, it all came back.

What had Austin said about money? About selling him and Carmelita to that doctor? Four grand? If he and Lefty got that, then Rocco got a lot more. That was why Rocco kept them alive. It wasn't for information he knew they didn't have. It was money. Wasn't that always what it was with Rocco? That fat fuck.

"Who did this to me? Who were those two men?"

Darlene brushed a strand of hair off his forehead. The good little nurse. "All in good time. Right now you need your rest."

CHAPTER 41

T-Tommy and I played a hunch. If Madison had begun her shift at six, then she just might get off at midnight. Worth a try, anyway. We sat in my Porsche and waited. The rain came a bit harder for a few minutes but then stopped abruptly. I nudged the wiper control, giving the windshield a swipe.

The parking area still contained nearly a hundred cars and trucks. A hooded light over a side door and three lampposts scattered through the lot offered the only islands of light, everything else shadowy. We were parked in one of the shadows, partially shielded by a jacked-up dually pickup.

Three girls came out of the side door and headed to their cars. A few minutes later, two more. None were Madison. I was about ready to admit our hunch was wrong when T-Tommy said, "Well, well, well."

Madison came out with another girl. She now wore jeans and a red sweater, loose, wide necked, one shoulder exposed, a small duffel bag slung over the other. I glanced at the dash clock—12:11.

She waved to the other girl and wound through the parked cars, avoiding the collections of rainwater, until she reached a Toyota SUV, one hand digging into her bag.

The side door opened again, and Lefty came out. He hurried across the lot, reaching Madison just as her vehicle flashed and barked, now unlocked. She opened the door, but Lefty closed it. They appeared to talk for a few seconds before he grabbed her arm. She tried to pull away, but he held on.

We got out of the Porsche and walked in their direction.

"I was you I wouldn't do that," T-Tommy said.

Lefty's head jerked toward us. "This is none of your business."

"Is now," I said. I looked at Madison. "He bothering you?"

"No," she said. "It's okay."

"Don't look that way to me." T-Tommy stopped within three feet of Lefty. "Let the lady go."

"Fuck you," Lefty said, a hand slipping inside his coat.

These guys seemed hell-bent on making bad choices. Even expecting it I didn't see it. In a heartbeat, T-Tommy had Lefty's gun in his hand and a fist buried into the man's stomach.

Lefty dropped to his knees, coughing, gasping, retching.

"You don't listen so good, do you?" T-Tommy said.

T-Tommy passed the weapon to me, while Lefty struggled to his feet.

"You got a habit of losing this thing," I said. Lefty had reloaded, so again I snapped the clip from the gun and ejected the chambered round. "Maybe I should just keep it." I stared at him as I thumbed the bullets from the clip. One by one they clicked against the asphalt. I handed the gun back to him. "Now, get your ass inside before T-Tommy gets really pissed."

"You'll pay for this." Lefty wobbled toward the door, massaging his gut, glancing at us a couple of times.

"You okay?" I asked Madison.

"Yeah." She opened the door to her Toyota. "You better get out of here. He'll be back in a minute with Austin and a handful of the others."

"How about some coffee?" I asked.

"Not a chance. You've already caused enough trouble."

I pushed the door closed with my hip and leaned against it. A little rainwater soaked through my jeans. It felt cool. I ignored it. "Okay. We'll just chat right here."

"No. You . . . I got to get out of here before he comes back."

T-Tommy crossed his arms over his chest and shook his head. "Don't see that happening."

"Who the fuck are you guys?"

"Coffee?"

Madison exhaled loudly. "Okay. If we leave right now."

"We'll follow you."

CHAPTER 42

ALEJANDRO NEEDED A PLAN. RATHER, ANOTHER PLAN. THE LAST one hadn't worked out so well. The one sure thing was that as damaged as he was, it was only going to get worse. More surgery until he was dead. He knew. He'd buried the bodies.

He was angry with himself for not seeing the entire picture. For simply doing as he was told. For taking the money without question. He knew the bodies had to come from somewhere. He knew Rocco was involved. He knew Rocco wouldn't do anything that didn't put money in his pocket. Rocco always had plans within plans. Yet it never occurred to Alejandro that Rocco was selling victims to these people, whoever the hell they were.

Of course, he also knew things could come back on him. That burying bodies could leave him vulnerable. Not to this—he would never have imagined this—but to something. That's why he had his insurance papers safely hidden. But to use them, to buy his way out, he needed to be on the street.

"What time is it?" he asked.

Darlene was behind the curtain, checking on Carmelita. "A little after midnight. Hard to tell day from night down here in the basement."

Good. It was night.

Alejandro tested the restraints. Very little give. He examined the straps that looped around his wrists and ankles. The same type of buckled, wide, leather bands that earlier had bound him to the surgical table. He had seen these before, anchoring his friend Pedro to a stretcher in an Arizona ER. Wild on peyote, Pedro had fought and strained and cursed and spit, but the restraints never weakened their grip. The nurses finally grew weary of his antics and sedated him.

Bottom line: Alejandro couldn't rip his way free and couldn't release the buckles himself.

A man walked by the windows, opened the door, and stuck his head in. He wore a uniform of some type. Gray and blue. No badge. A name tag, too far away for Alejandro to read. "Want some coffee, Darlene? I'm falling asleep out front, so I thought I'd brew a fresh pot."

"That'd be great."

"It'll take about twenty minutes. Everything okay here?"

"Just fine."

"See you in a few." The door closed, and the guard walked past the window.

Okay. Think. Twenty minutes to get free and set a trap. Alejandro twisted and tugged against the bonds. If he could get just one hand loose. Wasn't going to happen. He pulled his right hand against the strap until it squeezed his wrist. He held it there as he felt pressure build in his hand.

Darlene came around the curtain. "She's doing just fine."

"My hand's asleep," Alejandro said. "It feels cold and numb."

Darlene touched his hand. "It is a little swollen." She worked a finger beneath the restraint. "It may be tight, but it's okay."

"My hand's aching. It's too tight."

"Okay, okay." She unfastened the buckle and loosened the strap.

Alejandro wrenched his arm free and slammed the side of his hand against her throat. Darlene gasped, stunned. He clutched a wad of her hair and yanked her down on his chest. She tried to scream, but her throat apparently wouldn't cooperate, the blow having done some damage. She writhed against him and banged her fist on his face, chest, belly, anything she could strike. A fiery pain shot through his gut as his abdominal muscles tightened against her blows. She managed to turn her body, her back now to him, and stretched out a hand toward the nearby instrument tray.

He jerked her head back violently and then let go of her hair, immediately wrapping his hand around her throat. He pulled her tightly against him. Her thrashing and his struggles to control her sent a shock of pain through his belly. Stinging sweat leaked into his eyes followed by a wave of nausea and dizziness. *Hold on.*

Darlene attempted to pry him from her throat, but he held his grip. Her face reddened, then purpled. Her struggles became more frantic, but he only tightened his hold. Another minute and her eyes glazed over. Her struggles weakened, and finally he felt her muscles go lax. He held his stranglehold for another fifteen seconds and then let go. She slid to the floor.

Alejandro knew he had a minute, not much more, before she came around. He released the straps from his other arm and his ankles. Ignoring the pain that continued to burn in his gut, he slipped from the bed. The room felt cold against his bare skin. Another pulse of dizziness dropped him to his knees. He felt blood trickle down his arm and saw that the IV needle had been yanked free.

Darlene moaned and moved her head from side to side, natural color returning to her face. He swiped a roll of tape from the tray. Rolling her to her stomach, he pulled her arms behind her back and wound the tape around her wrists, binding them together, and rolled her to her back again. He then wrapped her ankles with tape.

Her eyes fluttered open and she looked around, at first unfocused, appearing confused, but then her gaze fixed on him. She opened her mouth to scream.

Alejandro clamped his hand over her face. "Listen to me. Cooperate. And you live. One sound, one move, and I'll kill you. Clear?"

She attempted to bite his hand, so he struck her on the side of the head with his other fist. "You want to die? Right here? Like this?"

Darlene shook her head, her eyes wide with terror.

"Then do what I say. Exactly what I say."

She nodded.

He took a stack of gauze from the tray, removed his hand from her mouth, and began stuffing the gauze inside. She resisted until he clutched her throat. "Don't move." He wrapped tape around her head, securing the gauze in place. Grabbing her feet, he dragged her beyond the curtain and to the far side of Carmelita's bed. The pain in his belly flared, and when he looked down, he saw that both bandages were soaked with fresh blood. Sweat frosted his face and chest. Placing his lips near Darlene's ear, he said, "Not a sound."

Alejandro stood, fighting off another wave of dizziness. He glanced at Carmelita. The only movement he saw was the rhythmic rise and fall of her chest as the ventilator cycled. He shook her arm but got no response. No time to deal with her right now.

He walked around the curtain, found a towel, and wiped the blood from his arm and hand, the IV site now barely oozing. He riffled through the instruments on the tray, searching for a weapon. He settled on a pair of pointed scissors. As he climbed back into bed, he saw that blood from the saturated bandages trickled down his belly and right leg. He stretched out and pulled the sheet up to his chest, making sure his right arm and the scissors were covered.

CHAPTER 43

T-TOMMY AND I FOLLOWED MADISON DOWN UNIVERSITY DRIVE, past the UAH campus, and then south on Jordan Lane. She parked in the side lot of a twenty-four-hour diner called Mac's. We took a red vinyl booth snugged against a wall of windows and ordered coffee. As the waitress filled our cups, I asked Madison, "Something to eat?"

"No thanks," she said.

I looked at the waitress. "Just coffee for me."

"Two over easy and some wheat toast," T-Tommy said. "Bacon. A couple of pancakes would be nice, too."

"So, who are you guys?" Madison asked.

"I'm Dub. This is T-Tommy."

"What kind of name is that?"

"Mine," T-Tommy said.

She was an even more attractive young lady in civilian clothes.

I'd guess early twenties, green eyes, a natural beauty. The stripper's life hadn't beaten her down yet. It would but not yet. I noticed a series of faint white lines on her left wrist. Palm side. Remnants from an unhappy time, no doubt.

Madison apparently followed my gaze and tugged the sleeve of her sweater down, clasping it in her hand. "Stupid, huh?"

"You probably didn't think so at the time," I said.

Her face softened a bit. "I was fourteen. Seemed like the only way out."

"Glad you missed the trip."

Madison smiled. "All hell broke loose. Mom had no idea what was going on with her new husband. My stepfather. At least I don't think she did." She sighed. "She took me to three different shrinks. I trashed them all. They were more messed up than me."

"Does seem that way, don't it?" T-Tommy said.

"So what happened then?" I asked.

"I decided he wasn't worth it. That he was the damaged one. Not me." She pushed her sleeves up to her elbows and propped them on the table. "I went back to school, got a part-time job, and bided my time. Took over a year, but I saved enough money to split."

"Sorry," I said.

The rain and wind kicked up, fat drops now slapping the windows. Lightning streaked the sky, and Mother Nature cleared her throat with rolls of thunder. A car pulled up, headlamps aimed at us. One of the waitresses, apparently completing her shift, hurried through the front door and around the corner of the building toward the car, a folded newspaper serving as an umbrella. She hopped in, and the car backed away.

Madison watched all this through the window, then leaned back, arms crossed over her chest. "So you guys got names. That doesn't tell me who you are."

"I'm looking for the person who killed the daughter of a friend," I said. "T-Tommy's a cop."

"Great. This is exactly what I need." She took a sip of coffee and then placed her cup on the table. "This involves me how?"

"You know Alejandro and Eddie."

"So? I know a couple of jerks who come in sometimes."

"What do you know about them?" I asked.

"They're poor tippers. Eddie tries to grab my tits all the time."

The waitress returned with T-Tommy's food. "Sure I can't get you guys something?"

Madison and I declined. The waitress turned and headed back to the kitchen.

"Do you know a girl named Noel Edwards?" I asked.

She shook her head and then picked up her cup and cradled it in her hands.

"Crystal Robinson?"

"Sure. She dances at the club."

"Not anymore," T-Tommy said around a mouthful of pancake.

Madison looked over her cup. "Why? Did she get a better gig?"

"Not exactly," I said. "She's dead."

Her face paled, and her pupils widened. "What do you mean?"

"She's dead. Murdered. Along with Noel. Our friend." I didn't want to come right at her like this, but I had to break through that wall. All strippers did that. Part of the job. I needed to find a sliver of light if we were going to get anywhere. I noticed a slight tremble in her fingers as she placed her cup on the table.

"I don't believe you."

I shrugged. "I could call the coroner. He did the autopsy."

Her eyes moistened. "I don't understand. What the hell are you two after?"

"The person who killed them."

"You think Eddie and Alejandro did it?"

"Maybe," I said. "But not likely."

"Then why are you looking for them?" Madison asked.

"We're only looking for Alejandro. We know where Eddie is."

"I'm not going to like this much either, am I?"

"Eddie is on the slab at the coroner's office. Bullet through his brain."

A tear slid down her cheek.

I grabbed a couple of napkins from the dispenser and handed them to her.

Madison wiped her eyes. "I knew something was wrong."

T-Tommy's fork froze halfway to his mouth. We both stared at her.

"Last Wednesday night. They were both there . . . at the club. Eddie had a hard-on for another dancer. A friend."

"Carmelita?" I asked.

She looked surprised. "Yeah."

"What's her last name?"

"Hidalgo."

"And?"

Madison pushed her hands through her hair and looked down. "I don't fucking believe this."

"Tell us about it," I said.

She dropped her hands into her lap. "Carmelita left with them. Around eleven. Took off early. She was going to screw Eddie for a couple hundred bucks and some cheap ring. Didn't make sense. She could make that in a few hours dancing and not have to put up with his shit."

"Then why?"

"She did it all the time. She liked the idea of screwing for money. Thrills, I guess. I don't know." Madison laced her fingers around her coffee cup. "She tried to get me to go along. For Alejandro."

"But you didn't."

"Some of us don't fuck the customers."

"That's not what I meant."

"Right." She started to say something else but hesitated, letting it come together. "Besides, this was different."

I waited. She needed to get her mind around it. Get it out her way. I could feel her tension rise, her gaze unable to find an anchor. Her pupils did a slow flare.

"Oh, fuck me." Madison shook her head, and tears pooled in her eyes. "Carmelita said Eddie was going to show her two dead bodies."

"What?" T-Tommy and I said at the same time.

She pressed the napkins against her eyes and sniffed sharply. "Eddie told her he was some big hit man or something. He's full of it. I told her he was. But she wanted to see the bodies. She'd never seen a dead person before." She shivered and wrapped her arms around herself. "I haven't seen her since."

"That unusual? Her disappearing for a couple of days?"

Madison nodded. "Carmelita's very reliable. Not like Crystal. She's a flake and a druggy. Carmelita missed her shift last night and again tonight. She never does that."

"Where does she live?" T-Tommy asked.

"Apartment near here. I called a couple of times but couldn't reach her."

"Did you call the cops?"

"No."

"We'll look into it." I finished my coffee. "You going to be okay?"

"You mean after you two stomped into my life? Pissed off those two gorillas?"

She was right, and I knew it.

"You guys have already made too many waves. If Mr. Scarcella finds out I talked to you, I'm screwed, blued, and tattooed." Madison took a deep breath and slowly let it out. "He'll turn that creep Austin loose. Jesus."

"Seems to me Austin's stuck on stupid," T-Tommy said.

"Maybe. But he's also stuck on mean."

"I'm sorry," I said.

"No, you're not." She tossed the napkins to the table, no longer needed, her face now stone hard. "You got what you wanted. That's what guys like you do. Take what you want, to hell with everything else. Dancers, hookers, all trash to you." Her jaw jutted at me, her eyes angry.

"Our friend Noel—the girl who was killed with Crystal—was a hooker. Seemed to be putting her life back together, and now she's dead."

Madison studied me as if trying to read my thoughts. After a moment, she said, "So what are you? Brother Love's Traveling Salvation Show or something?"

T-Tommy smiled. "Something like that."

"Bullshit," she said. "There's no such thing except in fairy tales, and High Rollers is about as far from never-never land as you can get."

"Why not leave?" I asked. "Pretty, bright girl like you could do anything."

"So, now you want to save me?" She fingered a strand of hair, pushed it behind her ear, and stared out the window, her gaze unfocused as if mentally picturing something. The rain had lightened, but drops still tapped the window. "Truth is, I've thought about getting out of here. Been doing this for three years. That's too long."

"And go where?" I asked.

"Indiana. Now that my stepdad's gone, Mom would let me come back."

"Do you need traveling money?" I opened my hands, palms up.

"I got money."

The waitress returned with the check, and I borrowed her pen. I scribbled my name and cell number on a napkin and gave it to Madison along with a pair of Franklins. "For your time. Maybe traveling money. Call if you need anything. If you do go home, please let me know how I can reach you. In case I have any more questions."

"I'm sure my mom would love to hear that I know someone who was murdered."

CHAPTER 44

ALEJANDRO LAY STILL AS THE MINUTES DRIPPED BY, SCISSORS clutched in his right hand, the sheet providing cover. Where the hell was the guard? More than once he considered not waiting. Simply get up, walk out of room, track down an exit, and see how it went. Deal with whatever came up. But he was in no condition to fight, and even if he slipped away unseen, he would gain only a few minutes' head start. Stick with the plan. Surprise was his only ally here.

From what he had seen earlier, the guard didn't appear to be much. Soft from a lot of sitting. Maybe three inches shorter than he was and not muscular like that goon Austin. Surely he was armed. Alejandro couldn't be positive of that last point but better to assume it. Which meant Alejandro had one shot.

Finally he saw the man walk by the windows and push the door open with a shoulder, a cup of coffee in his hand, a gun clipped to his belt. He stopped. "Where's Darlene?"

"Bathroom. She said leave her coffee on the tray there."

"She's not supposed to leave."

"Why? We aren't going anywhere."

He placed the coffee on the tray and turned toward the curtain that concealed Carmelita and Darlene. He took a step in that direction.

"Smells good," Alejandro said.

The guard stopped and turned back to him.

"The coffee. Wish I could have some, but Darlene said I couldn't eat or drink for another few hours."

The guard approached him and glanced down. "Jesus, you're bleeding." His gaze darted toward the door. "Where the hell is she?"

Alejandro looked at the guard's name tag. *Phil Dunlap, Security.* "You can handle it, Phil."

Phil's head jerked back to Alejandro, a surprised look on his face.

"Your name tag," Alejandro said.

Phil smiled.

That's it. Relax. We're friends. First name basis. "Just grab some fresh bandages," Alejandro said. "I think she put them up there. On top of the monitor."

Phil turned, looked up.

Alejandro didn't hesitate. He drove the scissors into the right side of Phil's neck. Phil recoiled. Alejandro yanked the scissors free. Blood fountained from the guard's neck. He spun, elbow knocking over the tray. Instruments clattered to the floor. Phil clutched at his throat. Blood gushed between his fingers. His other hand dropped to his gun. Too slow.

Alejandro rolled out of the bed and was on him before he could raise his weapon. He hammered the gun to the floor and then slammed the scissors into Phil's chest. The guard collapsed. His breath came in wet, bubbling rasps, and his life pumped away in ever weakening pulses.

Alejandro slid to the floor, sitting back against the bed, and watched until Phil bled no more. Only took a couple of minutes.

Dizziness and nausea rippled through him. He fought the sensations and took a couple of deep breaths before reaching under the bed and retrieving Phil's gun. He sat for another minute, gathering energy. He pressed a hand against his belly, now covered with blood. It felt hot and sticky. Fatigue pulled at him. He wanted to lie down and go to sleep.

Summoning what was left of his fading strength, Alejandro crawled to where Darlene lay. He stripped the tape from her face and tugged the gauze from her mouth. "Who else is in the building?"

"What did you do to Phil?"

"Just what you think I did. Now answer the question."

"You can't get out of here."

He pressed the muzzle of the gun to her cheek. "You better fucking hope I can, or you're going down with me. Now, one more time, who's here?"

"Two guards." She closed her eyes tightly and took a deep breath.

"Phil and one other."

"Where?"

"Up front. One stays there all the time."

"The two guys who did this to me. Where are they?"

"Gone. They won't be around until morning."

"I need clothes."

"There're some surgical scrubs over there." Darlene nodded toward a row of built-in lockers.

He looked at Carmelita. "Unhook her."

"Can't."

"You unhooked me. Unhook her."

"You were awake. She's not. She comes off the vent, who's going to breathe for her? You?"

"Fuck." He glanced around. "How long?"

"Couple of hours. Maybe more."

No way he could wait it out. "All right. I've got to go. You better keep her alive until I can get some help."

"Are you going to undo this tape?"

"No."

"Then how am I supposed to help her?"

"Pray it all works out." Alejandro managed to tape some fresh gauze over his two wounds, both now trickling blood, and put on a pair of scrubs. He dropped the scissors into the breast pocket and shoved the gun into the hip pocket.

He knelt beside Darlene. "What the hell is this all about? What are you people up to?"

"You know. You've been in it from the beginning."

"The hell I have."

"Don't play innocent. You buried the bodies."

"I didn't know about all this." He waved a hand. "This is fucking evil."

"No, Mr. Diaz. It's medical progress."

"That why you do this shit in the dead of night?" Alejandro glared at her. "Medical progress? The fuck it is. How many people have you killed already? Couple dozen?"

"Progress always has casualties."

"War has casualties. This is murder."

"You buried the evidence," Darlene said. "You took the money."

He hit her as hard as he could and square in the jaw. "You bitch. I should kill you right here."

She moaned. "You took the money."

He hit her again.

CHAPTER 45

AFTER T-TOMMY AND I LEFT MADISON AND STOPPED BY CARMELITA'S apartment, buttoned up, no one home, we drove back to Alejandro's. The storm had moved on, the rain now only a fine mist. I parked in the lot, and we walked to Alejandro's apartment. Still no answer to our knock.

It took a good five minutes to get Walter Moxley, the manager, to the door. His eyes drooped from sleep, and he wore the same robe he had had on earlier. I could still hear the TV inside and guessed he had probably fallen asleep in front of it.

"We need to take a look inside Alejandro's apartment," I said.

"Why?"

"Make sure Alejandro isn't ill or injured or anything like that," T-Tommy said.

"Why would you think that?"

"Can't say. Ongoing investigation. I'm sure you understand."

Moxley hesitated as if deciding what to do.

"As a police officer I have a duty to check it out. Just didn't want to break a window or jimmy the door." T-Tommy smiled. "Wouldn't want to do something you'd have to clean up."

Moxley looked past us at the wet ground and dripping trees. "I can't go out in this weather. Bad lungs. Wouldn't want to catch the pneumonia. That's what killed my daddy."

"Give us the key," I said. "We'll bring it right back."

"And you won't mess nothing up?"

"You've got our word."

He gave us a passkey.

Alejandro's place was small: living room/dining/kitchenette deal, a tiny bath, and a single bedroom. There was little furniture, and the walls were apartment white, no decorations.

Alejandro was neat, the only clutter a dish towel tossed on the countertop, a dirty cup and saucer in the sink, and several pieces of paper on the dining table. While T-Tommy searched closets and drawers, I shuffled through the pages: a letter in Spanish with a Mexican postmark from someone named Juan Fernandez; an electric bill for $61.42; and a coupon for a free burger at Hardee's. The phone sat at one end of the table, a folded piece of paper tucked beneath one foot. I pulled the scrap free, unfolded it, and read a handwritten list of phone numbers:

HR	*383-6722*
Eddie	*516-9932*
KR	*307-2200*

I guessed Alejandro didn't need to chat with too many people.

T-Tommy came from the bedroom. "Nothing. His clothes and bathroom shit are here, so it doesn't look like he split. What do you got?"

"Couple of phone numbers." I handed him the scrap. "That's it."

T-Tommy read it. "What's HR and KR?"

"Got me."

I looked underneath the sink, then went through the kitchen cabinets and drawers and the small pantry but found nothing of interest. The fridge contained a few beers and a carton of milk. Looked like Alejandro might find that Hardee's coupon handy.

As I walked around the kitchen counter and into the living area, something reflective caught my eye. I knelt by the central heat intake that was on the wall near the floor. The four screws that held the grate in place were scratched, paint missing. The exposed metal was what I had seen. "Look at this."

T-Tommy dropped to one knee next to me. "Here you go." He handed me his Swiss Army knife, screwdriver blade extended.

The screws took only a couple of minutes. I removed the grate and then bent down so I could see into the duct. Two feet in, I saw a single manila envelope. I had to lie on the floor to reach it. I removed it and stood. Inside, I found five pages and spread them on the table. Two proved to be maps of the greater Huntsville area. On them, locations were marked with either a one or a two, the numbers circled. Wait a minute. One was a three. Each had a date beside it. The marks were mostly west or north of the city. Three were in Maple Hill

Cemetery. Two up north just over the Tennessee line.

The other pages, neatly printed, contained a list of dates—military style—with what appeared to be directions by each. The dates were chronological. I read the final entry.

28 March

Maple Hill—McClung entrance

First right

On left, fifth row, 4th grave in

I checked the map pages and found the March 28 date beside a circled two. In Maple Hill Cemetery near the McClung Avenue entrance.

I looked at T-Tommy. "You thinking what I'm thinking?"

"This ain't no treasure map."

I picked up the other map page and located Jeff Road. My finger followed it north of Capshaw to the wooded area where Noel and Crystal were found. I didn't see a mark dated this week, but there were three others in the same area. A three and a couple of twos, with dates as far back as last August. I pointed that out to T-Tommy.

"Maybe he hasn't had time to update it yet," he said.

"That'd be my guess."

T-Tommy flipped open his cell and dialed the number listed as HR. He waited a second and then hung up, smiling. "HR is High Rollers." He dialed the KR. Listened for a minute and hung up. "Voice mail. Some dude named Karl Reinhardt, a security outfit I've never heard of. Sentinel Security."

"You think maybe Alejandro works there?" I asked.

"Good bet. I'll check it out tomorrow."

CHAPTER 46

ALEJANDRO CREPT INTO THE HALLWAY. IT WAS DARK AND QUIET, and he wasn't sure which way to turn. He chose left. His mouth was dry, and he felt cold and weak as if he might collapse at any moment. That wasn't an option. Not after coming this far.

The wall offered support as he moved down the hall. He came to the room where he and Carmelita had been held. Now empty, it looked as if they had never been there. It would also look that way to the police or anyone else who might come snooping. Neat and clean. The way Rocco liked it. Reinhardt, too, he suspected. He had to get out of here.

But now Alejandro knew exactly where he was and where he had to go. He continued down the hall to the bathroom where he had been taken each day. He went inside and eased the door closed. The window along the back wall was high but large enough to fit through.

He didn't hesitate. He pulled a handful of paper towels from the wall dispenser, held them against the window to smother the sound, and smashed the glass with the butt of the gun. He tapped away the remaining shards with the barrel, then stuffed the weapon into the back pocket of his scrub pants. He grasped the windowsill.

This would hurt. He lifted himself up and slithered through the window headfirst. Halfway through, he realized the floor he was on sank into the ground and, thank God, the ground was only a couple of feet below him. He tucked his chin and rolled through the window and on to his back. A ball of pain ripped through his belly. It felt as if something had torn loose deep inside. He curled on his side, knees drawn up, gasping for breath. Sweat erupted on his face. Consciousness began slipping away. *No, no, no. Not now.* He fought against the sinking sensation and managed to hold on.

Alejandro lay there for several minutes, letting the pain settle. He pressed his hands against his belly, now a sea of wet stickiness. He was bleeding again. More than before. Cold water from the damp grass soaked through the scrubs. It must have rained, he thought. He sat up.

He had no idea where he was. All he could see was a long building surrounded by a high chain-link fence. Beyond, nothing but darkness.

Time to move.

The thirty-yard run to the fence was a staggering, stumbling affair. He nearly went down several times before reaching the fifteen-foot-high chain-link barrier. Leaning against it, he glanced at the building. Still dark, no sign of activity.

He climbed. His fingers and toes ached as they clutched the metal links, and he felt as though the effort would rip open his gut. Fifteen feet seemed like a hundred, but he finally reached the top. He threw one leg over and balanced himself. The gun slid from his pocket and thudded to the ground, inside the fence. Climbing back down to retrieve it wasn't going to happen.

Alejandro hesitated, trying to gain some strength. His blood-slicked hands made gripping the metal bar along the top of the fence difficult. The gentle night breeze seemed icy cold. *Keep moving.*

He rolled over the bar and tried to jam a toe into the fence but lost his grip. He braced for impact. It seemed to take much longer than he expected, but when he hit the ground, air exploded from his lungs. He rolled into a ball and began retching. The pain in his gut was unbearable, and he faded away for a moment. At least it seemed only a moment. As consciousness returned, he tried to swallow, but his dust-dry mouth refused to cooperate. He began to shiver so hard his teeth clacked together.

Alejandro beat back another wave of nausea. The fence helped him regain his feet. Looking around he saw no signs of life anywhere. Only the faint line of a road, maybe a hundred yards away. He pushed away from the fence and moved toward the road, but when he finally reached it, he saw nothing but darkness in every direction. Which way? He chose left once more.

Time and distance lost all meaning. He walked, stumbled, fell, walked again. The rough surface tore at his bare feet. More than once he considered giving up. His cottony mouth, the bitter cold that seemed to well up inside him, and the blood that continually leaked from his wounds sapped his will. He continued forward, thinking only of the next step and then the next.

Alejandro noticed a faint glow in the distance. He squinted. Lights. A large building. To its left another. He recognized where he was. On the periphery of the Cummings Research Park. Had to be. Nowhere else had a collection of such large buildings spaced apart like this. Every major space-related company known. General Dynamics. Raytheon. Northrop. You name it. He didn't know who occupied the buildings he saw, and he didn't care. Get there. Find a guard. Set off an alarm. Anything to get help.

Problem was, they were half a mile away. Maybe more. The direct route would take him through a field. Recently plowed and prepped for planting. Probably cotton.

Head down, Alejandro trudged across the field. The soft, damp earth clung to his feet, but he made good progress. He just might make it. He stepped on a baseball-sized rock. His ankle twisted, and he tumbled into one of the shallow furrows.

The world dimmed.

Oh, Jesus.

CHAPTER 47

OUTRAGE AND DISBELIEF BALLED IN DR. ROBERT KINCAID'S THROAT. Incompetence. Lack of attention to detail. Pure stupidity. These always ramped up his blood pressure and drove him into a frenzy. Add to that a healthy dose of fear. Fear that this project could be exposed, that all his plans, the product of his genius, could be destroyed. His rage reached the boiling point. His hands shook, and he felt heat gather in his face as he looked at the body of Phil Dunlap. The deep gash in Dunlap's throat and the bloodstains that haloed his head and reached out in long fingerlike streaks across the floor only fanned his fury.

Kincaid turned to Darlene Montag, her pale face radiating her own fear. "How could you let this happen?" he said through clenched teeth.

"It was—"

"What? An incredible act of stupidity?"

"I didn't—"

"Shut up." Kincaid turned to Harmon Talbert. "We could be seriously screwed on this." He then looked at Karl Reinhardt. "Your guys fucked up big-time."

Reinhardt shook his head. "Wasn't my men. It was your nurse who screwed up."

"Really?" Kincaid stepped close to him. "Who's that lying on the floor with his throat ripped open? Isn't he one of yours?"

The muscles in Reinhardt's jaw pulsed. "Your nurse's incompetence set up the ambush."

"This is fucking insane." Kincaid paced back and forth. "Where's Rocco's men?"

"Right here."

Kincaid turned as Austin and Lefty came into the room.

"Broke out a window," Austin said. "The head. Down the hall. Crawled out, jumped the fence."

"Goddamn it," Kincaid said.

"Dropped this," Lefty said, holding up Phil Dunlap's gun. "So he's unarmed and on the run."

"Until he flags down a car or gets to a phone," Talbert said.

"Not much around here on a Sunday morning," Austin said. "Everything's closed. He'll have to cover a mile or more before he reaches a street with traffic. And he's bleeding like a son of a bitch. The fence was painted with blood."

"What are you going to do?" Reinhardt asked.

"As soon as you guys stop whining and bitching," Austin said, "me and Lefty'll track him down and kill him."

"Get going, then," Reinhardt said. "He can't get away."

Austin smirked. "Yes, boss."

Austin headed toward the door, but Kincaid grabbed his arm. "A word first."

Kincaid exited the room and moved down the hallway, Austin and Lefty following. He stopped and turned to them. "We're going to shut things down for a while. A few months, anyway. In case Alejandro has a chance to talk."

"Of course they do have the bodies of the two girls," Lefty said. "If they get Alejandro that'll make three."

"I'm well aware of that," Kincaid said. "The girls can't be connected back here. Alejandro can. If he does lead the authorities here, I want no hard evidence around. It'll be our word against his."

"What about the others?" Lefty asked. "Alejandro could give them all the burial sites."

Kincaid hadn't considered that. *What a fucking disaster.*

"He's the only one who knows there are other bodies," Austin said.

"Then you damn well better make sure he doesn't talk."

"He won't," Austin said. "We'll find him."

Kincaid wished he could believe that. The truth was he detested Austin and Lefty. Rocco Scarcella, too, for that matter. They were crude. Thugs. Not the kind of people he associated with. Right now he wished he'd never met them. But he couldn't undo what was done. Not yet, anyway. "Still, we'll clean things up here. Just in case." He glanced down the hall toward the ICU doors.

"Anything else?" Austin asked.

"Darlene," Kincaid said. "She's no longer reliable."

"Want us to fix it?" Austin said.

Kincaid nodded.

"It'll cost you."

"Everything costs," Kincaid said. "Just fix it."

"Carmelita?"

"She's served her purpose."

Austin shrugged and headed back toward the room.

Kincaid stopped him. "Not here."

"Why not? I got a minute."

Kincaid shook his head. "Later. Maybe at her home. Make it look like an accident."

"That takes time to set up. Time we don't have. We got a man on the run. Besides, we already got Dunlap's body to dump. A couple more won't make much difference."

Kincaid mulled it over. It did make sense. On some level, anyway. Maybe not light-of-day sense, but here in this dark hallway and in this even darker situation, he could see that Austin's solution might be the only solution.

Before he could say anything, Austin continued down the hall. He pulled something from his pocket and let his arm fall casually to his side. Kincaid saw Austin had a black-handled switchblade cupped in his hand. He flicked it open as he pushed through the door to the ICU.

Kincaid walked to the window and watched. Without hesitation Austin closed in on Darlene, and though she retreated and raised her hands for protection, she never had a chance. Kincaid jerked away from the window when Austin drove the blade into the pit of her gut, grinding it upward into her heart. Darlene collapsed against the knife, and Austin lowered her to the floor, her final few heartbeats pumping blood over his hand. Austin grabbed a towel off the tray table and wiped her blood from his hand and the knife. He dropped the bloody towel over Darlene's face, folded the knife, and slipped it into his pocket.

Lefty moved to Carmelita's bedside. He disengaged the ventilator from the ET tube in her throat. An alarm sounded. He and Austin stepped into the hall.

Kincaid felt as if the air had been sucked from the building. He couldn't breathe. Acid rose into his throat, followed by a wave of dizziness. He grabbed the window frame for support.

"That should take care of it." Austin smiled and clapped a hand on Kincaid's shoulder. "What's the matter, Doc? You look a little pale. Can't stand the sight of blood?" He laughed, brushed past him, and he and Lefty started walking away. He shot over his shoulder, "You clean that shit up and wrap all the bodies. We'll deal with them later. Right now, we got to catch a rabbit."

CHAPTER 48

THE SUN EASED ABOVE THE HORIZON AND THE EASTERN SKY GLOWED orange as Austin climbed behind the wheel of the SUV, Lefty riding shotgun. Exiting the parking lot, Austin turned on to the street and then into the open field that stretched alongside Talbert Biomedical's long building. He stopped near where Alejandro had scaled the fence, and he and Lefty got out.

"Lot of blood here," Austin said.

"He went that way," Lefty said, pointing.

The morning glow made the dark dribbles and drops of blood on the patchy grass and dry dirt appear more brown than red. The trail led across the field toward the street.

"You follow it," Austin said. "I'll pull around."

Lefty walked off, head down, meandering slightly as he followed the blood trail. By the time he reached the road, Austin had jumped from the SUV and stood near its front bumper. The engine idled with a soft ticking sound.

"This way," Lefty said.

They followed the few splotches of blood they could see for about a hundred feet, and then the trail played out.

"Must've stopped bleeding," Lefty said.

"Or someone picked him up," Austin said.

Lefty nodded. "Or that."

"Fuck," Austin said. "Let's search the neighborhood. Might get lucky."

"We better. Rocco's going to go off if we don't find him."

Rocco did. An hour later when Austin and Lefty told him they had found nothing.

They had zigzagged the streets, covering a dozen block area twice, and circled through the Cummings Research Park, but they found no sign of Alejandro. As if he had simply disappeared. They finally gave up and drove to Rocco's house, finding him on the poolside deck, coffee and an empty breakfast plate on the table in front of him.

"He didn't just fucking disappear. Somebody picked him up." Rocco slammed a fist down. His cup rattled against its saucer, and coffee sloshed onto the table. "First the bodies of the girls, then those two clowns looking for Alejandro. Not just a coincidence. They know something. Now Alejandro's gone. If he turns up alive, we're fucked. All of us."

"What do you want us to do?" Lefty asked.

"Find him," Rocco said. "Kill him. I'll get my ear to the ground.

See if the police or hospitals have anything."

"Kincaid's shutting everything down," Lefty said. "Just in case. You want us to set up things over on Pratt?"

Rocco stuck a toothpick in the corner of his mouth. "Yeah. Let's clean the slate. Tie a bow on this shit. It's been a good run, but Kincaid's right. Time to wind down. We can crank it up again in a few months. After the police solve the case."

"We'll get on it," Lefty said.

"I'll give our friend at HPD a heads-up. Let him know we're about to wrap up the case for him." Rocco laughed. "He'll love it. Make him a fucking hero." He snatched the toothpick from his mouth and wheezed out a wet cough. "This'll get him where he wants to be. Where he can be even more useful to us." He settled the toothpick back into the corner of his mouth.

"Walker and Tortelli?" Austin asked.

"Once the killer's found, they'll have no one to look for."

"And if not?"

"We'll drop the hammer on them."

Lefty nodded. "I like the way you think, boss."

CHAPTER 49

T-Tommy and I waited beneath a hickory tree near a gravel road that cut through the small rural cemetery. The sky was blue, with only a few cottony clouds, and the sun was just beginning to burnish the treetops of the adjacent wooded area where Noel and Crystal had been buried.

Last night after we left Alejandro's place, T-Tommy had put out a BOLO on Alejandro Diaz and Carmelita Hidalgo. He also arranged for Derrick Stone and a team of officers, as well as an excavation crew and a tech from the coroner's office, to meet us here. We had decided that even though Maple Hill Cemetery might be an easier place to search—just look for the freshest grave in the area indicated on Alejandro's map—it would also attract the most attention. Not to mention a court order to open up a grave that, at least in part, belonged to someone else. The bet was that the garbagemen had taken advantage of any fresh graves that popped up and simply buried a corpse or two on top of the casket. Who would think to look there?

We were now waiting for the cadaver dogs.

We didn't wait long.

A battered blue pickup crunched down the gravel road toward us and stopped thirty feet away. Two dogs and a man jumped from the cab. A dingy orange T-shirt hung from his bony shoulders. Spidery, sun-leathered arms dangled from the sleeves. He wore a blue cap that read Tilton Kennels. It seemed a bit large and sat low on his head as if supported by his ears. The band was sweat stained. A few cockleburs clung to the frayed cuffs of his jeans and the loosely tied laces of his boots. The dress of a man who knew hard work.

T-Tommy introduced me to Junior Tilton. His eyes were deep set and dark, and he looked me straight in the eye. His handshake was strong, and he smiled around the wad of chewing tobacco that pooched out his left cheek. The dogs sat at his side, no sound, no movement.

"Junior raises dogs," T-Tommy said. "Mostly hunting dogs. Spaniels, retrievers, beagles. These hounds are trained to sniff out cadavers."

Tilton launched a gob of tobacco juice to his left and wiped his mouth with the back of one hand. "You got bodies, Lucy and Frank'll find 'em."

T-Tommy unfolded the map we had found at Alejandro's. He pointed to it as he spoke. "If these are correct and mean what me and Dub think they mean, there are seven bodies out here. Two here and here. And three here."

Another wad of brown spittle and Tilton said, "Let's get at it."

Two of the deputies retrieved shovels from the trunk of one of the patrol cars, and we all followed Tilton and his dogs across the narrow open area and into the trees. Tilton gave a sharp three-note whistle through his teeth, and the dogs jumped into action. They rushed forward, heads low, sniffing whatever seemed interesting to them. A tree here, a rock there, but they soon locked on an area beneath a bright green sugar maple.

As we drew close, I could see that the ground was slightly sunken. The dogs danced around the depression, moaning and yipping, even giving an occasional growl. Tilton let out another three-note whistle, and Lucy and Frank backed away and sat, fidgeting a bit, but not moving.

The digging took a good twenty minutes before Stone, standing by the hole, said, "Got something."

A torn piece of plastic jutted from the dark, damp soil. As the deputies cleared away more dirt, two wrapped bodies appeared. Once the plastic was cut through, two corpses were revealed. One male, one female. Though seriously decayed, I noticed several wounds with metallic clips on the belly of each.

I glanced at T-Tommy.

"I hate it when we're right," he said.

"Me, too."

T-Tommy called Coroner Dreyer, told him what we had found, gave him the location, and said there were likely a dozen other sites. He requested that Dreyer contact Drummond and Cooksey and mobilize the crime scene unit. He also said that a couple of extra coroner's techs and excavators would be helpful. T-Tommy closed the phone and looked at me. "This is going to be ugly."

"I know. I did the math. If these maps are correct, we're looking at twenty-two bodies. Not counting Noel and Crystal."

T-Tommy forked back his hair. "The media will have a fucking field day."

"I'll call Claire," I said. "Let her get out in front of the story before all the wild speculation begins."

CHAPTER 50

THE TENNESSEE RIVER SAGGED INTO NORTH ALABAMA LIKE A slack guitar string, waiting to be tightened to the proper key. From its origins at the confluence of the Holston and French Broad Rivers near Knoxville, Tennessee, until it emptied into the Ohio River near Paducah, Kentucky, it covered over six hundred and fifty miles. The river was home to nine Tennessee Valley Authority hydroelectric dams, which supplied power to a large chunk of the southeast. The city of Huntsville, as well as the Redstone Arsenal/Marshall Space Flight Center, nestled against the river near the bottom of its Alabama swag.

Like most Southern cities, Huntsville was small. Though the population was around one hundred and sixty thousand and it was spread over one hundred and seventy-five square miles, you could drive fifteen minutes in any direction and be lost in rural America. No city lights. No traffic. Just fertile farmland where rabbits, squirrels, doves, and crows abounded. Land where cotton was king for so many years. Still was, though it had been joined by corn and soybeans and a handful of other food crops.

I stood at the back of my property and looked out over the city, the Redstone Arsenal, and the rolling green hills and thick patches of forest that surrounded both. The cloudless blue sky, the gentle breeze from the west, and the pink and white dogwoods that bloomed along the edge of my property offered no hint of the horrors that lay in those hills and forest patches. None of the people driving unhurriedly along Memorial Parkway could have guessed that at this very moment excavation crews were pulling body after body from the ground. Before sunset they would know, but right now life went on as if this were just another perfect April day.

Earlier, after we had uncovered the first two bodies, I cleared out. T-Tommy said that Furyk was going to swoop in, and it might be best if I made myself scarce. Good idea. He'd said he'd meet me here later.

I came home and went for a long run on Monte Sano Boulevard, a tree-shaded two-lane road that followed the spine of Monte Sano Mountain and stretched between Governors Drive to the south and the Bankhead Parkway to the north. I then hit the weights for an hour. I have a small shed toward the back of my property that I turned into a gym of sorts, complete with a treadmill, a stair-climber, a multistation weight apparatus, and a killer sound system. I pumped iron to the sounds of Buddy Guy, Eric Clapton, and Big Bill Broonzy.

The work and sweat felt good, but I couldn't shake off the images of Noel and Crystal and the young couple we had found this morning. Jill intruded a few times, too.

I sat at the table on the patio, and for the dozenth time read through all the information we had accumulated. Norton and Kramden showed up and harassed me for a while. I gave them some corn, they fought over it, and then, apparently bored with what I was doing, they took to the sky and disappeared across the valley.

I scanned my scribbled case notes, anemic on useful information, mostly questions. They were in no particular order, written as I thought of them.

Multiple surgeries over several days.

Medical skills. Type? How/where learned?

Special equipment required. Source?

Bodies disposed by punk—not the killer.

Why Noel and Crystal?

Who could do it? Group? How many?

Who killed Eddie?

Why? Why? Why?

Now I added:

Who is Alejandro Diaz? The killer? Garbageman?

High Rollers/Rocco connection?

Two dozen victims?

I looked up as T-Tommy came around the house. "What's the story?" I asked.

"They have eight of the twelve sites excavated. A body or two in each. Haven't been to Maple Hill yet. We'll do those last since they'll attract the most attention."

"What condition?" I asked.

"Half are either skeletal or severely decayed. Can't tell much about them. Those that aren't had similar wounds to Noel and Crystal. I guess surgeries would be more accurate." He took a deep breath and exhaled slowly. "I had to get away from it. Not much for me to do right now, anyway. This is the coroner's domain." He massaged the back of his neck. "I'm too old for this shit."

"You're not alone there," I said. "Want some coffee?"

"Sure."

I went inside and poured two cups and brought them back out.

T-Tommy sat across from me. "I had a little chat with Furyk this morning. Not really a chat. The real Furious Furyk came out. Mostly he screamed. I listened."

"What was his beef?" I asked.

"Ranted about you being at Eddie's murder scene last night. Talking to a witness. Going with us to Alejandro's place. I tried to explain that you might be helpful."

"Bet he was receptive to that."

"Oh yeah. What really put a weed up his ass was our little visit to Rocco Scarcella."

"He knows about that?"

"Furyk's got political ambitions. That takes money. Rocco's got a boatload of that."

"You saying your sergeant's dirty?"

He shrugged. "Rumors and innuendo."

"Which usually turn out to be fact. The cop grapevine usually knows the score."

T-Tommy nodded. "Anyway, he tore me a new asshole. Threatened to take me off the case."

"Sorry," I said.

"He wants this case he can have it. I hate psychos, anyway."

"You'll feel differently when all this is solved," I said.

He worked on a cuticle with his thumbnail. "No. I've been thinking about jumping ship for a few months. Just haven't overcome the inertia yet. Furyk may be the shove I need."

"Besides ranting and raving, what's Furyk's take on all this?"

"He's still focused on Eddie. Shotgunning it. Got guys working the drug angle. Busted a couple of meth labs. The lab guys are trying to match the seized product with what we found at Eddie's trailer." T-Tommy scratched an ear. "Of course it won't matter if they do get a match. Drugs got nothing to do with this."

"All these bodies didn't change his mind?" I asked.

"Not yet. We've got guys canvassing every hospital for two hundred miles, looking for unaccounted for patients, digging into the backgrounds of every surgeon in the state."

"They won't find anything. Liz Mackey was dead right on that. This shit isn't from some hospital or clinic. This is something else."

"Ain't that the truth." He stood. "Want some more?" He raised his cup. I declined. He went inside, refilled his cup, and returned.

"I'd suspect that whatever is going on Rocco and those two goons of his are involved. Know anything about them?" I asked.

"Tommy Austin and Lefty Bruno? Sure. A couple of years ago a witness saw Austin put a bullet through the head of a guy scheduled to testify against one of Rocco's buddies. A simple pandering rap, but his third strike. Funny thing. The witness committed suicide before he could testify."

"How?" I asked.

"Bullet to the head." He pointed to his right temple. "Full contact wound. Supposed to look like a suicide, but Austin was the triggerman."

"It was written off as suicide?"

"Almost. Austin and Lefty aren't that smart. Couldn't stage a crime scene for shit. The victim was found lying on a sofa. No GSR on his hands. Gun casually lying on his chest."

"So the case's still open?"

T-Tommy nodded. "Coroner listed the manner as undetermined. Wouldn't buy the suicide."

Claire arrived. Her mahogany-red hair—it moved around the red spectrum a lot, mahogany apparently this week's choice—was fastened into a ponytail and draped over one shoulder. She had her briefcase in one hand and a Starbucks cup in the other.

"Ain't this some shit?" She sat down at the end of the table. "I've filmed on-site pieces at three of the locations. Going to make for an interesting report tonight." She looked at T-Tommy. "When are you guys going over to Maple Hill?"

"After we finish the other sites."

"I want some shots from there. I have Jeffrey and the van staked out. He's going to call when the excavation crew shows up."

CHAPTER 51

"YOU TWO ARE FUCKING MORONS," ROCCO SAID. "THE COPS ARE DIGGING up bodies all over the place."

"What are you talking about?" Lefty asked.

Rocco leaned back in his chair and massaged his tightening neck. "I'm talking about all the goddamn bodies Alejandro and that jerk-off Eddie buried."

"How?"

"They have a map. Shows where they are."

"Where'd they get that?" Austin asked.

"Alejandro."

"They've got him?" Lefty asked.

Rocco was beginning to think these two were hopelessly stupid. He'd fix that once everything settled. "If they did, don't you think they'd be here arresting our asses?" He slid the cellophane wrapper off a fresh cigar and clipped the tip. "My guy says they found the map at Alejandro's place."

"We searched his house. Top to bottom," Austin said.

"Not very well." Rocco fired up the cigar.

"It was night. Had to do it in the dark."

"That your excuse?"

Austin shrugged. "Just saying."

"Should've popped that prick a long time ago," Lefty said.

"Too late now," Rocco said. "But we've got to find him."

"We went back over every street in Cummings Research Park," Lefty said. "Every alley. Every shrub. Even the garbage bins. Nothing."

"He wasn't beamed into some fucking spaceship. He's got to be somewhere." Rocco plucked a tobacco fleck from his lip and flicked it toward the trash can beside his desk.

"Somebody must have picked him up," Austin said.

"Who?" Rocco asked. "Someone who wouldn't call the police or take him to a hospital? Does that make any sense to you?"

"Guess not."

"He lost a lot of blood," Lefty said. "Bet he holed up somewhere and died."

"You better hope so. I know for damn sure he isn't in Memorial. I'd know."

"Could've taken him somewhere else," Austin said. "Out of the county."

Rocco shook his head. "Do I look stupid? You think I don't have that covered? He couldn't get into a fucking dog pound without me knowing. The word's out."

"What about Walker and Tortelli?" Lefty asked. "Could they be hiding him?"

Rocco gave his cigar a couple of long puffs. He stared at Lefty through a cloud of smoke, thinking that it was a stupid idea. Or was it? "Why would you think that?"

"I don't. But we can't find him. Cops don't have him. He's not in a hospital. Just trying to figure who else could know about him and who might be able to hurt us if they had him."

Rocco puffed out another cloud of smoke but said nothing.

"I mean," Lefty continued, "they were at Eddie's trailer. Talked to the sister. Went to Alejandro's place. Right?"

Rocco nodded.

"Maybe they found Alejandro. Maybe he isn't as bad off as we think."

"He's bad," Austin said. "You saw all the blood."

"Maybe they took him some place. A private clinic or something."

"Tortelli's a cop. He couldn't do that," Rocco said. "Besides, why would he? He's in charge of the murder investigation. Doesn't make sense that he would keep Alejandro holed up somewhere."

"Tortelli is a cowboy," Austin said. "Isn't that the word on him?"

Rocco dumped a long ash into the ashtray on his desk. "What's the payoff? Why would he take the risk?"

"Information," Lefty said. "Alejandro knows a lot. Too much, in fact."

"I don't buy it." Rocco shoved the cigar into his mouth and talked around it. "Alejandro's either dead or still on the run. Nothing else makes sense. Still, it wouldn't hurt to have another chat with Tortelli and Walker. Get a read on what they know."

"That'd be better than letting them decide when to play the card," Lefty said. "If they have a card, that is. We'll find them. Invite them over." He smiled.

Rocco flexed his neck, trying to get the kinks out. "What a fucking mess." He looked at Lefty. "You about ready to go over on Pratt?"

"Getting all the players lined up."

"Good. Time to pull the trigger on that deal."

CHAPTER 52

SUNDAY 1:01 P.M.

T-TOMMY HAD BEEN STANDING AT THE FAR END OF THE YARD, TALKING on his cell. He walked back to the table where Claire and I sat and flopped into a chair across from me. "Eddie's preliminary tox report. No meth. No amphetamines at all."

I nodded. "I figured that'd be the case."

"But there's something in his blood. Don't know what. They're sending samples to NMS in Pennsylvania."

"How long?" I asked.

"Depends on what it is. Maybe a day. Maybe a week. Maybe longer."

Claire stood, stretched, and then sat back down. She had been working on her notes for her broadcast. She looked at T-Tommy, her pen tapping the notepad in front of her. "Tell me about Alejandro Diaz."

T-Tommy flipped open his murder book and shuffled through the pages until he located what he was looking for. "Alejandro Diaz.

Age thirty-two. Originally from Juárez. Lived in El Paso most of his life. Didn't finish high school but got his GED. Did a stint with the Marines, then did eighteen months of a nickel rap for B and E, theft, and threatening a witness. That was in Miami. Apparently landed here about four years ago. Popped three years ago for grand theft auto. Charges dropped."

"Let me guess," I said. "The owner refused to press charges?"

"Yep," T-Tommy said. "Of course, he reported the car stolen and didn't know Alejandro Diaz from Adam's house cat, but after Diaz was released on a five-thousand-dollar bail, he refused to press the matter."

"Intimidation?" Claire asked.

"Most likely. The report I saw said the owner denied being threatened, said he was just glad to get his car back, yada, yada. You know how it works." T-Tommy shrugged. "Since that, he's been clean." He turned several pages. "His bank accounts show occasional paychecks from High Rollers. We know he worked there. He also made several larger deposits. All cash."

"Cash always means trouble," I said. "How much are we talking about?"

"Most of the deposits were a Grover or two." T-Tommy's finger ran down the page. "One. Two. Three, four, five . . . three more . . . five more. Eleven for a grand and ten for two grand. All in the past . . . let's see . . . fifteen months."

"That's thirty-one thousand," Claire said. "Pretty good side business. Wonder what he did for his thirty-one grand."

"Bury bodies," I said.

"And maybe whack punks like Eddie," T-Tommy said.

"They were buddy-buddy," I said. "He could get next to him. Even catch him in the shower."

"If we ever find him, we can ask him where the cash comes from."

Kramden and Norton returned. Apparently they couldn't find anything more interesting. Tried to steal some of Claire's papers. Latched on to her pen. She didn't back down and snatched it away. Indignant, they took to the trees and cawed their protest.

T-Tommy's cell chirped. He answered, listened for a minute, and then said, "You're sure?" He nodded and closed the phone. "Bingo."

"What?" I asked.

"Got the info on Alejandro's phone. He made or received over a hundred calls to High Rollers in the past two years."

"Yeah. He worked there."

"Right. But remember the other number? Karl Reinhardt and Sentinel Security? Alejandro made three calls to and received eleven from that number. All in the past ten months."

"Okay."

"Sentinel Security's an Illinois company. Privately held by Karl Reinhardt." T-Tommy stared at me. "Ready for the good part?"

"Let's have it."

"Reinhardt and Sentinel Security work for Talbert Biomedical. Reinhardt's the security chief there."

"What?"

"My thoughts exactly," T-Tommy said.

Twenty plus people buried after having buttonhole surgeries. Eddie and Alejandro buried the bodies. Eddie's dead and Alejandro's missing. Alejandro has the number for the security chief of a company that makes the instruments needed to do the surgeries. *Jesus.*

CHAPTER 53

T-TOMMY AGAIN WANDERED TOWARD THE BACK OF THE PROPERTY while he made phone calls. Claire worked on her notes. I stretched out on a lounge chair, the sun warm against my face. A dove cooed softly from a nearby tree. I closed my eyes and went over all that had happened in the past few days.

The movie in my head jerked from scene to scene. Noel's body resting on the dissection table, the smell of the place returning in waves. Rocco, Austin, and Lefty. Madison, Sin-Dee, Rosalee Kennedy. Always back to Noel. Her lifeless body hacked up and buried like so much garbage.

I looked over at Claire, seeing her in profile, remembering the first time I saw her. Coming out of a coffee shop. I had been at my lowest point, she stumbling out of a soured relationship. We went inside, had coffee, and arranged to meet for dinner that night. That led to our brief marriage, our divorce, and my trip to the Marines. My job at the Department of Forensic Sciences and FBI BAU stint followed.

I closed my eyes again, and the movie in my head cranked back up. Noel, Rocco, Madison, Sin-Dee, Rosalee, Noel again, and of course, Jill. The reason I never finished med school. The reason I walked the path I now walked. The reason my parents sank into despair. The reason I sank just as far. The hole Claire pulled me from. The reason I loved her and I always would even if we couldn't hang our toothbrushes side by side.

I pushed away these thoughts and focused on what we knew about Alejandro. Saw flash images of his apartment. Who was Alejandro Diaz? Was he capable of doing these procedures? Everything said no. Uneducated, no experience, career criminal. His only connection to the medical world the phone number for Karl Reinhardt at Talbert Biomedical.

So, who was he? Simply a garbageman like Eddie? No doubt that he helped Eddie bury the bodies. The map proved it. But for who?

Did he do Eddie, or was it someone else? Most likely Eddie was whacked because he fucked up or pissed off the wrong person. Became a liability. Had Alejandro been taken out, too? Was he on the run, fearing he could be next?

Was Carmelita Hidalgo running with Alejandro or planted somewhere? Was she part of this or another victim? Maybe she was simply on vacation. Without telling her best friend? I didn't buy that.

A shadow passed over. I opened my eyes and looked up, shielding the sun with one hand.

T-Tommy closed his cell phone, dropped it into his jacket pocket, and sat down at the table. "They're working on the last rural site. Said they'd be heading over to Maple Hill in a half hour or so."

"You going over there?" I asked.

He nodded.

"Me, too," Claire said.

"Do you think Alejandro could be the cutter?" I asked T-Tommy.

"Don't see it that way. Nothing about him says he has the skills or knowledge to do this stuff."

"I agree. Not quite ready to write him off, though."

"His connection to Talbert's a bit curious. I know for sure he's not on the company payroll or their workers' comp rolls. Just that he has the security chief's phone number."

"We're assuming it's Reinhardt," I said. "Could be someone else at Talbert."

Claire jumped in. "Maybe Alejandro does more than bury bodies. Like getting instruments for the killer. Buying them under the table from an employee."

"Maybe from Reinhardt himself," I said.

"You could be right," T-Tommy said. "These instruments aren't being lifted from any of the local hospitals. All theirs are accounted for. Same with the two medical equipment wholesalers in the area."

Claire opened her hands, palms up. "That leads us back to Talbert."

I liked where this line of reasoning was going. "After this morning, all the bodies, we know this deal's been going on for a while. Let's assume that Eddie and Alejandro grabbed the victims for the killer and then disposed of them afterward. Let's also assume that Alejandro gets the surgical tools from Talbert on the sly. Where does that leave us?"

"With a hell of a conspiracy," Claire said. "Why would the killer expose himself that way? Hire criminals to capture victims for him? Why not do it himself? Hookers aren't usually that difficult to isolate."

"About a third of the bodies are male," T-Tommy said. "Doubt that they're all hookers."

"They could be male prostitutes," Claire said. "Or simply loners. Easily abducted. Not likely missed. Like hookers."

"We'll know when we get the IDs done," T-Tommy said. "Might take a while, though."

Claire nodded. "Maybe the killer's not big enough to overpower his victims and too shy or too afraid to sweet-talk them. Maybe he can only relate to them after they've been restrained or immobilized. So he hires someone to do it for him."

That made sense on some level. The killer was smart. That was a given. He was skilled. Surgically, anyway. But maybe he was physically weak or socially inept. Wouldn't be the first serial killer to have such deficiencies. Perhaps Eddie and Alejandro were the hunters. The trashmen. The question was: for who?

I asked T-Tommy, "How many active missing persons cases do you guys have right now?"

"Don't know the exact number. I'd say a hundred and fifty or more."

"How many prostitutes you guess?"

"No way to know. Many aren't even reported. Most aren't really missing. Maybe hiding from someone or some situation. Parents, marriage, whatever. Some go home to try to fix things that can't be fixed. Others head to another city to work for a while. Most often they turn up."

"Except for the ones buried in the woods," Claire said.

"Maybe our guy isn't just shy," I said. "Maybe he has some physical defect that would make him stand out. Something memorable. So he gets Eddie and Alejandro to grab victims for him."

"What kind of defect?" Claire asked.

"Could be anything. A facial scar. A missing limb. A speech defect. Like David Carpenter."

"Who's that?" Claire asked.

"The Trailside Killer. Thirty or so years ago. Out in California. San Francisco area. The victims had all been hiking. John Douglas of the BSU did the profile. Told the local PD that the killer had some defect, but not one that would be obvious since none of the people who frequented the trails noticed anything. He suspected that the killer stuttered or had some other speech impediment. Couldn't sweet-talk his victims. Rather he would use a blitz attack to overpower them. When Carpenter was captured, he did indeed stutter."

"I guess our guy could look odd or have some noticeable physical problem," T-Tommy said. "Maybe a limp or one of those purple things Gorbachev had on his face."

"A nevus flammeus," I said. "Port-wine stain. It's a birthmark."

"You're thinking that Alejandro and Eddie are body snatchers for the sicko that's doing this?" T-Tommy asked.

"If so, Alejandro can identify him."

"If we can find Alejandro," T-Tommy said.

"Maybe his connection to Talbert will lead somewhere," Claire said.

"Let's hope." T-Tommy stood. "Time to head over to Maple Hill."

CHAPTER 54

THE OLDEST AND LARGEST CEMETERY IN THE STATE, MAPLE HILL WAS the final resting place of nearly one hundred thousand souls. Its gently rolling terrain, winding paths, and hand-carved headstones were shaded by trees of many sizes and varieties. There were simple, flat grave markers, elaborate headstones, huge crosses and statuary, a mausoleum or two, and even a section for the Civil War dead. Its parklike atmosphere attracted those looking for a quiet place to walk or contemplate as well as visit the dead.

Today it wasn't quiet. A crowd had gathered. Nothing like death to attract flies.

I leaned against the stone wall that surrounded Maple Hill near the McClung Avenue entrance, talking with Claire. The bodies had been excavated and carted off to the Department of Forensic Sciences. Claire had finished her on-site filming, and Jeffrey was loading his camera gear into the Channel 8 truck.

T-Tommy came from a cluster of HPD uniforms toward us. "Got the scoop on Talbert and Reinhardt. Talbert Biomedical was founded in 1998 by Harmon Talbert, the current CEO, and Dr. Robert Kincaid, the medical research director. It's a two-hundred-million-dollar company. Privately held."

I whistled. "Which makes Talbert and Kincaid very rich men."

"Looks like Mr. Talbert has started and sold several companies in his career. Most recently a surgical supply house. In Philadelphia. Sold it in '97 right before starting Talbert Biomedical. According to his company bio, Dr. Robert Kincaid practiced general surgery in Chicago for twenty years. Cook County Hospital. Professor of surgery. Research director. Bunch of honors."

"So, they probably hooked up through business connections, one making surgical instruments, the other using them, and moved here for their new venture," I said.

"Land and construction costs, taxes, unions. Lots of companies are moving here to avoid all that." T-Tommy opened his notebook. "Here's an odd little tidbit you're going to love. Talbert has a contract with a company called Gulf Coast Anatomical Supply. They purchased twenty-seven cadavers from them last year. Twelve so far this year."

"Why would Talbert need corpses?" Claire asked.

"I'd suspect to help design new surgical instruments," I said. "Medical schools and medical equipment designers purchase a bunch each year. If you just need a head or an arm, you can get that, too.

Burn centers buy skin from these outfits. Even auto manufacturers sometimes use real corpses instead of dummies for their crash tests."

"You're kidding," Claire said.

"No," T-Tommy said. "He's not. West Coast Anatomical's client list includes two car companies."

"Pretty morbid," Claire said. "I don't like the mental image of somebody's uncle Joe flying through the windshield of some goofy-looking concept car."

I laughed and then asked T-Tommy, "You think Talbert hooked up with Reinhardt in Chicago?"

"Good bet."

"What do you have on Reinhardt?"

"Chicago native. Master's in criminology from Northwestern. Chicago PD for ten years. Started Sentinel Security in 1994. Apparently joined Talbert in 2000."

"Criminal record?" Claire asked.

"Not even a parking ticket."

Claire glanced at her watch. "Got to get to the station and slap on a face before my six o'clock report."

"Maybe come by later?" I asked.

She laughed. "Feeling a little stressed?"

"Been a while."

Claire and I had been divorced for a decade. Though we couldn't hang under the same roof, the sex was always good, and we still played that game from time to time.

"I've got a cocktail reception to go to. Should be done by ten, maybe eleven. Think you can survive that long?"

"Should I pour a bucket of water on you two?" T-Tommy said.

"Funny." I looked at Claire. "See you then."

"I'm out of here." She headed to her car.

My cell phone rang. I recognized the displayed number as Ellie Elliott's. I had called earlier and left a message. "Thanks for calling back," I said. "Heard anything from Alejandro?"

"No."

"I have a few more questions about him. Would it be okay if we came by? It'll only take a few minutes."

She hesitated.

"It could be important," I said.

Ellie sighed. "I just got home. Been a hell of a day."

"I know. I wouldn't bother you if I didn't think it was important."

She hesitated again and then said, "Give me an hour."

CHAPTER 55

ELLIE ELLIOTT OPENED THE DOOR TO MY KNOCK AND LED T-TOMMY and me into her living room. She appeared tired but not as distraught as she had been last night. She wore gray sweatpants and a white T-shirt. We sat on a floral sofa, while she curled up into a blue wingback chair, a longneck PBR in her hand. She didn't offer us one, indicating the meeting would be short.

We had decided to keep it simple. Ask our questions and get out. No need to tell her everything. Unless it was absolutely necessary to get her to talk. If we did and Ellie leaked it, Furyk would have a fit if we were the source. T-Tommy would pay the price.

Before I could get out a question Ellie got right to it. "Did Alejandro kill Eddie?"

"It's possible," I said. "But I don't think so."

"Then who did?"

"Don't know."

She took a swig of beer, swallowing hard. "Then why are you looking for Alejandro?"

"He could be in danger," I said.

"From whoever killed Eddie?"

"That's one possibility."

"And the other possibilities?" Ellie asked.

"The bodies of two girls were found buried outside the city," T-Tommy said. "In an isolated wooded area. Murdered. Your brother's fingerprints were discovered at the burial site."

Her eyes widened. "My brother? You think my brother is a killer? Who the hell do you—?"

I raised a hand. "Relax. We don't believe your brother killed anyone. We do believe he buried the bodies, though. We believe Alejandro was involved, too."

Ellie put the beer on the table next to her chair. Her shoulders sagged. "Jesus."

"Tell me about Alejandro," I said. "Did he ever work in the medical industry?"

"What does that have to do with anything?"

"Maybe nothing," I said.

"Not that I know."

"What about for a vet or in a lab of some kind?"

"Alejandro isn't that smart. Thinks he is sometimes, but he's not."

"Not a science whiz?" T-Tommy asked.

She snorted. "You might say that."

"Never said he liked to cut up frogs as a kid? Anything like that?"

"What's this about?"

"Did he ever mention a place called Talbert Biomedical?" I asked.

"No. Never heard that."

"What about a Dr. Robert Kincaid or a guy named Karl Reinhardt?" T-Tommy asked.

"I heard Eddie use Reinhardt's name once. While on the phone. I didn't know who he was talking to. Probably Alejandro. Don't remember him using the name Karl. Just Reinhardt. Kind of an unusual name."

"When was that?" I asked.

"Two weeks ago. Maybe three."

"What did he say about Reinhardt?"

Ellie shrugged. "Nothing. Not that I heard, anyway. I just remember the name."

"Ever see Alejandro or Eddie with any tools or surgical instruments?" I said.

Her eyes moistened. "What the hell is this about? I'm not saying another word until I know what's going on."

She deserved at least that. I glanced at T-Tommy, who offered a slight nod.

"This goes no further than right here," I said. "You tell anyone and the HPD will be up all our asses. All of us. Understand?"

She nodded.

"You watch the news tonight?"

Ellie shook her head.

"The girls?" I said. "The two I mentioned? They aren't the only ones. There are a couple of dozen other bodies. Buried all around the city."

She blinked back tears and sniffed. "This is unbelievable."

"It looks like each of them had had surgery. Highly technical surgery."

"You think Eddie and Alejandro did it?" Another quick laugh escaped her lips. "I loved my brother, but he was an idiot." She picked up her beer and took a gulp. Then another. "He was smart on some levels, but overall he was a loser. I know that. I tried to help him, but the only thing he excelled at was being a punk. Same for Alejandro. We were hot and heavy for about six months. A year or two back. It was never going anywhere. Alejandro was never going anywhere."

I suspected we could eliminate Eddie and Alejandro as the killers. No real surprise there. "Did either of them ever mention a nurse, a paramedic, or maybe a military medic?"

"No. You know Alejandro was a Marine?"

I nodded. "He wasn't a medic, was he?"

"A grunt. A down-in-the-dirt grunt."

I looked at T-Tommy. "I guess that's all the questions we have."

"Do the police have any suspects?" she asked.

"Not yet."

Ellie walked us to the door. We thanked her and apologized for bothering her. Halfway down the walkway, I glanced back as Ellie closed her door. I heard her flip the lock into place. In the window of the apartment above hers, the curtain parted and a face appeared. Looked like an elderly woman, but I couldn't be sure. There was one in every neighborhood. The one nothing got by. I waved to her and headed for my Porsche.

Almost made it. A black Lincoln with blacked-out windows pulled to the curb. Austin and Lefty stepped out.

"What can we do for you two?" I asked.

"Boss wants to see you."

"About what?"

"You'll have to ask him." Austin twisted one fist into the palm of his other hand. His forearm muscles popped to life. "Follow us."

"We know the way."

CHAPTER 56

HIGH ROLLERS WAS PACKED, PROVING YET AGAIN THAT PEOPLE THINK about sex every day. Even the Lord's Day. The music thrummed against my chest as we climbed the stairs to Rocco's office. When T-Tommy reached for the door, the meat standing guard put a palm on T-Tommy's chest. Not a wise move. T-Tommy grabbed a handful of fingers and twisted them into an unnatural and what appeared to be a very painful position.

"You want your fingers back?" T-Tommy asked.

The man glared at him.

"Fuck with me I'll do this to your throat." T-Tommy torqued the man's fingers backward, dropping him to one knee. "That's better."

T-Tommy released his grip, and we entered Rocco's office.

Rocco looked up, surprise on his face, a chewed cigar in the corner of his mouth. An empty pizza box was on his desk.

"You didn't save us any?" I said. "T-Tommy's hungry."

"Told you we shoulda stopped," T-Tommy said.

Rocco tugged the dead cigar from his mouth. "Where's Lefty and Austin?"

"They'll be along," I said.

The door swung open, and Austin and Lefty came in.

"What'd I tell you," I said.

"Thought you guys were bringing pizza," T-Tommy said. "Haven't eaten since lunch."

Austin started to say something, but Rocco waved him into silence. He nodded toward the chairs that faced his desk. "Have a seat." He glanced at Lefty. "You guys wait outside."

Austin muttered something I didn't catch as he and Lefty headed out the door. T-Tommy and I sat down.

"You two are starting to piss me off," Rocco said.

"We don't mean to," I said.

"But we do hear that a lot," T-Tommy added.

Rocco clamped the cigar butt between his teeth, snatched a lighter from beneath the pizza box, and lit it. He gave it a couple of puffs. The end glowed red, and smoke swirled toward the ceiling. "What are you guys up to?"

"Looking for one of your employees. Alejandro Diaz."

"Never heard of him."

I leaned forward, forearms on knees. "We can fuck around, or we can get to it. I don't care which. We're not guessing here. We know Alejandro works for you."

"What if he does?"

"We're looking for him."

"Mind if I ask why?"

"You can ask."

"You guys may not be as clever as you think you are," Rocco said.

"Then again," I said, "we just might be."

Rocco blew smoke from the side of his mouth. "Let me make this as clear as I can. I don't want you two fucking around with my people."

"Just tell us where we can find Alejandro."

Rocco smiled. "Funny, I wanted to ask you the same thing. You guys are hot shit. Thought you might know where he is."

I smiled, too. "Wouldn't be here in this shit hole if we did."

Rocco's smile evaporated, and for an instant his eyes turned cold, and then just as quickly his face softened and the smile returned. A bit forced this time. He leaned back in his chair and scratched at one ear. "Don't know. Fired him a couple of months ago. Haven't seen him since."

"Then why has he called here so often in the last two months? The last time was . . ." I looked at T-Tommy.

"Four days ago."

"Didn't talk to me. Maybe he has the hots for one of my girls."

T-Tommy grunted. "That why you're still paying him? To entertain your girls?"

"I'm not."

"I'm disappointed," I said. "Thought you'd be clever enough not to leave a paper trail."

"Don't know what you mean."

"You write a check, Alejandro dumps it into his account, there's a record."

"Must be part of his severance package," Rocco said. "I'll have to check with my accounting people."

"Somehow I figure you're the accounting department," I said. "You ain't the type to let someone else watch the money."

Rocco shrugged. "Why are you looking for Alejandro?"

"Nothing big, just a few questions," I said.

"About?"

"Told you. We're looking for whoever killed Noel Edwards and your employee Crystal. And a couple dozen others."

Rocco aimed a cloud of smoke at me. "You think Alejandro might be that guy?"

I ignored the smoke. Wouldn't give him anything. "Don't know. But his friend Eddie Elliott is involved."

"Then why don't you talk to this Eddie guy?"

"We tried. Didn't have much to say. Being dead and all."

"Sorry to hear that."

I smiled. "Was that his severance package?"

Rocco's teeth ground the cigar butt. "I don't know anyone named Eddie."

"Is that why your two clowns were outside his sister's house?"

"They were following you."

"We're flattered," I said.

"Makes me all warm inside to know you care," T-Tommy said. "It truly does."

"So why are your two lapdogs sniffing around us?" I asked.

"To invite you here. For this little chat."

"Okay," I said. "Chat away."

"What's with you two? You come here looking for a hooker. She turns up dead. End of story."

I shook my head. "Beginning of story. We still haven't found the guy who did it."

"So I'll ask again. You think Alejandro is the killer?" Rocco said.

"Do you? Perhaps you know something we don't."

"All I know is that you guys've been sticking your noses where they don't belong."

"Why do you care?" I asked. "If this has nothing to do with you, what difference does it make?"

"I'm a concerned citizen."

I laughed and glanced at T-Tommy. "He look like a concerned citizen?"

"Not remotely."

Rocco thumbed a long ash into a thick green-glass ashtray and settled the cigar back into the corner of his mouth. He gave it a couple of puffs and smiled. "Since you guys are all big on missing persons, where's Madison?"

"Don't know a Madison," I said.

"The one you followed out of here the other night. Haven't seen her since."

"You know a Madison?" I asked T-Tommy.

"Not lately."

Rocco pointed his cigar at me. "Maybe I should file a missing persons on her. See if the HPD can turn her up."

"Why not call your buddy Furyk? I'm sure he'd help."

His eyes narrowed, now cold, with a steely edge. "Maybe I can find her myself."

Me: "Wouldn't suggest that."

T-Tommy: "Bad idea."

Me: "Something happens to her, and it'll look bad for you."

T-Tommy: "Real bad."

Me: "Wouldn't even want her to suffer a lightning strike."

T-Tommy: "If she did, we might have to come back out here."

Rocco shoved the cigar into his mouth and clamped down. "I'll try to remember to worry about that."

"I was you I would," T-Tommy said.

Rocco propped an elbow on the edge of his desk. "Let's get a few things clear. Don't fuck with my people. Don't fuck with me. My reach is far longer than you can imagine. So, why don't you two Boy Scouts head on out of here before something really bad happens."

I looked at T-Tommy. "Sound like a threat to you?"

"Sure does. Guess he don't know he can't threaten a police officer."

Rocco stood and leaned forward, palms flat on the desktop. "Call it a threat. Call it advice. Call it a lesson in how things work around here. Call it any fucking thing you want. But get in my way . . ." He shrugged.

I was no stranger to violence. Never sought it out but never backed away, either. Started with football, a sport that lent a certain toughness that never faded. Then a little boxing, mostly learned from my father. His philosophy was simple: hit first, hit hard, and keep hitting until the other guy doesn't move anymore. All in all a good strategy. Marine MP training solidified that.

T-Tommy was a different story. Linebacker's mentality. Loved contact. All kinds of contact. Not a big fan of the Queensberry rules, he'd fight you with everything and anything. His fists, his elbows, his head, a tire iron, a chair, even saw him rip a door off the hinges and waylay a couple of dudes. They shouldn't have pulled knives on him. His philosophy wasn't much different from my dad's: in boxing, second place was last place. No point in losing. T-Tommy could easily slide into that stomp-on-your-own-accelerator-and-fuck-it mode. I could feel that swelling up inside him right now.

T-Tommy stood. I did, too. If he was going to trash Rocco, I needed to cover his back. I could picture T-Tommy flipping the desk over on Rocco, then Lefty, Austin, and that door goon crashing in. I moved to the door and leaned against it. Not sure what that would do except maybe slow their charge. But if T-Tommy jumped into full rage that might be enough.

T-Tommy grabbed a handful of Rocco's shirt with one hand and snatched the cigar from his mouth with the other. He tossed the cigar into the trash can and pulled Rocco close. "Since we're making things clear here, let's try this one. You threaten me again, and I'll take it personal. You wouldn't like that. And don't think your jerk-off buddy Furyk will save your sorry ass. I got more friends than he does. Some of them are way above his pay grade."

Rocco tried to lean back, break T-Tommy's grip.

T-Tommy yanked him forward, his face only inches from Rocco's. "If you want, I can have the HPD crawl up your ass and bivouac."

A curl of smoke rose from the trash can as the cigar began to smolder the paper inside. Rocco glanced in that direction, but T-Tommy jerked his gaze back to him.

"And Dub here" —he nodded in my direction—"is plugged into the FBI, DOJ, DEA, the whole goddamn alphabet soup. So we can bring a shit storm down on your little fiefdom."

More smoke. The odor of charring paper filled the room.

"I know all about your lucky break," T-Tommy went on. "You know? The witness that committed suicide?" He shook his head. "Popping witnesses always attracts attention."

The trash was now sending up smoke signals. Rocco looked at it and started to say something.

T-Tommy cut him off. "Now, we're going to find whoever did Noel and all those others. If the trail leads here, we'll be back. If your goons get in our way . . . well, let's just say it won't be pleasant. I'm not big on rules and laws and all that shit. I'm sure you understand." T-Tommy let go of Rocco's shirt and gave him a push. He fell into his chair.

Not bad. No blood. No broken bones. Rocco got off easy.

T-Tommy nodded toward the trash can, now crowned with flames. "I was you I'd put that out."

I opened the door, coming face-to-face with Austin. I jerked my head toward Rocco. "Your boss needs you to piss on something."

CHAPTER 57

CLAIRE'S NIPPLES HARDENED AGAINST MY CHEST AS SHE SLID HER WET, warm body against me, the hot shower cascading over us. I lifted her chin and kissed her, her calf locking behind mine, as she pressed her body against me.

She moaned, breaking the kiss. "Take me to bed, and let's do this right."

No argument here. We quickly knocked off most of the water with a few swipes of a towel and moved to the bedroom, where she pushed me onto my back and straddled me. Neither of us lasted very long, and soon we were stretched out on the bed. She lay cradled in my arm, cheek against my chest.

"You're kind of fun," she said.

I laughed. "What wound you up?"

"Champagne. You know that always revs my motor."

"Glad the media dinner was fun."

"Had to do something while you guys were out looking at strippers."

"Part of the job."

"How convenient. Anyway, I had a great steak and a bottle of Dom."

"Let's see. That's champagne, wine, spicy food, the full moon, hot showers, silk sheets, and anything from Victoria's Secret."

Claire jabbed my ribs. "It's you that gets turned on by the Victoria's Secret catalog."

She had me there.

We started again. This time more slowly. A kiss, a caress, a murmur, and soon we were locked together. Me on top. Her legs wrapped around me as she pulled me into her, and we fell into a slow, sensuous rhythm.

Afterward, I stroked her hair as she drifted to sleep. Wish I could have, too, but sleep wasn't my friend. I tried to grab it, but it kept slipping away. The sheets seemed to bind me, and my pillow continually wadded into uncomfortable knots. My pancaking kept waking Claire. I think she kicked me a couple of times. She denied it. I didn't believe her.

When I did manage to doze, my dreams revolved around a ghoulish mad scientist who pumped people full of electricity, cut them open, and removed their hearts and kidneys and parts I couldn't recognize. There was a conveyer belt that carried the bodies to the mad surgeon, each one stopping in front of him so he could work. He wore a white surgical gown, sleeves bloody to the elbows. Shadowy assistants kept loading bodies on one end of the conveyer and taking the hacked-up corpses off the other. The victims were all alive and screaming, and the doctor howled fiendishly. He looked like Mr. Kirkland, my eighth grade math teacher. A mean SOB with a shock of wild white hair and a constantly foul mood. I always knew he'd come to no good.

I passed most of the night staring at the ceiling, the committee meeting in my head in full session. Each of the voices had an argument for who the killer was. None of the ideas made much sense, though. The only things we could all agree on were that neither Eddie nor Alejandro was the surgeon and that whoever was doing the cutting didn't learn it from a book. This guy had been schooled in medicine. Perhaps veterinary medicine, or even mortuary techniques, but he had some form of medical training.

Exhaustion finally won out, and I slid down the slope into sleep.

CHAPTER 58

I AWOKE FEELING FUZZY, FOGGY, STUPID, AND WITH A BUZZING IN MY head. A great start to the day. It seemed like I'd slept only ten minutes. I realized that the buzzing was my cell phone. Apparently I had silenced it, and it was now vibrating against the nightstand. I didn't recognize the displayed number, so I pressed the answer button and brought the phone to my ear. "Hello?"

"Dub Walker?" A woman's voice.

"Yes."

"This is Bobbie Hawkins at Memorial Medical Center ICU."

"ICU?" Not exactly what I was expecting. I remembered the nurse, though. She had helped care for Sammy after he was mugged by Brian Kurtz. If she was calling, it wouldn't be good news.

"Dr. Mackey wants to talk to you. Hold a sec and I'll get her."

Liz came on the line. "Dub?"

"What is it?"

"I thought I should let you know about a patient we got in early this morning. I'm not the doc on the case, but he has wounds similar to the ones you described on those two girls."

"He's alive?"

"Mostly. For now, anyway. Doesn't look good."

"Who is it?"

"No ID yet. The police are working on it. Took fingerprints and photos."

"I'll be right there."

Thirty minutes later, Claire and I entered the ICU. I had called T-Tommy as we left my house, and he came in right behind us. The nurses' station, a long counter topped with monitors, faced a row of glassed-in patient cubicles. Within one of the enclosures, several nurses and a doctor worked on a man. CPR, electrical shocks, the whole deal. Things didn't seem to be going well. I hoped it wasn't our guy.

"Mr. Walker, we have to quit meeting this way." Bobbie Hawkins smiled. "Let me get Dr. Mackey." She started to walk away but stopped. "Here she is now."

I followed her gaze. Liz came out of a cubicle and waved us to her.

We walked to where she stood. "What's the story?" I asked.

"This is John Doe," she said.

Through the glass I saw a man stretched out on the bed. A ventilator tube protruded from his mouth, half a dozen IV lines fed into his arms, and his belly was wrapped with bandages and tape. I stepped into the cubicle and looked down at the man. Alejandro Diaz. No doubt.

T-Tommy moved up beside me. "You've got to be kidding."

I turned to Liz and said, "His name's Alejandro Diaz. He's involved in the case we've been working. Not sure exactly how but—"

"Let's go where we can talk," Liz said.

We left the ICU and went down the hall to the doctors' lounge where we had met with Liz before. She poured a cup of coffee and sat. She pulled out several Polaroid pictures and handed them to me. "This is what he looked like when he came in."

I shuffled through the pictures, passing them to T-Tommy and Claire. Alejandro lay on a stretcher, unclothed except for a towel over his genitals, his belly coated with a large smear of dried blood. Six short, stapled wounds peeked through the crusty blood. Like those on Noel and Crystal.

"Paul Sammons, one of our trauma surgeons, operated on him. I happened to be in the ER with another patient when the medics brought him in around six this morning. I had the nurses take the photos. Sammons said when he got inside he found the gallbladder and the appendix had been removed. Both fresh surgeries. Probably done at the same time. A day or two ago at the most."

"What made you think he could be part of our investigation?" I asked. "I mean, he could have simply been a patient with post-op bleeding, right?"

"Sure." Liz set her coffee cup on the table. "Except he was found lying in a plowed field about five this morning by the farmer who owned the property. He planned to start planting today. When he first saw him, he thought he was dead so he called the police. They found a pulse, called the paramedics, and here he is." She bent over and began pulling fresh booties over her shoes. "I didn't see the girls, but this guy's procedures were done by the same technique. And with him running around in the middle of the night, I thought it was too much of a coincidence to let pass."

"Glad you didn't," T-Tommy said. "This could be the break we need."

"Where was he found?" I asked.

"According to the police and medic reports, out off Farrow Road."

I glanced at T-Tommy. Farrow Road was on the periphery of the Cummings Research Park. Very near Talbert.

"How's he doing?" Claire asked.

"He'd been in shock for quite a while before he got here. Kidneys and lungs are shot. Sammons pumped him full of blood and fluids and patched him up, but it doesn't look good."

"Did he say anything?" I asked.

"Been in a coma the entire time."

"Is he going to wake up?"

"Don't know."

"So how do you put this together?" T-Tommy asked.

"Not sure, but if I had to guess, the surgery went well. Then for some reason he was out in that field, ripped open his wounds, lost a ton of blood, bled himself into shock, and crawled to or fell where he was found." Liz stood. "I need to get to the OR. Got a patient on the table ready to go."

CHAPTER 59

CLAIRE, T-TOMMY, AND I STOOD IN THE HALL NEAR THE ICU entrance.

"Farrow Road," T-Tommy said.

"Seems like wherever we go we end up back at Talbert."

"Sure does."

"The question is, how did the garbageman become a victim?" I asked T-Tommy.

"Because garbagemen are expendable."

"This clears Alejandro as the cutter," Claire said. "He couldn't operate on himself."

T-Tommy nodded and then looked at me. "Makes what you said earlier seem more reasonable. That someone at Talbert could be involved."

"Or a friend of someone at Talbert. Someone who could get his tools from there and his victims from Eddie and Alejandro." I glanced at the ICU doors as they whooshed open.

A nurse came out. She smiled and walked down to the elevators.

"Let me carry it a step farther," I went on. "I haven't completely thought it through. Just came to me. What if these surgeries were done at Talbert?"

"Why would you think that?" Claire asked.

"Because Alejandro turned up bleeding and near death in the neighborhood. From what Liz said, he couldn't have gone very far from where he was cut on."

"Talbert's a manufacturing company," Claire said. "Not a hospital."

"We don't know that. We haven't been inside." Behind me I heard the elevator ding and the doors hiss open. I turned and saw Sergeant Furyk step out. His walk, his attitude, and the anger I saw in his face said it all. "Here comes trouble," I said.

T-Tommy whispered, "Great." He nodded in Furyk's direction. "Sergeant."

Furyk definitely had a mean-on. "What the hell is going on?" He glared at T-Tommy and then me. "I thought I told you to stay out of this."

"Did I do something wrong?" I asked.

Furyk's jaw barely moved when he spoke. "You know goddamn well what's going on."

"Maybe you could tell me. I'm confused."

"You've interfered with a homicide investigation. Stomped all over a couple of crime scenes. Interrogated my witnesses. Harassed one of our most influential citizens."

"You can't mean Rocco Scarcella," I said.

"Mr. Scarcella pays his taxes. Keeps his nose clean."

I doubted anyone would ever accuse Rocco of being clean. Except Furyk. Which meant that Rocco's reach did indeed extend right into the brass of the HPD. Political ambition was always corrupting. LA, New York, here, it didn't matter where. Once you got shit in your shoes, you were done. I also figured playing nice wasn't going to work. It was obvious Furyk wanted to lock horns, so what the hell.

"You must mean a different Rocco. That doesn't fit the one I know. He a friend of yours?"

Furyk ground his teeth.

I was in it now. No way to back out. Not that I really wanted to. "You running for office or something? Rocco a donor?"

Furyk's face reddened. His neck veins looked like two ropes. I loved this stuff.

"I want you out of here," he said. "Now."

"I was invited," I said.

"Now you're uninvited."

"By whom?"

"By me. I'm in charge here."

"Actually, you're second in command. I was invited by the person in charge."

His lips stretched tightly across his clenched teeth. "I'm afraid you're very mistaken."

"I guess you can cuff Mr. Diaz and drag his ass off to jail anytime you want."

"That's right. As soon as the doc says so."

"Like I said. Second in command." I honestly thought he was going to pull his gun and shoot me. Did I say I love this shit?

Instead he turned to T-Tommy. "Inside. Now." He spun on his heels and stalked into the ICU.

"That was fun," T-Tommy said.

"He was asking for it."

T-Tommy smiled. "Wanted to do that myself for a long time." He headed through the doors.

CHAPTER 60

"Do you have to piss everyone off?" Claire asked as she, T-Tommy, and I walked out into the sunlight. Claire and I had hung around outside the ICU, while T-Tommy endured an ass chewing from Furyk. Said this one wasn't too bad as Furyk's tirades go. Probably didn't want to go over the top in a hospital.

"Not everyone. Just the ones who need it," I said.

Claire shook her head. "You're a child."

"You didn't think so last night."

"Don't change the subject."

"He started it."

"Why didn't you just stick your tongue out and go nah-nah-nah-nah-nah?" Claire said.

"Thought about it."

She stopped walking and turned to me. "You think pissing off a police sergeant is a good idea?"

The morning sun lit up her red hair. She tried to put on an angry face, but it wasn't working. I knew her too well. She actually enjoyed me poking a stick in the eye of jerk weeds like Furyk. Would never admit it, but she did.

"Seemed so at the time," I said.

"Jesus," Claire said. "You're a moron."

I slipped an arm around her. "And you love me."

She slapped my butt. "Yes, I do. But you can be such an ass."

"Important thing is, this is the third time Talbert's popped up on the radar screen," T-Tommy said.

"Once is an event," I said. "Twice a coincidence. Three times a conspiracy. Let's give Talbert a drive-by."

We climbed into T-Tommy's car, the Porsche too small. Claire rode shotgun; I sat in back. We drove past Gate 9 to the Redstone Arsenal/Marshall Space Flight Center complex, through Cummings Research Park, and right past Talbert Biomedical. It was a long two-level building, half of the lower level sunk into the ground. A fifteen-foot-high chain-link fence embraced both the building and its adjacent parking lot. As we passed, I saw a black Lincoln parked near the front of the building.

T-Tommy rolled to a stop. "Well, well, look who's visiting."

We moved on. T-Tommy pulled off the road and rummaged through the center console. He pulled out his digital camera and handed it to me. He made a U-turn and gave Talbert another slow pass while I snapped photos. I saw two uniformed guards just inside the glass-fronted entrance. One slouched behind a desk; the other stood with a cup of coffee. They laughed as if sharing a joke.

Two blocks down, T-Tommy parked along the edge of Farrow Road near its junction with Slaughter Road. I held the camera over the front seat, giving T-Tommy and Claire a view of the small screen, and scrolled through the pictures.

"We need to get inside and look around," T-Tommy said. "Doubt we have enough for a warrant, though."

"Just as well," I said. "If the cops show up, anything incriminating would disappear."

I went through the pictures again. Talbert wasn't wide open, but it wasn't exactly a fortress, either. The chain-link fence was a hundred or so feet from the building. The upper floor windows were about four feet wide by six feet tall, the lowers similar in width but only two feet high. All were the metal-framed, push-out type. A small white sign with red lettering said, Protected by Gorman Security.

"I guess we could break in. Doesn't look very high-tech, and the guards seem disinterested."

"Might work," T-Tommy said.

Claire sighed. "You guys are low-functioning idiots."

"Because we want to dig into Talbert?" I asked.

"No. Because testosterone is a dangerous drug. You would butt a door down even if you had the key in your pocket."

"And you propose what?" I asked.

Claire rolled her eyes and took her cell phone from her purse. "What's Talbert's number?"

T-Tommy gave it to her, and she punched it in, waited a second, and then said, "Mr. Talbert's office, please. . . . This is Claire McBride, *Channel 8 News.* Is Mr. Talbert available? . . . I'd like to arrange a meeting with him. . . . I'm working on a story about minimally invasive surgery. I got Mr. Talbert's name from Dr. Liz Mackey over at Memorial Medical Center. I have a few questions I'd like to ask him if he has the time. I'll only need about fifteen minutes or so." She covered the phone and said to us, "She's checking." Then into the phone she said, "That would be great. I'll be there at three. Thanks." She closed the phone. "Now, that wasn't so hard, was it?"

She can be such a smart-ass sometimes.

CHAPTER 61

THE TWO GUARDS WE HAD SEEN BEFORE GREETED CLAIRE AND I when we pushed through the front door of Talbert Biomedical. Since I'd seen Austin's car here earlier, letting Claire go in alone was not open to discussion. She called me a ninny but gave in. I think she liked the fact that I was concerned. The cover? I was helping her with her story on minimally invasive surgery.

The guards were midforties, pizza and donuts lapping over their belts. The rounder of the two escorted us along a hallway, one wall windowed, security cameras near the ceiling at the far end. Halfway down, we entered Talbert's office.

Harmon Talbert, fiftyish, maybe five ten, one sixty or so, blue suit and red tie over a white shirt. Gray tinted his light brown hair at the temples, and his eyes were an intelligent blue.

We introduced ourselves and shook hands across his desk. We

sat in two straight-backed chairs facing him. His gaze floated over Claire. Pervert.

Elbows on his desk, fingers tented, he said, "Ms. McBride, I'm a big fan. Watch your segments on Channel 8 religiously."

"Thank you."

Talbert smiled. His teeth were perfect. His gaze kept dropping to Claire's chest. I didn't like him. "I understand you're working on a medical story and feel I might be able to help you."

"That's correct. Mr. Walker is assisting me with the story."

He looked at me. "I've seen you on TV and read a couple of your books. Very good. Even recommended them to my friends."

"Thanks." Maybe he wasn't a pervert after all.

"Dark stuff. Serial killers. Psychopaths."

I shrugged. My books were dark and definitely dealt with dark people.

"I particularly liked the new one," he said. "The one on how serial killers are made."

He meant *Multiple Murderers: Nature or Nurture?* One of my best if I said so myself. "I like it, too."

His gaze bounced down toward Claire's legs and back up. Pervert again. "You learned about us from Dr. Mackey over at Memorial?"

"That's right. When I interviewed her, she mentioned that your company makes many of the instruments they use over there. I thought seeing how they're made might add an unusual twist to my story."

Talbert nodded. "Is this for *Channel 8 News*?"

"That's right."

"I thought you'd have a cameraman or something. You know, get some footage for TV."

"This is a preliminary interview. Just to get a little background. That way we can streamline the process. Take up less of your time when we come back with a full crew."

"What's the slant you'll be taking on this?"

"This story concerns the post-operative, healing-phase psychological problems of people undergoing surgical procedures of all types," Claire said. "I want to compare the reactions of people subjected to traditional surgery with the reactions of those who have procedures done by the minimally invasive technique."

Where did that come from? She was good. Better than good.

"Fascinating." He stood. "Why don't we head over to the research area? My partner, Dr. Kincaid, is there. He can probably answer your questions better than I." He smiled warmly. "I'm the manufacturing side. He's the medical guy."

We exited the office and walked farther down the hallway until we came to a bank of windows that looked into a well-lit room where twenty or so people stood around a long metallic table. They were clad in head-to-toe white suits equipped with hoods, clear faceplates, gloves, the whole deal. They appeared to be sealing instruments into sterile packages.

Talbert stopped and gestured toward the window. "This is where we prep our products for shipment."

"Looks clean," Claire said.

"Completely sterile. The air is filtered, and there are laminar flow blowers near the door. Helps keep the bugs at bay." He laughed softly.

"Do you make the instruments here or just finish them?" Claire asked.

"After we perfect the design, they're made in Pennsylvania. Here we polish them, do our quality control, sterilize, package, and ship them."

"This building seems even bigger than it appears from the outside," she said. "I'm turned around. Are we on the first or the second floor?"

"Second. All our offices, design, and research areas are on this level."

"What's on the lower level?"

His gaze dropped to the floor. "Mostly storage. We also do the final crating and prep for shipping down there."

We moved farther to another bank of windows that also looked into a rectangular room. A tall man in surgical scrubs, mask, and cap stood over a cadaver that lay on a waist-high table. He appeared to manipulate a metal rod, twisting and angling it into the corpse's chest. A smaller man stood next to him and appeared to be assisting with the procedure.

Talbert rapped a knuckle on the window.

The tall man looked up, nodded, and then continued his manipulations. After a minute, he stepped back, examined his work, and said something to the assistant. He came around the table, tugged off his surgical gloves, cap, and mask, tossed them into a trash bin, and pushed through the door into the hallway.

"This is Dr. Robert Kincaid," Talbert said. "Bob, this is Claire McBride and Dub Walker."

"I understand you're doing a story on us," Kincaid said as we shook hands.

"That's right," Claire said.

Talbert excused himself, saying he had a couple of phone calls to make and would catch up with us shortly.

Kincaid faced me. "Harmon and I were talking about you earlier. We're both fans of your books. I find all that forensic and psychology stuff fascinating."

"Thanks."

"You and my assistant, Aden Slade" —he motioned in the direction of the younger man still working over the cadaver—"have something in common. Like you, he attended medical school but had to drop out due to a family crisis."

I had been three months from finishing when my sister was abducted. Jill was never seen again. I never returned to med school. I didn't like talking about it, so I didn't.

Claire jumped in and repeated the explanation of her story for Kincaid. She concluded with, "Besides the more rapid healing and less pain involved with the buttonhole surgery, there seems to be less depression, a more rapid return of self-confidence, and a stronger sense of well-being in those patients undergoing this less traumatic type of procedure."

Did I mention she was good at this?

"That's true," Kincaid said. "Those kinds of things plus fewer infections and shorter hospital stays are the reasons this approach has gained so much popularity."

Claire pointed at the window. "What's all this?"

"Aden and I are working on an improved chest cannula. It has a slightly different curve and is more easily manipulated. Better for reaching some lung lesions as well as the back of the heart during bypass procedures."

"You use cadavers for that?" Claire asked.

"Sure. We use a few dozen a year. It's the only way to make sure any new equipment does what we intend."

"I have a silly question," she said.

"Yes?"

"I've thought I might donate my body to science one day. Would I end up here?"

Kincaid laughed. "You might. We buy our cadavers from a company that supplies many medical schools and medical-related businesses."

"I heard they use them for crash test dummies, too."

Kincaid laughed again. Good. He was dropping his guard. "Yes, they do. Sounds awful, I know, but it saves lives."

"Can just anyone buy a corpse?" Claire asked. "I wouldn't want some perv to buy my body."

Kincaid flashed his pearly whites. Quite the charmer. "No. It's a tightly regulated industry. The procurement and disposal of cadavers are closely watched."

"So, you don't just toss them out with the trash when you're done?"

"No. As I'm sure Mr. Walker knows, they're treated as infectious waste. They have to be sealed in biohazard bags and then shipped to companies that dispose of them properly."

Claire glanced at the cadaver on the table. "This is all so cool. Maybe I'll donate my bod after all."

"I'm glad you like our facility." His gaze traveled down her body and back up to her face. "And we would welcome your body."

I wanted to shoot him.

"As soon as I'm done with it, it's yours."

"As young and healthy as you appear, it'll be a long wait. But it's the thought that counts."

"Does this mean I need a tattoo? You know, on the bottom of my foot or somewhere. One that says, Property of Talbert Biomedical."

Talbert laughed and clapped his hands together. "You are delightful. I'm so glad you came by. We need a little more humor around here." He looked at her cleavage.

Back off, slimeball.

Aden Slade came out of the room and walked toward us. Now, with his mask and cap removed, I could see a thin, angular face, framed by white-blond hair. His skin was pale as if he rarely ventured outdoors and never when the sun was up. Though he cast his gaze downward, I saw that his eyes were an almost translucent blue.

Kincaid introduced us. Slade was maybe five nine, one forty tops, and seemed nervous, never looking either of us in the eye. Maybe he was simply shy. Maybe he was uncomfortable around women. Maybe he was checking out Claire's cleavage. I wanted to shoot him, too.

"Dr. Kincaid was telling us about all the wonderful work you're doing here," I said. "Very impressive."

"Thanks." His voice was soft, almost a whisper.

"How long've you been here?"

He started to answer, but Kincaid stepped in. "As I said, Aden was in medical school but had to drop out. We were lucky enough to hire him. Sent him through surgical assistant training, and he's been part of the team for . . . how long now? Nearly six years?"

"That's right," Slade said.

Kincaid continued. "Aden is very gifted. Good hands, sharp mind. He would have made a fine surgeon had he been able to complete his medical training."

Slade offered Claire a quick nod and maybe a faint smile. I couldn't be sure.

"You ever try out your instruments on living subjects?" I asked Kincaid.

"No. We're not equipped for that."

"Then how can you be sure they'll work the same way in the operating room as they do here?"

"We have arrangements with several teaching hospitals—UAB, Mayo, Brigham, Duke, a few others. Once we're sure we have the instrument right, they try it out in their ORs. They then give us feedback, and we make modifications and back and forth until it's right."

"Sounds risky," Claire said. "To the patient."

"Not really," Kincaid said. "We have each instrument finely

tuned before we let the surgeons have it. The changes that follow are always minor. We don't begin manufacturing any instrument until it's perfect. And then only if the surgeons say it really makes their work easier. They're the final judges. If they don't like it, they won't buy it."

Claire smiled. "I've heard that surgeons can be a bit finicky."

Kincaid laughed. "Yes, we are."

Claire asked several more questions. How did Talbert Biomedical get started? What led them into the buttonhole surgery arena? How many innovative instruments had they brought to market? What projects were on the drawing board?

To that final question Kincaid responded, "We have several interesting things on the horizon. I can't talk about most of them." He smiled. "Wouldn't want to tip off the competition. One area is improved instruments for this buttonhole surgery. We see a strong future there."

"On that note," I said, "Dr. Mackey mentioned that many of the instruments used in these types of procedures are also used in robotic surgery. Are you involved in any of that?"

"No. We haven't entered that arena." He glanced at Slade. "We've talked about it, though."

"Dr. Mackey says it's a rapidly growing field. She wishes she had one."

Kincaid nodded. "That's why we're looking into it. We might consider developing some instruments for these robotic-type devices."

"Not the robot itself?" Claire asked.

"That's a huge and expensive undertaking. Not in our area of expertise. Not yet, anyway." Kincaid turned his palms up. "Who knows what the future might hold."

We thanked Kincaid and made our exit. Back in the car, I called T-Tommy. He had let us go in first, so Talbert and Kincaid would be relaxed and more open, but then he wanted to chat with them. Officially. Ask them directly if any of their instruments might be missing. How they accounted for them. Could an employee sneak them out? Mainly, he wanted to pressure them. Let them know they were on the HPD radar. Fear made people do stupid things. Let's hope.

CHAPTER 62

THE SUN FLATTENED ALONG THE WESTERN HORIZON AND PAINTED the bellies of the clouds that clabbered above it. I sat at the patio table, going over my notes again and shooing away Kramden and Norton. Attracted by the paper clip that held the pages together, they kept pecking and yapping. Relentless little bastards. I gave up. Kramden snatched the clip, and off they went.

Buddy Guy wailed "Feels Like Rain" from the outdoor speakers.

Claire worked on a glass of wine, her laptop, and her cell phone. She was digging into Talbert, Kincaid, and Aden Slade.

My notes were now officially boring. I had read them a dozen times, hoping something new, something I had overlooked, might jump out. Nothing did. I put them aside, picked up this morning's *Huntsville Times*, and reread the above-the-fold story on the bodies. Brief and mostly accurate, the piece contained some quotes from

Furyk. There was a photo of an excavation team working in Maple Hill. The byline was Blaine Markland, the city editor.

T-Tommy showed up. He had been meeting with the task force and with Drummond and Cooksey. He poured himself a Blanton's, refilled my now empty glass, and sat at the table.

"Any news on Alejandro?" I asked.

"I talked with Dr. Sammons maybe an hour ago. Still in a coma. Still on the vent. Said it didn't look good."

"We need him," I said. "He's the key to all this."

"I did get the prelim tox report on the two girls," T-Tommy said.

"And?" I asked.

"Both had traces of Valium, morphine, and fentanyl."

"Fentanyl?" I said.

T-Tommy nodded.

"Isn't that the stuff the Russians used on those Chechen freaks that took a theater?" Claire asked. "Bunch of the hostages died, didn't they?"

"That's right," T-Tommy said.

"Fentanyl's big-time," I said. "Take your ass right down. A spray in the face, a prick of the skin, and good night. Too much, you stop breathing, and . . . well, roll the credits. Story's done."

"Is that why Noel and Crystal died?" Claire asked.

"Cooksey thinks so," T-Tommy said. "The levels of fentanyl and morphine in each of them were high. There was no trauma or obvious bleeding, no other reasonable cause of death. He said as it stood right now it looked like asphyxia from an excess of those narcotics."

"What about the others?"

"Drummond sent off blood and urine on Eddie. Should know something in a day or two. The buried ones will take a bit longer since they're so decayed. A couple of weeks, maybe more. He said the skeletal ones we'll probably never know."

"Any of them IDed yet?" I asked.

"One couple. Disappeared two months ago while on a date. Reported missing the next day. Car found over at Madison Square Mall. Drummond's called in a forensic anthropologist to help ID the skeletal remains. That could take months."

"Where do you get something like fentanyl?" Claire asked.

"Pharmaceutical supply house," I said. "Hospitals. Pharmacies."

"We're contacting all the suppliers now," T-Tommy said. "See who buys it and how much. Could get lucky."

"Would Talbert have any of that on hand?" Claire asked. "I mean, if we're thinking there's some connection between Talbert and the killer, could he have gotten it there?"

"According to Talbert and Kincaid, they don't do surgery there," I said. "No reason for them to have it."

"But they could buy it if they wanted to?" Claire asked.

"Sure," I said. I looked at T-Tommy. "How'd your chat with Talbert and Kincaid go?"

"Looks like a legit organization. On the surface, anyway."

"What about that Slade dude?" Claire asked. "Get a chance to talk with him?"

T-Tommy took a sip of his bourbon. "Briefly. I agree with you. He's more than a little creepy."

Claire tapped the keyboard on her laptop. "Here's what I have on him so far. Aden Slade. Born November 12, 1986, in Baltimore. His father was Dr. Wilbert S. Slade. Taught at Johns Hopkins School of Medicine. Aden Slade got a degree in biology from Hopkins, bunch of academic honors, and then did a year and a half of med school. Also at Hopkins. Everything looked good. Then Daddy committed suicide."

"How?" I asked.

"From the newspaper stuff I could track down, it looks like he ate a bullet. Aden found the body."

"That's a tough one," T-Tommy said.

"It gets worse. His mother got the big C. He dropped out of med school to care for her. She died a year later, and Slade moved to Chicago. Worked for a surgical equipment company for a while and was then hired by Talbert. Apparently moved here when Talbert relocated."

"Could all this make Slade a deranged killer?" T-Tommy asked.

"Possible," I said. "Serials come from everywhere. The old paradigm that they gestate in abusive homes just doesn't work anymore. Not since Dahmer, anyway. His childhood wasn't that far out of line. Probably better than Slade's."

"Didn't Dahmer hack up some neighborhood pets?" T-Tommy asked.

I nodded. "Probably wired all wrong from birth. His family didn't do him in."

"Could Slade be the killer?" Claire asked. "Couldn't he be wired wrong?"

John Lee Hooker and Bonnie Raitt poured out "I'm in the Mood" from the stereo.

I shrugged. "What do we know so far? Someone is doing surgery on people, killing them, and dumping the bodies. This someone is not an off-the-shelf killer. He's skilled. He uses equipment that must be obtained from Talbert or some company like Talbert. Alejandro helped dump the bodies and had a phone number for Talbert's security guy."

"You're making a pretty good case for Slade being our boy," T-Tommy said.

"Maybe."

"If that's the case, why'd he kill Eddie and cut up Alejandro?" Claire asked.

I took a sip of bourbon, relishing the slow burn. "Maybe they threatened him in some way. Maybe they wanted more money. Maybe they found Jesus and wanted to repent. Could be anything."

"Money'd be my bet," T-Tommy said. "It's always money with dudes like Eddie and Alejandro."

"That's true. Slade could be crazy, but Eddie and Alejandro would want money." Claire turned to T-Tommy. "What does Slade make at Talbert?"

"I put someone on that. Let me see what he found." Tommy

pulled his cell from his pocket, punched a number, and talked for several minutes. Actually, he mostly listened, making notes in his notebook. He hung up.

"Salary is about $75K," T-Tommy said. "Plus bennies. Health insurance. Profit sharing. No large checks or cash removals from his bank account. Looks like he has about $110K in savings. Frugal boy."

"Means he could afford to pay Eddie and Alejandro," Claire said.

"What was it Alejandro got paid?" I asked. "The cash?"

"Thirty-one thousand," T-Tommy said.

"Where would Slade get that? That's a third of what he has banked. And that's just Alejandro. He'd have to pay Eddie, too."

"Unless Alejandro paid him from his cut," Claire said.

"Didn't see that in Alejandro's records," T-Tommy said. "Possible, though."

I drained my bourbon and refilled it, passing the bottle to T-Tommy. "Let me throw out something new." They looked at me. "What if this is some medical experiment?"

"What do you mean?" T-Tommy asked.

"To me, the odd piece of evidence, the one that needs explaining, is that Alejandro turned up very near Talbert. Talbert designs surgical tools. Experiments with them in the process."

"On cadavers," Claire said.

"As far as we know. There're things about Talbert we don't know."

T-Tommy gave a slow nod as if he was considering what I was saying.

"These surgeries were technically perfect. We heard that from both Liz and Cooksey. They're not the wild mutilations of some psycho. Why couldn't they be part of some medical experiment?"

"You think so?" T-Tommy asked.

"All I'm saying is that serials who perform ritualistic mutilations tend to have some well-orchestrated fantasy. Their mutilations reflect that. They damage faces and genitals. Something very personal. Or they pose victims in a certain fashion. Whatever stirs their chili. I guess our guy could have some doctor fantasy. Could think he's Herr Frankenstein or something." I took a sip of bourbon. "But what if the victims are the flotsam and jetsam of some medical experiment?"

T-Tommy nodded, obviously warming to the idea.

"Since Alejandro was found nearby, Talbert becomes the logical choice for where the surgeries took place."

T-Tommy swirled the bourbon in his glass. "They've got surgeons, like Kincaid, and assistants, like Slade, and a big ass building that could house ORs and ICUs and just about anything."

"Whoa," Claire said, holding up a hand, palm out. "You really believe that Harmon Talbert and Dr. Robert Kincaid are serial killers? That makes no sense."

It doesn't, I thought. "But if this is all part of some experiment, they could be behind it."

"They manufacture surgical instruments. You saw the plant. What do these things sell for? A couple of hundred bucks a pop? Why do all this to make a few tools?"

"Maybe there's more to it than we know," I said. "We haven't really dug into Talbert yet."

"Or spoken privately with Slade," T-Tommy said. "Even if he's not directly involved, I'd suspect that if something's going down at Talbert, he'd know. He looks like a weak link to me. Could fold under pressure."

CHAPTER 63

"IF HE TALKS, WE'RE DEAD."

Dr. Robert Kincaid sat behind his desk, phone to his ear, Rocco on the other end. This conversation would be better face-to-face, but going there was out of the question. Not that filthy, disgusting place. Having Rocco come here? Not a chance. The man was a living, breathing biohazard as far as Kincaid was concerned.

The past forty-eight hours had worn him out. The late night surgeries on Alejandro and Carmelita, Alejandro's killing of Phil Dunlap and escape, the cold-blooded killing of Darlene Montag by that Austin animal, and now Alejandro turning up alive in the hospital. His thinking wasn't clear, and if he was honest with himself, he was as scared as he had ever been.

How many deaths were on his hands now? He couldn't remember. Over twenty. Though technically Carmelita, Darlene, and Phil Dunlap didn't die by his hand. Of course, a jury wouldn't see it that way. If Alejandro died—*please let him die*—add one more.

"He'll never say a word," Rocco said.

"You know Dr. Paul Sammons is pretty good at his craft. He's saved sicker people."

"Not this one."

"How can you be sure?"

"I'm sure."

Kincaid sighed. "So you're a doctor now?"

"No. But I'm pretty good at my craft, too."

"What does that mean?"

How the hell did Kincaid get into this? With this scum? The project was righteous. He never doubted that. His motives were pure. Science above all else. Didn't millions die throughout history as doctors tried to grasp the science behind life and death? The first heart transplant lived a scant eighteen days. Early anesthesia did countless people in. Doctors used to bleed people to death, for Christ's sake. Progress always involved casualties.

Was it science that pushed him? Or greed? He honestly didn't know.

"It means you don't have to worry about it," Rocco said. "It means that last night's mess is cleaned up and this one loose end will be, too."

"A goddamn cop was here."

"What exactly did he ask you?"

"Wanted to know about our instruments. If we had any thefts

or missing tools."

"You don't. So no problem. Right?"

Kincaid shifted the phone to his other ear. "What if he comes back? What if he keeps digging?"

"There's nothing for him to find."

"Except Alejandro."

"That's covered. And soon we'll hand the police the killer. They'll be happy, you'll be happy, and life will go on."

Kincaid pinched the bridge of his nose between his thumb and forefinger, trying to dissipate the gathering headache. "Shit."

"Don't get wobbly on me here. It's all handled. Just like we discussed."

That was true. When this entire project began, they had planned for shutting it down. For covering their tracks. Of course, this wasn't how it was supposed to go. Alejandro, who could blow this whole thing up, lying in the hospital. The police sniffing at his door.

"Okay," Kincaid said. He rubbed his neck. "At least all the news isn't bad. Looks like Channel 8 is going to do a story on us. A little good PR can't hurt."

"What do you mean?"

"Claire McBride from Channel 8 interviewed Harmon and me this afternoon. Said they would come by later this week and do some filming—"

"You idiot." Rocco cut him off. "She's not doing a story. She's digging for information."

"No. She's the top reporter over at Channel 8."

"She's Dub Walker's ex-wife."

"He was with her."

"Jesus Christ. You know who his buddy is?"

"Who?"

"Tommy Tortelli. The cop who paid you a visit."

"Are you sure?"

"What planet do you fucking live on?"

Kincaid's mind swirled. Could this be true?

Rocco continued. "Walker and Tortelli aren't stupid. Neither is McBride. They're trying to figure out where the instruments came from. The ones used on the girls and on Alejandro."

"Jesus." Kincaid felt acid rise in his stomach.

"Alejandro turned up just down the road from you. Hard to waltz around that. That's why you've got to shut things down."

"We've taken care of it."

"Good. When Alejandro's gone, we should be clean."

"What do I do about Claire McBride and Dub Walker?"

"I'll take care of it."

"What does that mean?"

"It means I'll take care of it."

CHAPTER 64

Earlier we had swung by Sammy's for dinner. Claire and I had catfish, coleslaw, and hush puppies; T-Tommy had ribs and brisket and pecan pie with ice cream. We now sat in T-Tommy's car along Pratt Avenue half a block from Slade's house. Pratt was a divided street, its central esplanade lined with trees, their spring growth recently under way. The houses were older, most well over fifty years, but well kept. The street was quiet with only an occasional car rolling by. Most of the houses were buttoned down for the night. TVs glowed through a few windows, but no one roamed around outside.

Slade's place was white clapboard, single story. A slope-roofed, brick-corralled porch extended across the front, and two large windows flanked the front door. The curtains were open, and I saw no lights inside. T-Tommy had called his house and gotten no answer. Slade could be in there, not answering his phone, sitting in the dark.

Maybe his translucent blue eyes could capture light where there was none. Maybe he was watching us.

"Let's take a closer look," I said.

"I'll stay here," Claire said. "B and E isn't my thing."

"I guess you forgot about snooping around Dr. Hublein's office." She and I had broken in during the investigation of the Brian Kurtz case.

She stuck her tongue out at me.

T-Tommy and I climbed out and walked right up to Slade's door. Acting normal. I rang the doorbell. If he opened the door, I had no idea what I'd say. Probably should have thought that through. Moot point. He didn't answer my knock.

We snooped around the exterior, peered through a couple of uncovered windows, but found nothing unusual. I lost track of T-Tommy for a moment but found him working on the back door. He had it open in a minute, and we slipped inside.

We moved quickly from room to room, taking inventory. Living room, dining room, and kitchen were neat and orderly. Slade's bedroom had a made bed, nightstand, dresser, and a closet filled with clothes. Everything in the dresser drawers was also orderly—socks rolled, underwear stacked, T-shirts folded. The boy was definitely OCD.

The personality of a good surgeon.

Or a good killer.

Another bedroom had a desk and a computer, while the third was mostly empty, only a few boxes of books in one corner.

"Not much here," T-Tommy said.

We eased out the back door, locking it.

"If Slade's our guy, he ain't doing the work in there," I said.

"Maybe the garage?"

A double garage sat behind the house at the end of a cracked concrete drive. Its side door had a large window. The interior was dark. T-Tommy worked the lock open and flipped on his Mini Maglite, its beam cutting through the darkness. No car. No pile of boxes and trash like most garages. Everything clean and neat. Slade was consistent. Along the far wall, rows of tools hung on a large Peg-Board, and others lay in an orderly arrangement on a wooden workbench. A long metal table occupied the center of the garage. As T-Tommy swept the beam across the table, I saw at least two dozen shiny objects scattered on top. On closer inspection they became surgical tools of various types.

"Bingo," I said. I picked up a two-foot-long, hollow, curved metallic tube. It looked exactly like the ones Kincaid and Slade had been using on the cadaver. "He's got the tools."

T-Tommy handed me his flashlight, took out his digital camera, and began snapping pictures of the table, the tools, the entire garage. The flash seemed harsh.

I searched through the cabinets, drawers, even inside a large plastic drum. Empty. I half-expected a body or two. I directed the beam across the floor, beneath the workbench, along the walls, around the drain beneath the metal table, looking for any signs of blood. I found nothing.

"This place is immaculate," I said.

"Too clean," T-Tommy said. "Looks like it was scrubbed down."

I heard a car turn into the drive and saw light sweep across the gap beneath the garage door, go out, and then I heard the engine die. I killed the Maglite. A car door opened and closed. Footsteps faded toward the house.

"Let's get out of here," I said.

T-Tommy didn't argue. We slipped out the door and moved to the rear of the garage. None too soon.

I heard the back door open and then Slade's footsteps approach. The garage's side door lock clicked open, and the door closed. Interior fluorescent lights stuttered on. I could hear Slade moving around inside and music. Jazz.

I eased around the corner, approached the door, and peered through the corner of the window. Slade sat on a stool at the end of the table, his profile to me. He took a bite of a Big Mac, set it aside on its wrapper, and washed it down with a gulp of Heineken. He picked up and examined one of the instruments, a tubular-looking thing. Then with a piece of what appeared to be very fine steel wool he went to work on one end of the tube. He seemed relaxed, eating, sipping beer, working on the tool, his head bobbing in time with Wynton Marsalis' "Hesitation."

CHAPTER 65

"ZEKE?"

Zeke Reed turned to see Charge Nurse Bobbie Hawkins coming toward him. One of the RN types. One of the ones that climbed the ladder, browned her nose, made it all the way to ICU charge nurse. BFD.

"Run this down to the lab and then clean four. Dr. Sammons just put a new central line in Mr. Diaz and left a mess in there." She motioned toward the cubicle where a bedside tray was stacked with used instruments, gauze, drapes, and other trash. "You'll need a biohazard bag for most of that stuff."

Like he hadn't done this a million times.

She handed him two tubes of blood, turned, and walked away. No please, no thank you, no nothing. *Bitch.*

Taking the stairs, Zeke dropped down two floors to the lab, delivered the blood tubes, and then ducked into the men's room. The last of three stalls. He punctured the rubber stopper on the bottle of potassium chloride and filled the syringe. He capped the needle and settled the syringe into the pocket of his short white coat.

Back in the ICU, coast clear, he wiped his prints from the bottle and returned it to the drug cart behind the nurses' station. Almost home free now.

He went to work on Diaz's room. He filled the biohazard bag with the disposable trash, put the instruments into a metal basin for transport to Central Supply for re-sterilization, and began to mop the floor. Diaz's ventilator rhythmically whooshed through its cycles.

Zeke mopped slowly, waiting for the right moment. When Nurse Hawkins left the nurses' station and headed for cubicle one, he quickly removed the syringe, popped off the needle cover, and slid the needle into the rubber-capped injection port of Diaz's IV line. Had to move fast now. One more glance over his shoulder and he plunged the potassium into the line, yanked the needle free, capped it, returned it to his pocket. He went back to swiping the mop across the floor.

Ten seconds. That was all it took. The EKG monitor went flat. The alarm sounded. Three nurses rushed into the cubicle. Charge Nurse Hawkins told him to leave. Gladly. He backed out of the cubicle as another nurse rolled the crash cart through the door. He moved behind the nurses' station as "Code Blue ICU, Code Blue ICU" blared from the ceiling speakers. Nurse Hawkins began barking orders.

Why did they always put the women in charge and never the men? Of course only two male nurses worked here, and they were both losers. Neither was an RN. Maybe one of those other degrees. LVN, LPN, he couldn't keep them straight.

Zeke didn't have any letters on his name tag. Didn't need them. He was smarter than all of them. He'd already done in six people, and none of them had a clue. Fact is, he'd gotten one of them fired. Well, moved out of the ICU, anyway. She should've paid more attention. Shouldn't have left a dangerous drug like morphine lying around. Should've noticed the vent alarm was turned off. Then the old man would be alive and she would still be here in the ICU in the limelight, not shuffling bedpans up on 6A.

They were all that way. This . . . this ICU . . . the goal of their miserable little lives.

He had bigger things in mind. Ezekiel James Reed. Angel of Death. Front-page stuff. The others had been. Charles Cullen, thirty or so in New Jersey. Donald Harvey, eighty in Kentucky and Ohio. Richard Angelo, convicted of four, but he must have done more out on Long Island. Efren Saldivar in California. Zeke couldn't recall his final body count. He had newspaper articles on them and others. Many others. Tucked away in the bottom drawer where he kept such secrets.

One day, he'd be bigger than them all. The really fun part? He'd actually been paid to do a couple of them. Counting this guy. The other he'd made only five hundred bucks. That was a year ago. This one? Two thousand. Inflation was a good thing.

That old man, the five-hundred-dollar one, was his first. Zeke had never seriously thought about killing any of the patients. Maybe once or twice he had wanted to but nothing he ever did anything about. Then he met that guy—what was his name?—at that strip club. Guy seemed interested in the fact that he worked at a hospital. Said he might have a job for him someday. Said it would pay well. About a year ago the guy found him. Called him at home. Never said how he got the number. Offered the five hundred if he'd off the old man. Piece of cake. A bit of potassium chloride in the IV and *adios*.

He'd now used potassium three times, morphine once, and Pavulon twice. Saldivar liked Pavulon. Zeke preferred potassium, though. Clean, effective, and fast. They said it was a bitch to trace, too.

The feeling he got from the old man was . . . He couldn't think of a word for it. *Thrilling* didn't seem strong enough, but it was the best he could come up with. The ones that followed were done to recapture that thrill. A thrill he never knew lived inside him. A thrill that once exposed needed feeding.

Besides, Zeke could use the two grand. That was more than he made in a month. Maybe he could get that new car, after all. The red Mustang convertible. It had been sitting on the lot for a month, but the price was too high. By a grand and a half. With the cash he'd make for this, he could cover the difference and still fold five hundred into his pocket. Life was good.

CHAPTER 66

TUESDAY 7:11 A.M.

"Damn it. That's just great." I sat on the side of the bed, phone to my ear, while T-Tommy told me that Alejandro Diaz had checked out during the night. "There goes our best lead."

"Maybe our only lead," he said.

I ran my fingers through my hair. "Let's hope Slade pans out."

"See you guys in about forty-five."

I hung up the phone and sat there, listening to the hiss of the shower as Claire got ready for her day.

After our visit to Slade's house last night, T-Tommy, Claire, and I had sat down to plan the next step. Another talk with Aden Slade was the consensus. He seemed the one most likely to slip up or crack under pressure. Whether he was the cutter or not, whether he was involved in all this or not, if it was connected to Talbert, he'd likely know something. If the surgeries had actually occurred there, he'd have to be aware of them.

We had kicked around ideas on how to approach him. The one thing that was easily decided was that it should take place at his home, not at Talbert. Just in case. Would Slade react violently? Would he break down and confess? Maybe implicate others at Talbert? Whatever happened it would be best if he was alone, isolated.

A search warrant came up but was rejected. That'd put Slade on the defensive. Besides, a warrant based only on a few surgical instruments lying on a worktable just wasn't going to happen. No judge was that friendly. Slade worked with these gadgets. Had every reason to have them around. Then there was the fact that this information resulted from trespassing. I could almost hear the judge laughing as he issued a warrant for our arrest.

Claire suggested that she talk with him again. Make up some story about needing more information for her newscast. Slade had obviously been attracted to her and might talk more freely, even brag. Maybe try to impress her. Never underestimate the power of sex.

Not a chance. No way would I let her enter Slade's house alone. Even with T-Tommy and me nearby.

It was finally decided that T-Tommy would visit him. Alone. No uniforms. No patrol cars. Just a friendly chat. A few routine questions. Put a little more pressure on him. T-Tommy decided not to run this by Furyk or anyone else. He wasn't in the mood to listen to Furyk's bullshit or defend the decision. Better to ask for forgiveness than permission.

Besides, if Furyk knew, Rocco would know. That would complicate things big-time.

Claire and I would be the cavalry. Nearby in case things didn't go as planned.

CHAPTER 67

T-TOMMY PEERED THROUGH THE OPEN GARAGE DOOR.

Slade sat on a stool at the long metal table T-Tommy had seen last night, back to the door. A white T-shirt hung loosely on his narrow shoulders as he hunched over something he was working on. A pile of wood shavings, half a dozen hollow metal tubes, and several clusters of steel wool lay on the table in front of him.

T-Tommy rapped a knuckle on the doorframe.

Slade spun in his direction. In his left hand he held a slender, curved piece of wood and in the other a finely honed knife.

"Sorry to bother you this early," T-Tommy said. He flipped open his badge and extended it to Slade. "I'm Investigator Tortelli. HPD. We met yesterday."

Slade seemed to stare at T-Tommy's chest as if raising his gaze higher was physically impossible. "I remember. What can I do for you?"

"Just a couple of follow-up questions, if you don't mind."

Slade hesitated.

"Only take a few minutes."

"Sure." Slade stood. "You want some coffee? Just made a fresh pot." He motioned to a coffeemaker that sat on a corner table.

It did smell good. "Sure. Thanks."

Slade poured some coffee into a big-handled brown mug. "Cream? Sugar?"

"Black is fine."

He handed the mug to T-Tommy and then returned to his stool.

T-Tommy circled the table until he faced Slade. He took a sip, then another. It tasted even better than it smelled. "This is excellent."

Slade smiled. Sort of. More a quick widening of his lips, barely visible. "I order the beans from a company in Miami. Grind them myself."

"Not much better than a good cup of coffee." T-Tommy nodded toward the piece of wood Slade had been working on. "What're you doing here?"

"A new design. Trying to smooth the edges."

"Not going into Talbert today?"

"Later. Got stuff to do around here."

"You do a lot of your work at home?"

Slade appeared nervous, his gaze darting around, never staying on any one thing, brushing over T-Tommy a couple of times before moving on. "I'm sure you didn't come here at this time of day to chat about my work."

T-Tommy shrugged. "Actually, Mr. Slade, I find what you do very interesting. Never knew much about this kind of stuff until yesterday. Impressive work."

"Thanks." His eyes seemed to brighten a bit.

T-Tommy picked up the piece of wood. "What's this?"

"Working out a new shape for one of our instruments."

"You whittle them out of wood?"

"That's how I work out the design." A quick smile. "Wood's a little easier to work with than steel. Doesn't dull the knives." Another slight smile.

This kid was charming in his own way. No doubt intelligent and creative. T-Tommy couldn't help but like him. Still, if he turned out to be the killer, he might revise that assessment. But here, in his own backyard, talking about his work, he seemed more relaxed. This just might work.

"Once you have it carved, what happens?"

"We send it to a company that uses the carving as a template to make a mold and then stainless steel copies." Slade held up one of the metallic tubes. "Like these. Then I polish off the rough edges, and they're ready for a trial run."

"Clever." T-Tommy spread his hands on the end of the table, leaning a little. "We didn't get a chance to talk much yesterday. What I wanted to ask is, do you know Alejandro Diaz?"

"Never heard of him."

"He's tall, dark hair, Hispanic. Ever seen anyone like that around Talbert?"

"No." He inspected the metal tube. Despite his nervous nature his hands were steady. His fingers lean and delicate. "Why're you looking for him?"

"I know where he is. Just wondered if you knew him."

"Never met him."

You never will. T-Tommy placed his coffee mug on the table. "What about Eddie Elliott? Ever heard of him?"

Slade hesitated as if thinking and then flicked a strand of hair from his eyes. "I don't think so."

"Don't think or don't know?"

"It's a common sounding name. I may have heard it, but if so I don't remember when or where."

"Have you heard of any thefts at Talbert?"

He rolled the tube back and forth on the table with his palm. "No. Other than this stuff, that is." He waved a hand at the instruments on the table.

"You steal those?" T-Tommy asked.

"With permission. Mr. Talbert and Dr. Kincaid are good employers. They let me do much of my design work here."

"How did you hook up with them?" T-Tommy asked.

"I sold surgical instruments. Years ago. When I lived in Chicago. I called on Dr. Kincaid. A few years later, after they had formed the company, they called me. Paid for my education. Gave me a job."

"Now you assist Dr. Kincaid with testing the equipment?"

"More than that. I design most of the tools. Dr. Kincaid is a very gifted surgeon, but he's not an artist. Design requires a certain artistic ability."

"You have that? Artistic ability?"

"I've always seen things a little differently."

T-Tommy leaned more of his weight on the table. "I understand you attended medical school?"

"You've researched me?"

"I'm an investigator. That's what I do."

Slade sighed. "Made it halfway through my sophomore year before Dad died and Mom got cancer. Had to drop out and get a job." He picked up another instrument, a long tubular affair with a pistol grip and trigger on one end and what appeared to be tiny scissors on the other. He squeezed the trigger, and the jaws of the scissors opened and closed.

"Must have been disappointing," T-Tommy said.

"It was. But I like where I am now. Dr. Kincaid gives me a great deal of freedom."

"You just assist him, or can you do all those surgical things, too?"

"Surgical things?" His gaze bounced up to T-Tommy, held him for a second.

T-Tommy laughed. "I don't know what any of that stuff is called. The words are too big."

"After working with Dr. Kincaid for so many years, I could probably do almost everything he does."

"Really?"

"Well, I have to. If I'm going to design new instruments and improve on others, I have to know how they work. What they feel like."

T-Tommy nodded. "Never thought of that. Makes sense."

"But I'm no surgeon. Not trained like Dr. Kincaid. I just copy what I see him do."

"So you're not qualified to operate on the living?"

"Oh no. I couldn't do that. Why do you ask?"

"Dr. Kincaid told me that he thought you would have made an excellent surgeon. Good hands was the way he put it."

"He's kind. But, no, I've never done any kind of surgery." Slade looked at the ceiling, brow furrowed, and then smiled. "Unless you count teasing a piece of glass from my dog's paw when I was eight."

"Did the patient survive?"

"For many years."

Though Slade's shyness and inability to look anyone in the eye was a bit unnerving and he was a touch weird, T-Tommy sensed nothing menacing or dangerous in his demeanor. Sitting right here, right now, anyway. Of course, Bundy and Dahlmer were polite and shy, too.

"How do you come up with new designs? I mean, do you just dream them up out of thin air?"

"Not exactly. The design follows the need. Our customers will make a suggestion. Or a complaint. Maybe they need an instrument of a different shape or size or angle. Whatever makes their surgery easier. I'll take what we have and modify it. Or sometimes I'll have to start from scratch and design an entirely new tool."

"Sounds difficult."

"I have a knack for seeing things spatially. I find it interesting. That's why I don't regret not finishing med school. I like what I do."

"Is this all Talbert Biomedical does?" T-Tommy waved a hand across the table. "Make these types of instruments?"

Slade shook his head. "We make all kinds of stuff. Scalpels, scissors, hemostats, clamps."

"Just instruments? No mechanical devices?"

"Such as?"

"I don't know. Maybe those electrical saw deals. Like they use to take a cast off."

"No. Just stainless steel tools. The ones with few moving parts and no motors."

T-Tommy picked up a hollow tube and examined it. He placed it back on the table. "Does Dr. Kincaid do any surgery on patients anymore?"

"No. He doesn't have a practice or go to any of the hospitals. He's purely research now."

"No actual surgeries are done at Talbert?"

His gaze jumped right, left, to the floor. "We're definitely not equipped for that."

CHAPTER 68

WE LEFT SLADE'S, HEADED DOWN PRATT, THROUGH FIVE POINTS, and swung by Mullins for breakfast. Mullins had been a Huntsville institution for decades. A low brick and metal building with a bright blue and yellow checkerboard sign out front and a noisy crowd inside. Pictures of old Huntsville decorated the faux brick interior walls.

We settled in a corner at one of the Formica-topped tables. Claire had a bagel. I had scrambled eggs and wheat toast. T-Tommy went for the Country Boy Special: three eggs as you like them, T-Tommy going for over easy, four strips of bacon, four link sausages, hash browns, pancakes, and toast.

"He's got the tools and the skills," T-Tommy said. "I'd put Slade at the top of the list."

"He's not alone up there," I said. "He's too shy to con someone into his car. He's small and seems frail. Doubt he could overpower anyone. Definitely not Alejandro or Eddie. Maybe not even the two girls."

We sat quietly for a minute, and then T-Tommy said, "If Alejandro grabbed girls for him, then how did Slade, or whoever the cutter is, take down Alejandro? I'd bet Alejandro was a pretty tough customer. And, as you said, Slade doesn't look like a warrior."

"Fentanyl?" Claire asked. "Like the two girls?"

"Good thought," T-Tommy said. He grabbed his cell and made a call. Lasted about two minutes. He snapped the phone closed. "That was the lab in Birmingham. They were just finalizing their report. Eddie had fentanyl on board, too."

"Well, well," I said. "We have a pattern."

"They'll check Alejandro, too, won't they?" Claire asked.

"Unfortunately, tox testing on Alejandro is worthless," I said. "I'm sure he had a ton of drugs of all types during his surgery and his resuscitation. It would be a pharmaceutical soup."

"What about the other victims?" Claire asked.

"They're testing the ones with enough tissue left. It'll take weeks if not months."

T-Tommy took a gulp of coffee, the cup hidden in his massive hands. "Slade might be the cutter, but he didn't do it at his place."

"Everything points to Talbert," I said. "No other explanation for Alejandro turning up nearby. Which means that Talbert and Kincaid are involved."

"Hell of a conspiracy," T-Tommy said.

"You saw that place," Claire said. "Looks like a tight ship. Don't think any of them could pull this off without the others knowing."

The waitress swung by and refilled our coffee cups. "Anything else?"

We all declined, and she headed off to the kitchen.

I added some cream to my coffee and took a sip. "What I can't get my head around is why? What's the payoff for Kincaid and Talbert?" I glanced at T-Tommy. "As you said before, it can't be for a handful of two-hundred-dollar surgical tools."

"Then what?"

I shrugged. "No clue."

"Only one way to find out," T-Tommy said. "Answer's somewhere inside Talbert."

"Break into Talbert?" Claire asked. "I thought you'd decided that was a bonehead idea."

I looked at T-Tommy.

He smiled.

CHAPTER 69

TUESDAY 12:13 P.M.

"BECAUSE THAT'S WHAT COPS DO," KINCAID SAID. HE SAT AT THE conference table with Harmon Talbert and Aden Slade. "They ask questions. Sniff around. Mostly waste the taxpayers' money."

"Do you think he knows?" Slade asked. "About the project?"

Slade was shaken. Kincaid could see it in his face, his body language, hear it in his voice. He needed to calm him, hold it together for a few more hours, and then it wouldn't matter anymore. He smiled and spoke in his most soothing voice. The one he had used with frightened patients for years. "They're investigating a couple of dozen murders. They think it's the work of a deranged serial killer."

"How do you know that?"

"I have my sources." Again Kincaid smiled. "Relax, Aden. They have nothing." He leaned forward and looked into Slade's eyes. "Nothing."

"Then why did they come here? Come to my house?"

Kincaid folded his hands. "I'll admit it was unfortunate that the bodies were found. But the wounds on them only prove that someone, not us, just someone, had done things to them. We make tools. They were simply looking under every rock."

Slade shook his head. "I don't like this scrutiny."

Talbert stepped in. "We're in the clear. There's no way they can connect those bodies to us."

"That cop knew all about me."

"Cops have access to all kinds of information," Kincaid said. "He could find out about anyone. Me. Harmon. You. Anyone."

"But . . ."

"In fact, when he was here yesterday, he knew everything about us." He waved a hand in Talbert's direction. "About the company. I saw that immediately. The questions he asked? He already knew the answers to most of them. That's how they work."

Slade sighed. "Why didn't he just talk to me when he was here yesterday? Why come to my house?"

Kincaid glanced at Talbert and then turned to Slade. "Probably forgot something. What'd he ask you?"

"If I knew some guy named Alejandro. And some other guy."

"What did you tell him?"

"That I didn't know either one of them."

"Did he seem satisfied with that?"

"I guess." Slade fiddled with the pen in his breast pocket. "Who are these guys? The ones he was looking for?"

"Nobody. They don't exist."

Slade looked at Kincaid, then Talbert. "What does that mean?"

"Just that," Talbert said. "They don't exist."

Slade dropped his gaze but said nothing.

"Anything else?" Kincaid asked.

"Wanted to know if any of our surgical tools were missing. He treated me like I was a suspect or something."

"You are," Talbert said. "We all are."

Slade stared at him. "You seem calm about this."

"There's no need to panic," Talbert said. "Just go about your work, and we'll handle the police."

Slade nodded, got up, and walked to the door. He hesitated as if he had something else to say but pushed through the door and left the room.

"What do you make of that?" Kincaid asked.

"There are very few threads that lead back to us. Actually, there's only one left, and our friend will take care of that."

"Some friend." Kincaid twisted his head one way and then the other. The tightness in his neck didn't retreat. "He's a damn criminal."

"But he can fix all this."

"I hope you're right."

"Trust me," Talbert said. "It's covered. We've shut everything down. Tonight the police will get their deranged killer, and then there's no one left who can hurt us."

"No way this could come back to us?"

"None. Not ever."

Kincaid settled back in his chair, shoulders falling a bit. "How long will we be down?"

Talbert shrugged. "Six months. A year at the most. Until things settle. Then we'll gear up again."

"That's a long time."

"Not really. Besides, didn't you say you needed to work on a few things? Smooth out some of the gears? Change out the laser like we discussed?"

Kincaid nodded.

"Then this downtime will help us." Talbert tugged at the cuff of his shirt. "After tonight, no more loose ends."

"Unless Ms. McBride keeps snooping."

"She won't. Our friend's going to fix that, too."

"How?"

"Don't know. Don't want to know. Just want to get it behind us."

Kincaid moved to the door and turned. "Let's hope."

"Hope's got nothing to do with it. It's not like we dreamed this up. We've planned for it. Knew it might come to this."

Kincaid sighed. "I'll just be glad when it's done."

CHAPTER 70

"YOU'RE VERY BEAUTIFUL," ROSALEE KENNEDY SAID AS SHE BRUSHED A wayward strand of hair from the girl's face.

"Thank you." Katie Fuller blushed and smiled.

The words *young* and *naïve* came to Rosalee's mind.

Rosalee sat on her living room sofa, Katie next to her. Max leaned against the bar, arms crossed over his massive chest. Sin-Dee lounged in a chair, facing them across the coffee table. Rosalee had opened a bottle of wine, Katie quickly accepting, trying to calm her nerves, no doubt.

Timing is everything, Rosalee thought. Yesterday she had been fretting over finding a pair of girls. Then as if God herself had intervened, Sin-Dee called, saying she had a new girl who needed work.

When Rosalee first saw Katie, she had had second thoughts. This girl was special. She had green eyes, the kind that could light up a room, full lips, model-like cheekbones, and rich black hair that framed her face and curled just beneath her jawline. She wore little makeup. Didn't need it. Everything about her—her face, her body, her walk—exuded an athletic purity. Like a high school cheerleader. Just what every man wanted. She could demand the highest fees. Make Rosalee a fortune. Work for years before the toll wore her body out and Rosalee passed her on to Miss Sally or someone else farther down the food chain. Unfortunately, another matter needed attention, and it required two girls. No time to find anyone else.

"I'm a little scared." Katie cupped her wineglass with both hands, took a sip.

"You're going to do just fine." Rosalee patted her leg. "Max will take care of you. Sin-Dee, too."

"I know. She told me she would."

"We all will," Rosalee said.

Earlier, on the phone, Sin-Dee said she had met Katie in some bar off University. Said Katie was nineteen, broke, running from a bad place, living in a piece of shit motel, hoping the city would be her salvation. Maybe scrub away painful memories. Sin-Dee listened to her story, took her in, told her she could get her work, making a ton of money, and called Rosalee.

"So, what do you think?" Rosalee asked. "Want to work for me?"

"I need to do something. I asked for a job at some bars, but they weren't hiring. They said I could fill out an application and they'd call." Katie smiled at Sin-Dee. "Sin-Dee came to the rescue."

Sin-Dee returned a glassy smile. Obviously she had already been in the medicine jar. Kept rubbing her nose and fidgeting with the strap of her purse.

Rosalee placed her wineglass on the coffee table. "You know what kind of work I'm talking about, right?"

Katie nodded. "I'm just not sure I'll know what to do."

"You ever had a boyfriend?"

"Sure. Lots of them."

"Sex?"

"Of course." A nervous smile.

"How many?"

"Seven. If you count the next-door neighbor."

Rosalee raised an eyebrow.

Katie stared into her wineglass. "My mom was screwing him. He thought that made me fair game, too." She looked up, eyes slightly moist, lower lip with a faint tremble. "I put up with it for a month and then split. Hitchhiked here." She took a sip of wine. A drop dribbled down her chin. She wiped it away and smiled at Rosalee.

"Relax." Rosalee added a bit of wine to Katie's glass. "I know what you're worried about. I'll never ask you to do anything you're not comfortable with."

Katie sighed. "I didn't know what to expect."

Rosalee laughed. "Everything will be fine." She squeezed Katie's hand. "In fact, I have a job for you tonight."

"Tonight? I'm not sure I'm ready."

"This is an easy one. A twofer. You'll work with Sin-Dee. Max will drive you and take care of things."

"How will I know what to do?"

"This'll be a good warm-up for you. Young guy. At his home. Not one of the motels. Sin-Dee will be with you the entire time. Show you how it works."

The girl still looked unsure. As if things were moving too fast. Rosalee knew she needed to reel her in. Couldn't afford to have her balk now.

"Pays a thousand," Rosalee said.

"A thousand dollars?"

"I'll throw in an extra five hundred for each of you. My way of welcoming you to the family."

"Fifteen hundred dollars?" Katie said, apparently unable to comprehend the number.

Rosalee nodded. "This is just the beginning. Soon you'll have more money than you can spend, and you'll forget all about home and the shit that went down there."

"That would be nice."

Rosalee tapped her wineglass against Katie's. "To a beautiful future."

Katie's eyes glistened with tears. "Thank you." She looked at Sin-Dee. "Both of you are lifesavers."

CHAPTER 71

"IF YOU WANT TO SEE THIS CRIME SCENE, GET YOUR ASS OVER HERE."

It was T-Tommy. I was sleeping when he called. I did that a lot at six in the morning. I was still mostly sleeping when I answered the phone and first heard T-Tommy apologizing for calling so early. I snapped to full wakefulness when he told me that Aden Slade was dead and that there were three other bodies. That the entire scene was unnerving. His word.

I swung my legs around and sat on the side of the bed. "Where? Slade's house?"

"Yeah. Hurry it up. I haven't called Furyk yet, but I can't hold off on that much longer."

"I'm on the way."

I took a quick shower, slipped on jeans and a black T, grabbed the gray sports coat I found hung over a chair in the kitchen, and was out the door in ten minutes flat. I wound the Porsche down Bank-head Parkway, which plugged right into Pratt Avenue. I pulled to the curb half a block from Slade's place by 6:35. Three prowlers, two un-marked cars, the crime scene truck, and a van from the coroner's office were parked out front. Yellow tape embraced the property, keeping the smattering of neighbors away.

I told one of the uniforms who guarded the perimeter that T-Tommy expected me. He lifted the tape for me to pass beneath. Several other uniforms milled near the garage's open side door. I nodded to them, went inside, and looked around. Two crime scene techs, a coroner's tech, and three bodies that I could see.

T-Tommy was right. The scene was unnerving.

The metal table we had seen a couple of nights earlier now held the nude corpse of a young, raven-haired woman. Several clean slashes marked the flesh of her chest and abdomen. A metal tube projected at an angle from her belly. No blood. Looked as if she had been washed clean.

Along the far wall, the large trash can I had examined the other day now rested on its side. Near its mouth lay the body of another young woman. She had been wrapped in plastic, the sheeting now sliced open. My gaze fell on a third body. Crumpled in a corner. Sidau Yamaguchi knelt beside the corpse. He looked up at me and then stood.

"What you got here?" I asked.

"Slade. Gunshot to the head."

Aden Slade's corpse half-sat against the wall, the left side of his head matted with blood, a nickel-plated S&W .357 lying on the floor next to his open hand. I moved closer. Entrance wound near the left temple, exit wound high on the right side, the wall spattered with blood, bone, and brain tissue. Looked like a distorted slug had wedged into the wall in the middle of the mess.

T-Tommy came in. "That was quick."

"You said hurry."

He led me around the head of the table to where a fourth corpse lay. Another nude female, on her back, head turned away, blonde hair splayed across the floor. I saw several gaping wounds over her chest and abdomen. Again no blood. Ligature bruises circled her neck. I looked back at the girl on the table. Similar neck bruises.

"They were strangled," I said. I was intuitive that way. I carefully stepped around the girl on the floor, now seeing her face. "Jesus. It's Sin-Dee."

"I know," T-Tommy said.

"Somebody want to let me in on it?" Sidau asked.

"Noel and Crystal were the first two bodies found. Sin-Dee lived with them."

"Really?" Sidau asked.

I nodded. "She worked for Rosalee Kennedy. Danced for Rocco Scarcella."

"Everything keeps leading back to Rocco, don't it?" T-Tommy said.

"'Cause he's in this. Up to his ass."

"Good bet he had this done," T-Tommy said.

"That'd be my guess, too." I walked around Sin-Dee's body. "Covering his ass."

"Then there's this." T-Tommy turned to the corpse near the trash can. "She has wounds exactly like those on Noel and Crystal."

I moved closer, detecting the faint odor of decomposition. Not bad, just noticeable. The girl appeared young, Hispanic. She had several abdominal wounds, each closed with the same metallic clips we had seen on Noel and Crystal. I looked back at Sin-Dee and the girl on the table. No clips, just gaping wounds. "Why no clips on these two?"

T-Tommy shrugged. "Maybe he wasn't finished."

"So in the middle of the surgery he just up and decided to kill himself?" I asked.

"Someone wants us to think that." T-Tommy glanced at Sin-Dee. "This ain't right. None of it's right."

Sidau pointed to the corpse on the table and then to Sin-Dee. "The wounds on those two appear to be postmortem. No bleeding in or around the wounds. I'd suspect the cause of death is ligature strangulation. Need to wait for Drummond and Cooksey's autopsies, but that's what it'll be. The wounds are actually quite superficial. I probed them to no more than four centimeters. Only this one" —he motioned to the instrument protruding from the raven-haired girl's belly—"actually entered the abdominal cavity."

"So neither had any organs removed?" I asked. "Anything like that?

Sidau shook his head. "Doesn't look that way."

I looked at T-Tommy. "You find a knife or a scalpel?"

"Nothing."

"Well, Slade didn't do it with his fingernail," I said.

"He didn't do it at all," T-Tommy said. "This is a setup. Saw it from jump street. We're supposed to think he did all this, then shot himself in the left side of his head when he's right-handed."

"You sure?" I asked.

"He whittles right-handed. What do you think?"

"I think I can't remember the last time I saw someone shoot themselves with their nondominant hand."

"Like never," T-Tommy said. "I got a good idea who could do such a shit job of staging a crime scene."

"Austin and Lefty?" I said.

T-Tommy grunted.

I turned back to the girl who had been wrapped in plastic. "This girl's been dead a day or so. Any estimate?"

"Very odd." Sidau indicated Sin-Dee and the girl on the table. "These girls died recently. Based on body temp, lack of significant rigor, and the lividity, I'd guess four to six hours max." He gestured to the girl on the floor in the plastic sheeting. "Here rigor has passed and the lividity is fixed. The body was definitely moved more than eight hours after death. Lividity pattern doesn't match the body position."

"Which was?" I asked.

"Stuffed in that drum."

"There's more, isn't there?" I asked.

Sidau smiled, and his eyebrows bobbed a couple of beats. "Oh yes, there's more."

Sidau was an old movie buff. We had had a long talk about it one night a couple of years ago. He liked the old black and whites. Anything with a cliff-hanger. He liked to make everyone cliff-hang a bit. Like now. Save the best for last.

"What's the punch line?" I asked.

"Her core temp is nearly ten degrees less than the room temp. According to the weather service, the low was fifty-eight at four this morning. Currently in this garage it's sixty-two. She's at fifty-three. Core temps can't fall below ambient temperature."

"You're telling us she's been in cold storage?" I asked.

"Had to be."

"What the hell is going on?" Furyk's voice was unmistakable. He stepped into the doorway, looked at me and T-Tommy. "I should have known." He turned to the uniformed officers who followed him. "Get these two out of here. If they refuse, arrest them."

"Listen—," I began.

"No, hotshot. You listen. This is a crime scene. You have no authority here. I'm in charge."

"Sergeant," T-Tommy said.

"And you," Furyk said. "This is your doing. You're off the case. Now. And suspended."

"But—"

"Get back to the department. Turn in your gun and badge. I'll file the paper later."

"Don't you think you're overreacting a bit here?" I said.

His jaw pulsed. "Where were you when this went down?"

I saw where this was going. I could play the game. "When exactly did this go down?"

Furyk's face reddened. "You better have an alibi. One that's fucking titanium."

"I do. What about you? Where were you?"

I thought he would crack a molar. Maybe rupture an aneurysm. I loved this shit.

He moved close, his voice like air seeping from a punctured tire. "Get the fuck out of here. I won't ask again."

I walked past him to my car. I leaned against it and waited. In a couple of minutes, T-Tommy ducked beneath the tape and walked in my direction.

"Sorry," I said.

"Fuck him." He glanced at the garage. "Something's wrong here. He goes to the gym every morning from six to eight. Every day. No one calls him or bothers him during that time. Regardless of what's going down."

"So, who called him today?" I asked.

"That's what I'd like to know."

CHAPTER 72

T-Tommy left his car at the scene and rode with me. He wanted to swing by the South Precinct and drop off his badge and gun, muttering something about how Furyk could run off and fuck himself. I told him I understood, but maybe a couple of days to cool off might be wise. Give it some thought, anyway. He grumbled but finally agreed.

We rolled toward Sin-Dee's. On the way, I called Claire and told her what was up and that she might want to go over to Slade's place. She said she'd grab a camera crew and head that way. Now she owed me. I liked that.

As expected, no one answered my knock at Sin-Dee's. They were all dead. I noticed Martha Godwyn peeking through her curtain and waved to her. She opened her front door and stepped onto her porch. She wore the same kimono I saw her in last time we were here. A cigarette hung from her lip. No drink. Maybe she waited until noon to start. Maybe she left it inside.

"If it isn't the Hardy Boys," she said. She nodded at Sin-Dee's door. "She ain't there."

"I know."

Martha cocked her head and angled her gaze at me. "So, why're you here?"

No time for BS. "Sin-Dee's been murdered."

She stumbled back. I thought the cigarette might slip from her now slack mouth, but it hung on somehow. Seemed to defy gravity. She scissored it between her fingers, took a quick hit, and pulled it from her lips. "What do you mean?"

"She was killed last night."

"The other girl, too? The new one?"

"Who?" I asked.

"Don't remember her name. Kay or Katie. Maybe Kathy. Just met her in passing. Only been here a couple of days. They left together last night."

"What does she look like?"

"Cover of *Vogue*. Has a face you won't forget. Hair like a raven. That blue-black color."

"You saw them leave last night?"

"Around ten. Big, bald black guy picked them up."

T-Tommy and I looked at each other, and I knew he was thinking the same as me. Max.

Martha lit a fresh cigarette from the remnant of the one she held and then ground the butt into the soil of an ornate pot on her porch. The scraggly plant didn't seem to mind. She took a long pull and with smoke trailing from her nostrils said, "You going to look inside again?"

"Yeah. Hopefully find something that will help us figure out who did this."

T-Tommy had the door open in a couple of heartbeats, and we slipped inside. Martha took up a position at the door, leaning against the jamb, sucking smoke into her lungs.

The place was neat and clean, no sign of an altercation. Didn't suspect there would be. It looked as it did when we had seen it a few days ago. The pile of coke was gone, but the razor blade and mirror lay on the coffee table, a few grains of white powder clinging to the glass. In the kitchen, two wineglasses, a small puddle of red wine in the bottom of each, and a half bottle of Merlot were next to the sink.

In the upstairs room where Noel had stayed we found a small suitcase, empty, a handful of clothes in the closet, and a purse on the nightstand. The wallet inside contained no money or credit cards, only an Alabama driver's license issued to Kathleen Amanda Fuller, twenty in two weeks, Russellville address. The smiling face belonged to the strangled and sliced-up girl I had seen on the table in Slade's garage.

I handed the license to T-Tommy when he walked into the room.

"Sin-Dee's purse is in her room. Means they went out on a job."

Hookers rarely took much personal stuff with them when they were working. Just the essentials. A little cash, lipstick, mouthwash, condoms. A credit card if absolutely necessary.

We left everything as it was and went back downstairs. On the kitchen counter beside the phone I found a slip of paper. A list of six items, four checked off.

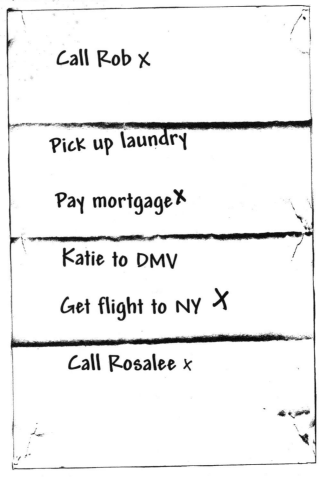

Call Rob X

Pick up laundry

Pay mortgage X

Katie to DMV

Get flight to NY X

Call Rosalee x

I didn't know who Rob was or what the trip to New York was about, but I was dead solid sure that Katie's license renewal and Sin-Dee's laundry wouldn't happen. The call to Rosalee apparently had. Well, well.

CHAPTER 73

T-TOMMY AND I REACHED ROSALEE KENNEDY'S IN ABOUT TEN MINUTES.

Max answered the door. "The fuck you guys want?" He wasn't as pleasant as last time. Couldn't imagine why.

"Rosalee," I said.

"She's busy."

"So are we." I pushed past him.

He grabbed my arm, squeezed. "Don't you hear so well?"

In an earlier life—right after Jill's abduction and my spiral into depression and my brief marriage to Claire—I was a US Marine MP. They teach you how to handle these situations. How to take down bad guys with minimum effort. Eyes, neck, balls, fingers, whatever was available. I chose a thumb.

I fisted Max's left thumb and cranked it back. Hard. Max dropped to his knees. He didn't resist when T-Tommy snagged his gun from the holster on his belt. I let go.

God bless the USMC.

"I hear real good," I said.

We found Rosalee in the kitchen, sitting at a table in a nook that had views over the pool. She wore a loose silk robe and scanned the newspaper spread on the table before her, narrow reading glasses settled low on her nose. A phone and what appeared to be a black leather appointment book lay nearby. Ready for business. She looked up, shock on her face, and fumbled with her coffee cup, spilling some on the paper. "What the . . . ?"

I waved her into silence and sat down across the table. "I'll ask the questions."

Max came in, shaking his hand and rubbing his thumb. "Sorry," he said.

Rosalee tugged off her glasses, dropped them on the paper, and glared at me. "You can't come in here and—"

I pointed to the phone. "The number's 911 if you want to call. Or I have Investigator Tortelli right here if you want to file a complaint. Maybe you want to call your buddy Rocco. Or your guardian angel."

She settled in her chair, regaining her composure, and dabbed at the spilled coffee with a napkin. "I don't need a guardian angel. I can take care of myself."

I smiled. "I'd bet Sergeant Furyk would be disappointed to hear that."

"Who's that?"

"The guy you've given . . ." I looked at T-Tommy. "What is it? Ten thousand?"

"Closer to twelve."

"The guy you've given twelve Grovers to so he can be your next mayor or whatever cushy job he's looking for."

"I don't know what you're talking about."

"Sure you do." I leaned back, starting to enjoy this. "I find it odd that the top homicide cop gets money from you, Rocco Scarcella, and Harmon Talbert."

Her gaze darted around. Max, the floor, me, T-Tommy, the floor, back to me. I could feel the wheels turning inside her head.

I pressed on. "Quite a confederacy. So I ask myself, why is this dirty little group killing so many folks?"

"I'm afraid you're misinformed." Rosalee stood, but I motioned her back into her seat.

Max began to move forward, but T-Tommy gave him a look that convinced him to stay put.

"Relax, Rosalee," I said. "We might be your shining knights. Might be able to pull your bacon from the fire."

She sat and crossed her arms over her chest.

I went on. "The thumbnail is that we know that Alejandro and Eddie supplied bodies for someone. We know they dumped the bodies after this person was finished. We know Alejandro worked for Rocco. We know Crystal, Sin-Dee, the new girl, Kathleen Fuller I believe, and our friend Noel were likely set up by you. We know that you and Rocco think that you're bulletproof because of Furyk. What I'm telling you right here, right now, is that ain't so. We're going to take down

Rocco. Furyk, too, if necessary. You'll get flushed in the deal. Max, too."

"That's a wild theory you have there," Rosalee said. "Problem is that it isn't true. None of it."

I caught her gaze, held it for a minute, waiting for things to ripen in her mind. Then I said, "The only piece we're missing is who's the cutter. Who chopped up these folks? And why?" Her eyes never wavered. Neither did mine. "If you know, you might be able to buy your way out of this."

"You guys are behind the curve." She refilled her cup from a coffee carafe on the table. Took her sweet time about it. Didn't offer us any. Sort of rude, but under the circumstances I understood. "They got the killer this morning."

"On the news, was it?" I asked her.

"I have my sources, too."

"Better check them," T-Tommy said.

I nodded. "They're a little off base here."

She took a sip of coffee. Another. Drawing it out. The cup made a soft ping when she returned it to the saucer. "We'll know soon. There's a press conference at noon. Furyk's holding it."

I didn't ask how she knew. Furyk? Rocco? It didn't matter. She was in the loop. I stood and looked down at her. "The offer stands. You can still buy your way out of this."

Rosalee smiled. "This what?"

I picked up the pen that lay next to her appointment book and scribbled my cell number on a dry edge of the newspaper. "Eddie

Elliott knew. He's dead. Alejandro Diaz knew. He's dead. Aden Slade knew. He's dead. You and Max know. Do the math."

CHAPTER 74

I LEANED AGAINST THE CHANNEL 8 VAN, TALKING WITH T-TOMMY AND sipping the coffee we had picked up at The Coffee Tree Books & Brew, a cool book, coffee, and sandwich shop at the south end of the strip mall that housed the South Precinct. Besides being T-Tommy's office, the South Precinct was home to the Major Crimes Unit, which handled homicides and other crimes against persons, and the HPD crime lab. It was easy to miss, occupying the middle unit of the mall, wedged between a discount store and a sports and fitness center. The only sign that it was a governmental agency was the American flag out front and the white lettering on the double glass doors.

Claire was doing a pickup interview of one of the HPD uniforms who had been at Aden Slade's house this morning.

We were all killing time, waiting for Furyk's press conference. He had set up a podium near the precinct's front doors.

While I waited, I called Miranda.

"How are you?" I asked when she answered.

"Been better."

"Anything I can do?"

"More than you've already done?" She sighed heavily. "No. This'll just take time."

I brought her up to date on everything and then said, "Sergeant Furyk, head of homicide here, is holding a press conference at noon. I'm sure it'll be carried down in Birmingham. If you watch, it's all BS."

"What do you mean?"

"He's going to say that he got the killer. That it's some guy named Aden Slade. That Slade committed suicide."

"Did he?"

"Not even close. He didn't do himself, and he ain't the killer."

"Then who is?"

"Don't know yet. Slade's probably involved, but he ain't the brains behind it. He's just the fall guy."

Miranda sighed. "When will this be over?"

"Soon. Very soon. I'll call when I know more."

As I expected, Furyk was late. Didn't hurt to appear busier than you really were. By 12:10 the crowd was growing restless. Finally, Furyk came out, camera lenses and microphones aimed at him, and exchanged a few words with a uniformed officer who stood beside him.

He then approached the podium and faced the reporters. "Thank you for coming. This has been a tough case, and I'd like to thank all the dedicated officers who have put in many hours of hard work. I'd particularly like to thank the lead detective of the task force, Investigator Tommy Tortelli."

"At least he's giving you some credit," I said.

T-Tommy shook his head. "He's covering his ass. If this little charade goes south, he's got me to blame."

Furyk continued. "This case began nearly a week ago when the corpses of two young women were found buried in a wooded area just north of the city. They had been horribly mutilated by a very sick and sadistic killer. Then another mutilated victim, now identified as Alejandro Diaz, was found in a field where the killer had dumped his body. He obviously thought Mr. Diaz was dead. But he was alive and was transported to Huntsville Memorial Medical Center where, despite heroic efforts by the doctors and medical staff, he died early yesterday morning."

He cleared his throat. "Over the past few days the bodies of nearly two dozen other victims have been unearthed, and this morning the corpses of three more young women were found. Each and every one of these victims had been similarly mutilated." He took a deep breath, stuck his chest out, and put on a serious expression. "I should point out that it appears that these mutilations occurred while the victims were still alive."

A murmur swelled and rolled through the gathering.

Furyk waited for it to die down. "Today's victims were discovered at the home of the killer, Mr. Aden Slade. His body was also found at the scene. He died from a self-inflicted gunshot wound." He looked over the crowd. "I'll answer a couple of questions."

Hands shot up, and voices called out.

Furyk pointed at a woman near the front.

"What are the names of the other victims?"

"The initial two young women are Noel Edwards, age nineteen, and Crystal Robinson, age twenty-four. We can't release information on any of the others since our identification process is ongoing and we are still attempting to locate next of kin of those we have been able to identify." A grim look again. "Many of the victims are young women who appear to have been prostitutes. That makes ascertaining their true identity more difficult. It may take a while." Now his face softened. "We want them returned to their loved ones. Even the most weak and vulnerable among us deserve the same respect that each of us is entitled to."

"He's quite a humanitarian," I said.

T-Tommy grunted.

The next question came from a *Huntsville Times* reporter. I recognized him but couldn't remember his name. "What can you tell us about the perpetrator?"

"Aden Slade was a troubled young man. His father was a brilliant physician who committed suicide, and his mother died after a long illness. Mr. Slade had been enrolled in medical school but had to drop out to care for his mother. I'm certain that was an embittering experience. He was apparently a loner with few friends, which seems to be common with these types of sociopaths. He worked locally for a medical equipment manufacturing firm. Apparently he stole instruments from his employer, and it was these that he used to torture and mutilate his victims. That's really all we know about him at this time."

If nothing else, Furyk was smooth. The reporters seemed to eat this up, not sensing that it was complete bullshit.

Except for Claire. "Any idea how Slade managed to keep his victims imprisoned yet still go to work every day?" she asked. "Why none of his neighbors noticed anything?"

"Mr. Slade was very clever." Furyk pointed to another reporter.

Claire wasn't that easily brushed aside. "Are you sure that Slade acted alone? Seems like all this would require more than one person."

Furyk set his jaw. "Aden Slade is the one who did this. The only one. We found him with his final victims. In his garage where he tortured his victims. All his victims. There is no evidence that anyone else was involved."

Claire was now in full Claire mode. "Didn't murder victim Eddie Elliott work for Alejandro Diaz? Weren't his fingerprints found at one of the burial sites?"

I could tell by Furyk's expression that this wasn't going the way he had hoped. He was losing control of the situation. "Needless to say, there are many unanswered questions about this investigation. I'd rather not get into the details at this time."

A young man in the middle of the pack yelled, "Do you think there might be more victims? Bodies you haven't discovered yet?"

Furyk seemed relieved at the interruption of Claire's hammering. "That's possible. Since Slade took the coward's way out, shooting himself, we can't ask him. So, yes, there could be other victims, and unfortunately we may never know." He held both hands up, palms toward the crowd. "That's all for now."

Shouted questions followed him as he walked inside, enveloped by officers.

"I should've resigned," T-Tommy said.

"Where do you want to sniff around next?" I asked.

"We know Slade ain't the cutter." T-Tommy raised his left thumb, counting it off. "We know someone staged the scene at Slade's." Index finger. "We know the girls passed through Rosalee. We know Rosalee and Rocco are the same species. We know that special tools are needed to do this shit and that Talbert makes them." A fistful now. "We know that Slade worked at Talbert and that Alejandro had Talbert's number." Right thumb and index finger. "We know that Furyk just lied his fucking head off." Middle finger. "We know that Rocco, Rosalee, Talbert, and Furyk are bound together by money and power. Crack one of these nuts, and you get them all."

"We tried Rosalee," I said. "I don't think Furyk will cop to a lesser charge. So that leaves Rocco and Talbert. Who do you like?"

"Don't know how deep in this Slade was, but someone wants us to think he's the whole deal. Means that Talbert his ownself must have helped set up Slade."

I nodded. That sounded good.

T-Tommy smiled. "We need to get inside Talbert. Something ain't right over there."

"Front door or back?" I asked.

"We've been through the front."

CHAPTER 75

AFTER THE PRESS CONFERENCE BROKE UP, CLAIRE HEADED TO THE station to work on her six o'clock report. T-Tommy and I drove to my house and settled on the back deck. T-Tommy reached out to a contact at county records, and she agreed to put together recent construction permits and plans on the Talbert building.

My cell phone rang, and I answered.

A male voice said, "Rosalee wants to talk."

Fifteen minutes later, T-Tommy and I climbed from my Porsche and walked up Rosalee's driveway. An uneasy feeling blossomed in my gut as I approached the front door. It stood open. An invitation. Come on in. No sign of Max, no evidence of forced entry.

"Rosalee?" I called.

Nothing.

"Rosalee?"

T-Tommy pulled his Glock. "I'll take the back."

I went through the front. Nothing in the foyer. Nothing in the living room. The kitchen was a different story.

The open newspaper, coffee cup, phone, and Rosalee's glasses were on the table exactly as they had been earlier. The leather phone book wasn't. Rosalee's chair had tipped over, and she lay on the floor, a bloody stain over her chest, a round entry wound in the middle of her forehead. Dry and clean, obviously delivered after death. Just in case. Eyes black and glassy. A pancake of dark purple clot surrounded by a halo of yellow serum fanned across the floor. The coppery smell of blood hung in the air.

T-Tommy came through the French door that opened to the pool deck. He settled his gun back in its holster.

"Been dead awhile," I said. "Blood's already separated."

He looked down at Rosalee and sighed. "Why aren't I surprised?" He moved around the kitchen counter. "At least we know Max didn't do this."

I rounded the counter. Max lay on his back near the refrigerator. Three dark circles patterned his chest, and, as with Rosalee, a dry, clean entry wound stared up from his forehead. "This must have gone down right after we left this morning."

The sound of approaching sirens came through the open front door.

"Wonder who called the cops," I said.

"The one who put the holes in these two."

"Lefty and Austin?"

T-Tommy nodded. "Which means Rocco's trying to set you up.

Thought maybe you'd come here alone."

I heard tires screech outside and car doors slam. We moved to the foyer just as four uniforms came through the door, guns in hand.

The first officer stopped, surprise on his face. "Investigator Tortelli? We got a call about a shooting." He put away his weapon. "You call it in?"

"No. Two victims." T-Tommy jerked his head toward the kitchen. "Back there."

Two of the officers headed that way.

Another car pulled up, and Furyk got out. *Great.*

"Hello, Sergeant," I said as he marched into the house. "What a pleasant surprise."

He ignored me and snapped at the two uniforms. "Place Mr. Walker under arrest."

"What charges?" I asked, knowing the answer, just wanting him to say it.

"Murder. Two counts."

One of the officers started to move. T-Tommy froze him with a glare. The young man looked at Furyk, obviously unsure what to do.

T-Tommy held up a palm toward the uniform. "Just a minute." He turned to Furyk. "He's been with me all day."

Furyk glared at him. "You looking to get arrested, too? I gave you an order. Take this man into custody."

T-Tommy stepped forward. "Sergeant, this is a mistake."

"Why are you here? You've been suspended. I'd suggest you back off."

I moved close to Furyk. "A word?" I brushed past him and walked through the door where I waited for him. I led him out into the circular drive, away from the door, out of earshot. "Knowingly making a false arrest would just about do in your little mayoral run, wouldn't it?"

"Unless you're guilty."

"Which I'm not, and you know it."

"I'm afraid I don't know any such thing."

"Then maybe you better call your suck buddy Rocco."

"He's not my buddy, and I doubt he knows anything about this."

"Really?" I smiled.

Furyk didn't respond.

"Rocco and his two clowns are going to bring you down."

"I have nothing to do with them."

I sighed and waited for his gaze to leave his shoes and rise to meet mine. "You know me. Know what I do. Know I've consulted on cases all over. Even overseas. Know I have friends from here to DC. Marine Intel, the CIA, NSA, FBI."

"I'm impressed." He didn't do sarcasm well.

"You should be. I can have a line of attorneys from here to DC in a heartbeat. I can have an FBI forensics team in here before the sun sets. I'm sure they might turn up a thing or two. Like maybe Aden Slade didn't shoot himself."

"Only the HPD can get them in here."

"Try me. You forgetting that two of the victims were buried in

Tennessee? Crossing state lines makes it a federal beef. I make a call, the feds pop in here, find out you fucked this thing all up, and there goes your trip to the mayor's office." I kicked at a loose stone. It clattered across the drive and settled in the dirt beneath a pink azalea.

Furyk stared at me but remained silent.

"More to your future aspirations, I can also drag in a few news reporters. I'm sure you know my ex, Claire McBride. If you thought her questions today were tough, wait until she really gets focused. The woman has no manners and no brakes, and blood in the water drives her loony. Trust me on this one. I know."

"Are you threatening me?"

"Just giving you the lay of the land. Claire is only the beginning. I can drag TV and print reporters from coast to coast in here. The kind who love dirty cops. The kind who sink political futures. The kind who crush balls."

"Modesty isn't your strong suit, is it?"

I couldn't suppress a brief smile. "Not really. And discretion isn't yours."

He raised an eyebrow.

"Take Wendy Morland for example."

Got to love Claire. She had dug up this tidbit. Furyk had been pumping old Wendy—actually twenty-three-year-old Wendy—for a couple of years. Claire sniffed it out over a year ago but never ran the story. I hoped this might be the push Furyk needed to turn his rudder in another direction.

"Bet your wife and your future voting public don't know about her. A trip to Cabo? On the taxpayers' dime? You and little Wendy? Wendy who used to dance at High Rollers."

His chest heaved, and I thought he might hyperventilate. Sweat beaded on his neck and forehead. Must have been the heat.

He didn't have a comment about Wendy, so I went on. "You hooked up with her when you were doing vice and narc over at the West Precinct? Maybe Rocco made the intro?"

His fists balled at his side, but he still had nothing to say. I was a bit disappointed. I expected better.

"Then there's Francisco Flores."

Furyk straightened his shoulders. "Never heard of him."

I put on a face of mock surprise. "Really? I'd bet he would be disappointed to hear that. After he was kind enough to donate ten Grovers to your campaign. Lot of money for a gardener. Even Rocco's gardener."

"How did you . . . ?"

"I confess. It wasn't me. It was Claire. See what I mean about staying on her good side?"

Furyk worked his neck, glanced back at the door, and let out a long breath. "I'm listening."

Bingo. Just had to find the right buttons. "Rocco's going down. If my suspicions are correct, Talbert and Kincaid, too."

"And?"

"Play it smart. You'll lose a couple of donors. But if you don't cut them loose right now, you could lose the whole deal. It's like a cat with a ball of string. Once he starts clawing at loose ends, things tend to unravel."

"What exactly are you proposing?"

"Walk away. Let me and T-Tommy handle it."

I could almost see the wheels in his head turning. Finally, he said, "What about me?"

"I want the guy who did Noel. That's it. When I get him, I'm done. So, unless you were involved in that, I don't give a shit what happens. You can take credit for solving the crimes. Pad your fucking résumé. Become mayor and live happily ever after."

"What are you planning?"

"Can't say."

"Can't or won't?"

"Same thing. All you have to do is walk away."

"That's it?"

"Give T-Tommy his shield back. Stuff a letter of commendation in his jacket about his stellar work on this case."

He hesitated, brow furrowed, then nodded.

CHAPTER 76

WE SWUNG BY THE COUNTY RECORDS OFFICE. T-TOMMY RAN IN AND returned in a few minutes with a roll of plans. When we got home, I called Claire. Got her voice mail and left a message. I tried her at the station but was told she wasn't there yet.

I grabbed a bottle of Blanton's and two glasses, and T-Tommy and I moved to the patio table. For the next half hour, we dissected the plans, going back and forth between the blue-line drawings and photos we had taken.

I pointed to one of the photos. "This lower floor window corresponds to this one." I indicated the same window on the plans. "The new construction is just inside there. See this hallway? Runs most of the length of the building. These two rooms are new."

"They're each about twenty by thirty," T-Tommy said.

"Each is wired heavily. Both standard and 220 outlets, two

banks of overhead lights. And these . . ." I flipped to another page and pointed out several symbols. "Here, here, and here are oxygen and suction ports."

"You sure?"

I nodded. "The only reason I know is that when I was in school I saw some plans for the UAB expansion down in Birmingham. I didn't know what these symbols meant, either."

"Don't need oxygen for cadavers," T-Tommy said.

"Looks like Talbert and Kincaid set up their own hospital," I said.

T-Tommy let out a low whistle. "So the surgeries were done there."

"It all fits. Talbert runs the show, and Kincaid's the cutter. Got to be. Has the skill, the equipment, and now apparently the location. Eddie and Alejandro, with Rocco's blessing, were the garbagemen. Furyk provided protection . . . just in case."

"And they filled up Furyk's campaign coffers," T-Tommy said.

"I'd suspect Rocco's pockets, too."

"Makes your medical research theory seem more likely," T-Tommy said. "But I still don't see why they would do all this. I mean, using people as guinea pigs to perfect another tool? Doesn't wash."

"We don't have the whole picture yet," I said. "Could be they're working on something bigger than a few new tools."

"Like what?"

"Don't know."

T-Tommy leaned back in his chair. "A little recon work seems to be in order."

The phone rang, and I walked to the bar and answered it.

The voice was masculine, muffled a bit. "Walker?"

"Yeah."

"Want to see your ex-wife again?" The voice was harsh with a Germanic accent.

"Who is this?"

"Stay close to this phone. Call your buddy Tortelli, and then both of you sit tight. Don't fuck up. We'll be in touch."

The line went dead.

CHAPTER 77

I LAY ON THE BED AND STARED AT THE CEILING. IT HAD BEEN OVER three hours and still no call. What if they never called? What if I never found Claire? What if she was buried somewhere?

Earlier I had called Channel 8. Maybe it was a hoax, and Claire was really there. She wasn't. They were worried. Said Claire was never late. I knew that. Said they were going to call the cops. I told them I'd handle it.

I then tried to help T-Tommy collect more info on Talbert, make a plan to get inside, but I couldn't concentrate. Or sit still. I paced the room, gazed out the window, stared at the phone.

The big question was why had they grabbed Claire? The case had been solved. At least to the satisfaction of Furyk and the gullible public. Slade was the killer. Eddie and Alejandro accomplices. All dead. Case closed. Let the sun shine, the flowers bloom, and the birds sing.

The world was perfect again, and the citizens of Rocket City could go about their lives without fear. Rocco could peddle his sleaze. Furyk could run for mayor. Neat. Clean.

But why grab Claire?

Only one answer. Rocco. He knew that T-Tommy and I had the goods on him. Knew everything. About him. About Furyk. About their little marriage of money and power. He also knew we wouldn't simply walk away. We'd made that clear. His first shot? Rosalee and Max went down, and we got set up for the murders. But he hadn't figured on us buying our way out of that deal. Knowledge was rich currency.

It also made Claire, T-Tommy, and I liabilities. The only remaining loose ends. Without us, Rocco was home free. Who could tell the truth then? Furyk? Talbert or Kincaid? Get real.

So, Rocco hatched a plan in that greasy little head of his. Take Claire, draw us in, whack all of us, and the package was complete.

Which meant we had to find Claire.

T-Tommy and I agreed that she was likely being held at Talbert. They'd already imprisoned a couple of dozen victims there, so it made sense. Problem was, we weren't sure. She could be anywhere. Storming Talbert might put Claire in the line of fire. And if she wasn't there? That was the real problem. She would be in even more danger. Bottom line: if we knew for sure where she was, we'd go in. Not knowing left us with nothing.

At one point I suggested we snatch Rocco. Just go into High Rollers and grab him. Kick his fat ass around. Make him talk. Make a trade. T-Tommy loved the idea but said only as a last resort. I hated it when he was rational. Usually I had to hold him back. I brought that fact up, but he said I wasn't exactly thinking straight right now. That was when he suggested I go lie down so he could get some work done.

Claire, where are you?

In the quiet room I could almost hear the seconds ticking by. Slowly. I glanced at the clock beside the bed—7:34. Exactly two minutes since I last checked.

My thoughts ran the gamut. Claire was already dead. She was being tortured, raped. She was strapped to a table, and Kincaid was cutting into her. She had escaped and was on the run. Like Alejandro. Bleeding, weakening by the minute. Around and around I went from image to image.

I must have dozed off because Jill made an appearance. I only saw her in my dreams. Could never pull up her face when I wanted to. Not sure why, but that was the way it was. Jill was screaming for help. I could almost reach her but not quite. She sank into something deep and black. Water? A well? Her face and cries and whimpers faded. She slipped away. I jerked awake.

I got up, headed to the bathroom, and splashed water on my face. Didn't help much. I looked in the mirror. Could I survive losing Claire? Jill's abduction almost did me in. Depression, anger, self-incrimination, a ton of other shit pulled me from med school, from life. Only Claire and the USMC saved me. A fear rose deep inside that if Claire was gone I could easily circle that drain again. This time I might not find a rope. I liked to think I was a stronger person now. That such a descent wasn't possible. Truth was, I simply didn't know.

I went out on the deck, and T-Tommy handed me a fresh bourbon. I took a long drink. I needed it.

Mississippi John Hurt sang "I Been Cryin' Since You Been Gone" through the outdoor speakers.

I sat at the table across from T-Tommy. "What've you got?"

"I had some guys contact medical and pharmaceutical supply companies in the area." He slid a piece of paper to me. "Here's some of the shit Talbert's bought over the twenty-four months."

The list went like this:

Oxygen cylinders, masks, and tubing

Surgical drapes

Bandages

EKG paper

Sutures

IV lines and fluids

Urinary catheters and bags

Two ventilators

Antibiotics, potassium chloride, morphine, fentanyl, and
several other anesthetic agents

"Smells like a surgical setup to me," I said.

"Looks that way." He turned the plans toward me. "I think I

know where they're holding Claire."

I studied the schematics. It was always amazing when something you'd looked at dozens of times suddenly took on a new meaning. You saw it differently. Made connections that should have been obvious. "Here?" I pointed to a small interior room.

T-Tommy nodded. "Plans say it's got a steel-reinforced door. Walls are solid cinder block. No windows. Pretty tight prison."

"That's got to be it."

T-Tommy flattened his palms on the table, leaning on them. "You want to slip in and sniff around or go straight at them balls to the wall?"

I hated these kinds of decisions. Ones where the information at hand was fractured and fuzzy and you could only guess the right path. Ones where the wrong choice could be a disaster. Ones where errors in judgment could haunt you forever. I lost Jill because I didn't show up where and when I said I would. I failed her. I couldn't fail Claire.

"Where do we go in?" I asked.

T-Tommy smiled and slid another of the blue-line drawings toward me. A floor plan for the lower floor. He pointed to a series of windows along the side of the building. They opened into a hallway that fronted the newly constructed ORs or ICUs or whatever they were and the room we believed to be a holding cell. "This is a ventilation grate. It's four by four. Opens right into the hallway. Probably easier to open than one of the windows. Probably no locks. Few screws around it."

If we made it into that hallway undetected, we might be able to get Claire out without a fuss. Even if we ran into a couple of bad guys, it could still work. But if we ran into an entire posse, this deal could go way south.

The phone rang. We exchanged glances, and I walked to the kitchen counter and answered.

"Walker?" Same voice.

"I'm here."

"Good boy. I want you—"

"I want to talk to Claire."

"Not a chance."

"I want proof she's still alive."

"Want me to send you one of her tits?"

"Listen, you—"

"No. You listen. You want to see her again you shut the fuck up." I did.

"I want you and Tortelli walking down David Douglass Road. Out off Kelly Spring Road. Like Tweedledee and Tweedle-fucking-dum. Ten sharp. Don't be late."

"We won't."

"Unarmed. If I even smell the cops, she's dead."

"I believe you."

"You fucking better." He waited for my response, but I didn't give him one. "Ten sharp. Clear?"

"We'll be there."

He hung up.

CHAPTER 78

T-Tommy and I walked north on David Douglass Road, an uneven, patched-up blacktop. We passed a sleeping farmhouse. Behind it a windmill squeaked and ticked against a soft breeze, rich with the aroma of honeysuckle. A layer of clouds shut out the moon, and the stars and the darkness deepened. The words *completely isolated* came to mind. The guys waiting for us could be anywhere. I imagined the red dot of a laser site on the back of my head. It burned.

The plan was simple. T-Tommy and I would do exactly as they said. Walk right into their trap. Let them take us wherever they wanted. Hopefully to where Claire was being held. That would put us next to her where we could protect her when the shit went down.

The last instructions from that German-sounding dude changed everything. Had he jerked us around some more, not arranged a meet, then slipping in the side grate at Talbert made sense. But when he told us to come here, north of the city and miles from Talbert and nowhere near civilization, we had to scrap that idea. Claire could be out here somewhere. In the trunk of a car. In some abandoned farmhouse. Maybe even the dark one we had just walked past. Maybe she was tied to a tree in one of the many wooded areas. Maybe she was already dead. I didn't believe it and still held to the notion that Talbert was the best bet. Couldn't be sure, so we needed a more flexible strategy.

T-Tommy reached out to Furyk. Furyk, seeing a way out of this, agreed with the setup we had devised. One thing about Furyk, he always did what was best for him. Right now, that was just what T-Tommy and I needed.

HPD officers Derrick Stone and Glenn Stanhope sat in an unmarked car back near the junction of Kelly Spring Road and the Ardmore Highway. To leave this area we'd have to go right past them. They would follow. Make sure we were going to Talbert and if not lead the cavalry to wherever we ended up. The cavalry was Furyk, a handful of uniforms, and a SWAT team. They were waiting half a mile away just off the Ardmore Highway, ready to move when Stone called.

Of course, if this went badly, Furyk would lay it off on Tortelli. If it went well and his troops stormed the bastille and saved the maiden, Furyk would be a hero. We didn't particularly like either choice, but what the hell. Getting Claire out was all that mattered. If Furyk got to play hero, then so be it.

As we walked deeper into the darkness, we both knew this could go sideways in a heartbeat. We were sitting ducks. Birds on a wire.

Canaries in a coal mine. Take your pick. They could take us down at any time, and we'd never see it coming.

But it didn't feel that way.

Too bad life didn't have background music. If it did, would we now be hearing the dirgelike droning of impending doom or something brighter? Something indicating that the conquering heroes were triumphantly entering the bad guy's lair? Could go either way. We were betting on the hero's march.

The road crossed a narrow creek, embraced on each bank by a thick hedgerow. Not far from the end now. When we crested a modest rise, we were suddenly bathed in light as headlamps and a roof-mounted light bar from a vehicle a hundred feet away sprang to life.

"Hands where I can see them." The voice was that of the caller. Same guttural Germanic accent.

I shielded my eyes and could just make out a shape near what appeared to be some kind of SUV. No, two shapes. One thin, the other large and thick. Lefty and Austin.

"Fancy meeting you guys here," I said. "Rocco come with you?"

"Shut the fuck up," Lefty said. "Hands on top of your heads, fingers laced."

We did.

Another shadow emerged from the darkness to our left. "Don't move." The German stepped behind us and patted us down. "Clean," he said.

Austin and Lefty came forward, the light behind them casting them in silhouette. Austin stopped a good twenty feet away from me and pointed a gun at my head. Lefty did the same to T-Tommy.

"Nothing cute now," Lefty said. "Go ahead, Karl."

Karl Reinhardt. Security at Talbert. Looked like we had it pegged right. It also meant that when this went down it wouldn't be some slappy fight. This was the real deal. Austin, Lefty, Karl, probably Rocco, and God knew who else. Not good odds, but it was what it was.

Karl nudged my shoulder. "Hands behind your back."

I did, and he bound my wrists together with a plastic loop. He then moved to T-Tommy and did the same.

They loaded us into the middle seat of a Chevy Suburban. Lefty drove, and Austin rode shotgun. He twisted in the seat, gun aimed at my face. Karl sat behind us, his gun resting against the back of T-Tommy's neck.

CHAPTER 79

AUSTIN LED US THROUGH THE FRONT DOOR OF TALBERT BIOMEDICAL and down a dark hallway. We were now on the clock. We had exactly thirty minutes to find Claire, set the stage, and wait for the cavalry to surprise the bad guys.

Finding Claire turned out to be easy. They took us right to her.

She was in the newly constructed operating room. Her ankles and wrists were strapped to a table beneath a circular bank of surgical lights. Kincaid, Talbert, and Rocco stood over her completely nude body.

"You okay?" I asked.

"What the hell is going on?"

"Be cool," I said. "It'll be all right."

Austin shoved me toward the far wall where two metal folding chairs sat side by side. "Sit down. Don't say a fucking word."

I dropped into one chair, T-Tommy the other. I went to work on the plastic cuffs, moving my wrists back and forth, creating a little play.

Kincaid stood before us. "You two have proven to be a problem. That'll end tonight."

"What do you want?" I asked.

"Nothing. I have everything I need." He waved a hand at Claire. "Another subject for my work." He turned back to us. "And the only two loose ends."

Flattening my palms together, I levered my wrists apart. The plastic dug into my flesh, but I could feel it loosening, stretching. Not much, but I didn't need much.

Kincaid smiled and rubbed his hands together. "So, let's get to work."

He and Talbert moved to the corner and tugged a plastic cover off some mechanical device. It was the size of the chair I sat in and seemed to be constructed of a haphazard arrangement of metallic tubes. It rested on a rolling platform, which the two men wheeled to where Claire lay. Austin helped them lift the device and attach it to the edges of the table. It straddled Claire's body.

I could feel the fear grow within her, her eyes wide, her chest heaving. "What the hell is this?" she asked.

Kincaid gave her a fatherly pat on the shoulder. "All in good time."

I wanted to kill him. Actually I wanted to hurt him. Bad. Then kill him.

I continued working on the cuffs. The band cut deeply into my flesh, and I felt blood trickle down into one palm.

It took about five minutes for them to set the device up. The contraption was straight out of the old black-and-white sci-fi movies I used to watch on late-night TV. It looked like a giant mechanical spider, four legs grasping the edges of the table and as many as six others pointing directly at Claire. I almost expected a drooling, metallic-toothed mouth to begin devouring her at any minute.

Kincaid connected electrical and computer cables to it, then moved to the computer that sat on a desk along the wall. He made a few keystrokes, dramatically tapping the last one. He moved toward Claire.

The device jerked into motion. Claire flinched. One of the metal spider legs lowered and brushed against her flesh. She recoiled from the contact.

"Once Robbie begins his work, I'd advise against any movement," Kincaid said.

I saw sweat slick Claire's skin. "What the fuck is that?" I asked.

Kincaid turned to me. "An Automated Robotic Surgical Device. Or ARSD, if you prefer. We call him Auto-Rob. Sometimes Robbie. Isn't he beautiful?"

No, he's not, I wanted to say. *He's a hideous-looking monster.* "What is it?"

"He's my creation. And Ms. McBride's surgeon."

"You're crazy."

Kincaid stepped closer and looked down at me. His eyes cold, his jaw fixed. "Do you think a crazy man could build such a device that will alter medicine forever?" He smiled. "The truth is that you are all lucky. Your lives will actually be worth something. Like the others, you'll help perfect this amazing device." He moved over to Claire. "Don't worry. We'll numb things up for the actual operation. Most of it, anyway."

"What the hell are you talking about?" she asked. Her voice was high-pitched, filled with fear.

"Leave her alone," I said.

Lefty stuck the muzzle of his nine against my cheek. "All I need is an excuse."

"Twenty-two minutes," Stone said to Stanhope. He punched a number into his cell and waited for an answer. When it came, he said, "Going in now."

"We're all set," Furyk said.

Stone approached the fence that surrounded Talbert. He took a last look around, scaled the fence, and dropped to the ground on the other side. Stanhope followed.

CHAPTER 80

KINCAID TURNED TO T-TOMMY AND ME. "YOU ARE ABOUT TO WITNESS a true miracle of modern medicine. I'm sure you'll find this quite fascinating."

When neither of us responded, he frowned.

Good. Get angry, asshole.

His frown faded, and he smiled. As if he were a college professor, I was an underachieving student, and he was attempting to explain something I should be eager to learn.

Fuck you, Professor.

"Robbie is getting very good at the surgery." Kincaid caressed one of the device's metallic legs. "He can execute many different procedures without my help. A truly revolutionary invention." With dramatic flair he paused as if awaiting some flash of divine wisdom. "Imagine if you will that you are in darkest Africa. Or perhaps at a research station in the Antarctic or in a remote war zone. Maybe even an outpost on the moon. I assume you know that NASA is planning to return there and establish permanent settlements."

I knew but said nothing. *Just keep talking.*

"And when they do, we'll be ready." He was getting into it now, adopting the professorial walk. The one every overly tenured professor I ever saw used. Back and forth, occasionally glancing at the ceiling as if recalling something from his brilliant mind, glancing now and then at the class. That would be us. "I want you to further assume . . ."

Further assume? What kind of crap is this?

". . . that you needed some lifesaving surgical procedure. It could be an appendectomy, a gallbladder removal, or a tumor resection." Kincaid opened his arms toward us, as if inviting us into his world. "Would you have a surgeon with you? Not likely."

T-Tommy's face remained expressionless, his jaw fixed. Austin and Lefty seemed to be wrapped up in Kincaid's tale, so his lecture wasn't a total waste.

I guessed we had another fifteen minutes. I could sense T-Tommy working on his cuffs. I grasped the tail—the leftover part of the plastic after it had been pulled tight around my wrists—between the index and middle finger of my left hand. This would prevent it from falling to the floor when it broke, giving away the fact that I was free. I nestled my right fist into my left palm. Keeping my left hand firm, I levered my right forearm upward. The plastic band gave a little more. Again I pressed against it and felt it weaken. I relaxed. One more good crank, and it would snap.

Stone spun out the last screw, lifted the ventilation grate from its mooring, and placed it on the ground behind him. He stuck his head inside and looked both ways. The corridor was dark except for light spilling from somewhere about a hundred feet to his left.

He slipped through the window and dropped to the floor. After Stanhope did the same, they crept down the hall until they neared the source of the light . . . a window. Stone crouched and moved toward it.

CHAPTER 81

"Auto-Rob is the best surgeon in the world," Kincaid said. "And he does the entire procedure on his own. So, you can carry your surgeon with you in a suitcase wherever you go."

"You mean this thing actually cuts on people?" T-Tommy asked.

"Yes."

"On its own?"

Kincaid smiled. He obviously thought T-Tommy was actually interested. Divert and conquer.

"Auto-Rob can perform seventeen different procedures. Flawlessly, as you will see. Soon he'll do many, many more."

"I have a question," I said.

Kincaid's eyes lit up. "Yes?"

"Why all this? Why torture innocent people this way?"

"We're not the only ones working in this arena. It's a race. The winner, the one who creates a truly self-contained robotic surgeon, will make hundreds of millions."

"Are your competitors kidnapping young women, too?"

"That's why they will lose." Kincaid frowned. "You, of all people, should know how the feds and the FDA can fuck up research. Put hurdles and regulations in the way. Stagnate the process. We'll cut ten years off the R and D time. Save a fortune in the process. Flash past the finish line before our competitors even know we're in the race."

Megalomania just didn't seem strong enough.

Kincaid turned to his creation. "Robbie uses lasers to do the actual cutting. Cleaner and less bleeding. The problem we are having is with anesthesia. Right now we need an anesthetist present to put the patient to sleep."

"That sort of limits its use, doesn't it?" I said. *Keep him talking.*

"Right you are." Kincaid smiled at me. I was his favorite student now. "We're working on a system. Sort of anesthesia as you go." He touched the end of one of the spider's legs. "Using a combination of micropicolated drugs, basically an aerosol or mist, and high-frequency sound waves. The sound waves confuse the nerves, alter their ability to transmit pain signals. The drug does the rest, completely blocking the transmissions. The chemical we use is an analog of lidocaine. Soaks into the tissues and goes to work almost instantly. The patient doesn't have to be put to sleep."

"Until you're through with them," I said.

His face hardened. "Progress always comes at a price."

That's it. Focus on me. "Just so you aren't paying it, right?"

Lefty slammed his fist into my temple, knocking me against T-Tommy. As T-Tommy shouldered me upright, I felt more than heard the plastic snap. He was free.

"Enough talk. It's late, and we have work to do." Kincaid returned to the computer and tapped a few keys.

Again the metal creature came to life. Another one of the legs came down close to Claire's abdomen, not touching but moving one way and then the other. I saw her skin twitch slightly.

"Robbie is mapping the area. Using high-density ultrasound to create a three-dimensional picture of the skin, muscles, and internal structures. Once this is completed, we can begin."

I saw Stone. One eye peeked through the corner of the window, and then he ducked from sight.

The robot kept up its work, Kincaid patiently waiting. He turned to me. "Sorry we have to slice up Ms. McBride. But it is in the interest of science."

"Is that what this is?" I asked. "I thought maybe it was greed."

Lefty hit me again.

This time I was ready and didn't budge. Instead I looked at him and said, "You hit me again, and I'll kill you."

He laughed. "You're not in a very good position here."

Me: "I kind of like it."

T-Tommy: "Me, too. Where else can you get an education and entertainment?"

Me: "A professor and two clowns."

T-Tommy: "Three clowns."

Me: "Sorry, Rocco. Didn't mean to leave you out."

Rocco pushed himself away from the wall. "You guys are real comedians. But I'll have the last laugh. See, I get to decide how you die. I can make it easy or . . . ?" He shrugged. "Austin and Lefty are pretty good at both."

Me: "I thought they just did whores."

T-Tommy: "Sort of specialized in them."

Me: "Found their niche."

T-Tommy: "Something they could handle."

Me: "Of course there was Aden Slade."

T-Tommy: "He was a little puny."

Me: "And albino."

T-Tommy: "Almost."

Me: "Yeah, almost."

Lefty clenched his fist.

"That's enough." Kincaid waved Lefty away and glared at me. "You two think you're clever. Not for long. As soon as I finish with Ms. McBride, you guys are next." He turned to T-Tommy. "I'm really looking forward to getting you on the table. We've never had a subject your size. And when I'm finished, Mr. Scarcella will deal with you both."

"You mean his lapdogs," T-Tommy said. "Boss Scarcella don't get his own hands dirty."

Austin slammed his fist into the side of T-Tommy's head.

T-Tommy didn't move, showed no reaction, except a grin directed at Austin. Austin rubbed his knuckles.

"I was you I'd have that looked at," T-Tommy said.

"What?"

"Your hand. Felt like something broke in there."

Austin hit him again. High on the side of his head. "Seems to work okay."

"Goin' to be fun crushing your ass," T-Tommy said.

Austin shoved the muzzle of his gun against the side of T-Tommy's head.

"Stop it," Kincaid said.

The spider contraption made a beeping noise.

CHAPTER 82

"ALL SET." KINCAID RETURNED TO THE COMPUTER, AND AFTER A few more taps, the spider creature jumped into motion. One of the legs contacted Claire's flesh and made a slight hissing sound. She recoiled with a quick intake of breath.

"That's the anesthetic spray," Kincaid told her. "It's a bit cold at first. You'll also feel a slight tingling when the ultrasound kicks in."

I coughed for cover and snapped the plastic band. I wadded it in my hand, my fingers searching for the tip. Finding it, I gripped it between my thumb and forefinger, a quarter inch protruding. A weapon of sorts.

"Don't worry. For this first part Robbie will only make shallow cuts. He's set to go a quarter of a centimeter deep."

The tip of one of the spider's legs seemed to glow a red-orange color. It moved several inches down and across Claire's abdomen.

"See. Didn't feel a thing."

Claire looked down. "I'm bleeding. It cut me." She bucked against her restraints. "Get this thing off me, you psycho."

"Don't you know you should never call your surgeon names?" Kincaid shook his head as if he were a disappointed father scolding a child.

"Use me." I slid to the front of my chair.

Kincaid turned to me. "Where's the fun in that? Fear of loss is much worse than fear of pain."

Stone peered through the window once more, and I gave him a slight nod. He sank below the window frame.

Kincaid tapped something into the computer. "See what happens if we turn the anesthesia off."

Again the laser moved across Claire's belly. This time she jerked and screamed.

"Leave her alone," I yelled.

Lefty leaned toward me. He drew back his gun to hit me with the butt. In one motion I knocked the gun from his hand and slashed my makeshift knife across his face. The gun clattered to the floor, and Lefty backed away. Blood erupted from his cheek.

T-Tommy leg-whipped Austin's feet out from under him. He hit the floor hard. T-Tommy was on him in a flash and slammed his fist into Austin's throat. I heard a loud crack.

Stone and Stanhope burst through the door. Reinhardt pulled his weapon. Too late. Stone shot him in the face, along the jaw. In the enclosed room, the sound concussed against my ears. Reinhardt went down on one knee and tried to lift the gun. Stanhope put two in his chest, and Reinhardt collapsed forward.

Lefty wiped blood from his face and reached for the gun on the floor. The chair I had been sitting in stopped him. I swung it against his face, felt the bones crack, and stepped back as he collapsed to the floor unmoving. I kicked the gun toward the corner.

Austin, still clutching his throat, still unable to draw a breath through his crushed larynx, tried to get to his feet. Should've stayed down. He got as far as his knees before T-Tommy chopped his right fist into the side of Austin's head. Austin's face hit the floor with a sharp crack. He lay motionless, no longer struggling for air, no longer needing it.

By that time I had Rocco backed against the wall, my hand flattened against his chest. He offered no resistance. Didn't matter. He wasn't going to escape undamaged. Not a chance. I hit him with a solid left hook. His head thudded against the wall, and he staggered. The second left was pretty damn good, too. Rocco's legs folded beneath him, and he slid down the wall to the floor.

Kincaid and Talbert hadn't moved, their backs against the window, eyes wide.

I grabbed the device that hovered over Claire and twisted it until I managed to rip it from its moorings. I tossed it across the room.

"No," Kincaid yelled.

"Shut up, or you're next," I said.

I loosened Claire's restraints and pulled her into a sitting position.

She hugged me tightly for a moment and then pushed me away. She was off the table and on Kincaid in a flash, swinging her foot up into the V of his legs. The thwack made me wince. It buckled his knees. I thought his eyes might jump from their sockets. Claire drove the palm of her hand into his chin. His head smacked the window behind him. It bowed and vibrated but didn't break. Kincaid dropped to his knees. She spun and drove her heel into the side of his head. It jerked sideways. His body followed. He didn't move.

"You sick motherfucker," she screamed at him. Blood from her two wounds trickled down her bare belly. She kicked him in the gut.

I came up behind her and got her in a bear hug.

"Let me go," Claire said, "or I'll kick your ass next." Her legs bicycled in the air.

I held on and laughed. "Glad all those kickboxing lessons finally paid off."

She started to laugh and then to cry. I turned her around and drew her close.

T-Tommy wrapped a surgical drape around her shoulders. I helped her back up on the table and examined her wounds. Two four-inch long lacerations. Both shallow.

Furyk and half a dozen uniforms burst in.

CHAPTER 83

AFTER FURYK AND THE UNIFORMS TOOK EVERYONE INTO CUSTODY and called in the coroner's team to deal with the late Karl Reinhardt and Tommy Austin, we gave brief statements to one of the officers. Furyk said that was all he needed and we were free to go. He was such a nice man. Very giving. Concerned about us. I was sure he never gave a thought to the fact that the less we said the better it was for him. I also suspected that he had dusted any trail that might connect him to Rocco. The good sergeant was definitely not going down with this crew. Pissed me off, but there you go.

Now we were in the ER at Memorial. Dr. Charlie Beck was on duty. We had met him during the Hublein-Kurtz-Pearce case. He had already seen Lefty. Said he had half a dozen fractured facial bones. I probably should have felt bad about it. I didn't.

Beck looked at Claire's wounds. "Not bad. Very superficial."

"So you can just use some of those little tape things?" Claire asked.

"Steri-Strips?" He shook his head. "They're not that superficial. They'll need a few stitches."

"Come on. Just tape them."

"I can charge more for stitches." He laughed.

"I knew it," she said.

"I've been following your reports on these murders," Beck said. "I hear they caught the guy."

"Wrong guy," I said. "We got the real ones tonight. That's how this happened."

"Oh?"

I told him the story while a nurse set up a suture tray, painted Claire's belly red with Betadine, and draped her with one of those sterile blue sheets. The two wounds peeked through a hole in the middle. Beck put on a pair of gloves and went to work.

The nurse cleaned the blood from my wrists. The plastic cuffs had scraped away a little flesh, but Beck said all it needed was antibiotic ointment and time. No big deal. I continued my story as she patched me up.

When I finished the tale, Beck asked, "How could Dr. Kincaid and Mr. Talbert get involved in something like this?"

"Once you step off the tracks, the end of the line can go all the way to murder. Out there off the rails you have secrets. Secrets get heavy. They need protecting, or they just might bring everything down. What will a man do to protect everything?"

Beck looked at me. "Anything."

I nodded. "You got that right."

Beck shook his head. "Unbelievable."

I watched as he finished closing the first of Claire's wounds and began work on the second. "Can I ask a question?"

"Of course."

"You know anything about robotic surgery?"

"Sure. It's an up-and-coming procedure."

"I know that the surgeon still does the work. Just remotely."

"That's right."

"If someone invented one of those gadgets that could do the whole thing by itself, even the anesthesia stuff, what would that be worth?"

"You mean a totally self-contained robotic surgeon?"

"Exactly."

"Very *Star Trek*."

"But if it could be done?"

Beck hesitated as if thinking about the question, then said, "Millions. Hundreds of millions. If it could be done, that is."

"That's what I thought."

"Is this what Kincaid was up to?"

"Yeah."

He gave a low whistle. "Ambition has no bounds."

"Neither does greed."

"This planet is full of crazy folks." Beck tugged another stitch tight. "Tonight was the topper."

"Are you talking about me?" Claire asked.

He laughed. "No. We had one of those twilight zone moments earlier."

"That why all the cop cars are out front?" I asked.

When we had pulled into the ER parking area earlier, there had been four patrol cars. T-Tommy stopped to chat with a couple of the uniforms he knew, while Claire and I went in to get fixed up. I assumed all the black-and-whites meant that there had been a traffic accident or maybe an injured suspect. Or sometimes cops just liked to hang around ERs. Probably had to do with coffee and nurses.

"Yeah. Bobbie Hawkins, one of our ICU nurses, caught an employee trying to inject a patient with potassium chloride."

"An angel of death deal?" I asked.

He nodded. "Our security guys held him until the police got here."

"Put up a fight?"

"No. In fact he seemed happy that he got caught. Said he'd be in the paper now." Beck shrugged. "Weird."

"How's the patient?" I asked.

"Fine. Last I heard, anyway."

"Who's the guy?"

"An orderly named Zeke Reed. I'm sure he's right. You will see his picture in the paper tomorrow."

"Did he say why he did it?"

"Haven't heard. Maybe the police know." Beck tied the last suture, slid the drape off Claire, dropped it into a trash bucket near his feet, and peeled off his gloves. "We'll get a bandage on that, and you're out of here. Stitches come out in a week."

CHAPTER 84

"Six total," T-Tommy said as Claire and I walked up.

"Six what?" I asked.

"Victims. Some orderly has whacked six people. Tried again tonight."

"We heard about the one tonight," Claire said.

"Perp's name is Ezekiel James Reed. People call him Zeke. Worked here for a few years. Whacked his first patient maybe a year ago. Couldn't remember exactly."

"I take it he confessed?" I asked.

"Apparently they couldn't shut him up. Told the whole story. Wants to be famous. Even wanted to talk to news reporters before going down for booking." T-Tommy shook his head. "But that's not the good part. He got paid for a couple of them."

"What?" Claire said. "Angels of death aren't contract killers."

"This one is," T-Tommy said. "One of the people he got paid to do was Alejandro Diaz."

Which made the source of the cash obvious. "Rocco?" I asked.

"You got it."

"He said that?"

"No. Didn't know the name of the guy who paid him. Big muscular guy. Met him at High Rollers."

"Austin," I said.

"Yep."

"Who was the other one he got paid to do?" Claire asked.

"Guy named Joe Samuelson. He was suing one of Rocco's buddies over some land deal. Gallbladder acted up, had to have surgery, never made it out of the hospital. This Reed dude said that was his first."

"And the others?" Claire asked. "Why'd he kill them?"

"He liked it," T-Tommy said. "Got a taste of it. Couldn't let go."

CHAPTER 85

I HAD FINISHED PACKING WHEN T-TOMMY STOPPED BY. CLAIRE WAS in the shower. We were going down to Birmingham for the weekend to see Miranda and help put her daughter in the ground.

"This case is really heating up," T-Tommy said.

"What's happening?"

"Lefty's cutting a deal. Going to bring down Rocco and Furyk." He smiled. "After they put his face back together."

"Furyk been arrested?"

"Did it myself. About six this morning. Right as he was heading to the gym. You should have seen the look on his face."

"Wish I had. What about the hospital orderly? Any more from him?"

"He IDed Austin from a photo as the guy who paid him for Alejandro and the other guy. Gave us names, dates, the whole deal. Kept records of everything."

"Bet his lawyer'll love that."

"Didn't want one. Asked for Claire. Wants her to interview him."

"She can't until next week. We're out of here in about fifteen minutes."

"He'll keep."

I shook my head. "Guess the book deal's next."

"This is one fucked-up planet," T-Tommy said.

He had a way with words.

STRESS FRACTURE

DUB WALKER SERIES, BOOK 1

D·P· LYLE

Dub Walker, expert in evidence evaluation, crime scene analysis, and criminal psychology, has seen everything throughout his career—over a hundred cases of foul play and countless bloody remains of victims of rape, torture, and unthinkable mutilation. He's sure he's seen it all . . . until now.

When Dub's close friend Sheriff Mike Savage falls victim to a brutal serial killer terrorizing the county, he is dragged into the investigation. The killer—at times calm, cold, and calculating and at others maniacal and out of control—is like no other Dub has encountered. With widely divergent personalities, the killer taunts, threatens, and outmaneuvers Dub at every turn.

While hunting this maniacal predator, Dub uncovers a deadly conspiracy—one driven by unrestrained greed and corruption. Will he be able to stop the conspirators—and the killer—in their bloody tracks?

ISBN# 978-160542134-6
Hardcover / Thriller
US $24.95 / CDN $27.95
AVAILABLE NOW
www.dplylemd.com

OTHER BOOKS BY D.P. LYLE

FICTION

Stress Fracture
(Dub Walker Series, Book 1)

Royal Pains: First, Do No Harm
(The First Royal Pains Tie-In Novel)

Devil's Playground
(A Samantha Cody Novel, Book 1)

Double Blind
(A Samantha Cody Novel, Book 2

NONFICTION

Murder and Mayhem: A Doctor Answers Medical and Forensic Questions for Mystery Writers

Forensics for Dummies

Forensics and Fiction: Clever, Intriguing, and Downright Odd Questions from Crime Writers

Howdunit Forensics: A Guide for Writers

MEDALLION
P R E S S

Be in the know on the latest Medallion Press news by becoming a Medallion Press Insider!

As an Insider you'll receive:

· Our FREE expanded monthly newsletter, giving you more insight into Medallion Press

· Advanced press releases and breaking news

· Greater access to all your favorite Medallion authors

Joining is easy. Just visit our website at www.medallionpress.com and click on the Medallion Press Insider tab.

MEDALLION
P R E S S

Want to know what's going on with
your favorite author or what new releases
are coming from Medallion Press?

Now you can receive breaking news,
updates, and more from Medallion Press
straight to your cell phone, e-mail, instant messenger, or Facebook!

For more information
about other great titles from
Medallion Press, visit